Proven Innocent

Liza Finch

Contents

PROLOGUE

I knew I was never meant to be a mother. The blood that runs through my veins is anything but maternal. The atoms and molecules that my body are comprised of simply aren't equipped for such a task.

For some women it comes naturally, as though they were destined for such divine greatness. At the mere age of eighteen, girls around me were longing to produce offspring. They described the feeling as natural and womanly. As though being a woman comes with this inherent prerequisite to nurture a child. It is instilled in us from birth. We are raised with this one goal in mind: to be mothers. I mean, what other purpose could we possibly serve in this world? We are women, after all. We are maternal. We are motherly. But apparently, I am not.

I didn't want to have children. That was a phrase that often left my mouth when I was young. "I don't want kids." The statement that somehow invites listeners in, automatically giving them permission to respond: "You're still young! You'll change your mind once you get older!"

My mind didn't change. Not when I turned twenty-six and my friends politely reminded me that my biological clock was ticking. Not when I took the pregnancy test and saw the double pink lines. It didn't change when I felt my stomach expanding for nine months, growing this new formed life inside of me that I didn't ever think would be possible. My mind didn't change when she came out of me, slimy and screaming, demanding my undivided attention at all times.

Some women just aren't meant to be mothers. But that doesn't mean I killed my child.

Let me rewind.

CHAPTER ONE

A FTER Cordelia Waters Thursday May 18, 2016

I'm lying on the couch in the living room, drifting in and out of consciousness. I smell the burning candle from the kitchen, filling the air with artificial apricot. I'm comfortable, which is rare considering our couch is anything but. I maneuvered my body in between the cushions, my legs dangling over the edge. I'm relishing in this tranquil feeling of serenity, which seems to be an uncommon occurrence these days.

I'm awakened to the sound of Weston calling my name. At first I don't move. I simply keep my eyes closed and hope he finds whatever he's looking for. He yells again, and it's then that I realize his tone is that of panic. I open my eyes and sit up quickly, my pupils adjusting to the bright light. Weston rushes into the room, his jacket still on from work, and comes to an immediate halt upon seeing me.

"Where is she?" he asks, catching his breath. My lovely husband, standing there demanding answers. I stare at him for a moment, trying to decipher his words. "Who?" "Emerald! Who do you think?" "In her crib." "No, she's not." He looks around the room, then focuses his attention back on me. "Were you sleeping?" he asks, as though this has just become apparent to him. "I must have dosed off." "So you don't know where our daughter is?" "I just told you, she's in her crib." I stand up, straightening out my shirt and brushing the strands of hair out of my face. He stares at me with focused eyes, silently willing me to listen to him. "I just checked her crib, Cordelia. She's not there." It is at this moment, finally – as though my natural motherly instincts had failed before when the warning lights should have been going off – that I feel my heart sink in my chest. "What are you talking about?" I rush past him and hurry down the hallway into the nursery. I flick on the light and peer into the crib, only to discover that my husband was correct: Emerald is not there. My mind is blank and my words do not come. The thoughts in my head escape me, and I can't seem to form a proper sentence in what I intend to say. The first thing that comes out of my mouth: "She was just there!" Seeing my inception of panic allows Weston's façade to fall and turn to total chaos. "Call nine-one-one," he turns and heads back towards the living room. I pry my eyes away from the vacant crib and watch him disappear down the hall. "You think somebody took her!?" "I don't know, Cordelia!" he yells back. "She's a six-month-old baby. Where the hell else could she have gone?"

Unsure of whether it's the sharpness of his words, or the fact that what was just a moment of uncertainty has now turned into a full reality of mayhem, I start to cry. My husband does not approach me or comfort me in any way. I head back to the living room and he rushes past me towards the kitchen to grab the landline. I hear him dial, wait, then say: "My daughter is missing."

He tells the 911 operator what happened – he came home from work, found me sleeping on the couch, and went to check on Emerald. But when he looked in her crib, she wasn't there. He recites our address and pleads for them to hurry. He hangs up the phone and it's silent for a moment before I hear him start to cry. It's always difficult hearing the one's closest to you cry, especially men, who pride themselves in being strong and shedding no tears. I've only seen Weston cry on one or two occasions. He's trying to be quiet, trying to accomplish one of those silent cries in hopes that I won't hear. But I do.

I walk over to him. "She was just there." He raises his head and looks at me. It is then that I see the anger in his eyes. He turns his head and walks into the other room. "Weston!" I follow after him. "Save it, Cor." I catch up to him and reach for the back of his shoulder, gently. He turns around to face me, that look still in his eyes. "I'm sorry!" I cry. "For what? Losing our daughter? Or... is there something else you're sorry for? Did some stranger come into our home and take her? Or did her own mother do something to her?" "What are you talking about!?" "You know you have issues, Cordelia! You have ever since she was born." He pauses, catching his breath. "Did you snap? Did her crying finally get to you? What the hell did you do?" I flinch backwards, struck by his accusations. More tears stream down my face. "I didn't do anything to her! You know me, Wes!" "Do I?" "Of course!" I cry. "Believe me!" "Yeah, well that's a little difficult, given the circumstances." "You honestly think that I would hurt my own daughter?" My heart is aching inside my chest. I'm offended and mortified all at once, not only for the fact that my husband is accusing me of hurting our daughter, but because at one point during these past six months, his words may have actually made sense. "I don't know what you'd do. Honestly. And that frightens me."

I stare at him, unable to say anything else. I hear the sirens blaring in the distance. They're getting closer. I step away from him and walk back into Emerald's room. Perhaps I'm hoping that if I check once more, she will be there. That we somehow missed her the first time and this was one huge misunderstanding. Oh what a pleasant surprise that would be. But when I look down into the crib, it's still empty.

CHAPTER TWO

B EFORE Cordelia Waters November 13, 2015

I was a devilish child. The phrase 'never judge a book by its cover' could be accurately applied to my life. Everyone I knew was hoodwinked by the white blonde hair and Bambi eyes, thinking I was this innocent angel who could do no wrong. That couldn't have been farther from the truth.

I used to roam around the neighborhood with a hardy look of malice in my eyes. To this day I'm still not able to pinpoint the exact origin to the madness that was in my soul. While the rest of my friends played contently with their dolls, I had a craving for trouble and conflict. I got high off the fumes of disaster and punishment. Something about the feeling of rivalry and revolt left me almost intoxicated, constantly wanting more.

I would plan out events in my little pink diary, noting which of the neighborhood children were going to suffer the wrath of little Cordelia each week. Thinking about it now, perhaps it was my looks that were the core driving force to my behaviour. I was small and petite, the subject of ridicule, the one easily pushed around. When you're small and a female, people assume things about you – that you're gentle and kind. That you can do no harm. I guess I wanted to prove that I was more than just a stereotype.

My family lived in a rural-suburban neighborhood where everyone was accessible and easy to locate if you needed them – usually lounging on the front porch with a drink or two in hand. In the summer time, our house was the meeting place for stray cats. Numerous felines would wander into our yard, squat out for a while, breed, reproduce. My emotions were fairly neutral towards the strays. I didn't despise them, but I wasn't fond of them either.

This one day, a stray who we called Tim-Tam, had somehow made his way into our house. He was an orange tabby – a brave little thing. The rest of the clan remained outside, afraid of the trouble that loomed if they dared enter our home. But like I said, Tim-Tam was a brave one. He was clearly oblivious to the lack of authority he possessed. He strutted inside and perched himself on our kitchen table. I remember walking into the kitchen one afternoon only to lay my eyes on the orange tabby sitting there, staring at me. Squinting his beady eyes at me in defiance, it was a show down, determining who possessed more power. I must admit, I had to give the cat some credit for challenging me out of all people. Me! The one relatives referred to as the craziest of the Cruz children.

After moments of periphery battle, I lunged forward and grabbed him, his tiny body struggling as I held him tight. His claws lurched towards my face, aiming for my eye. I swung open the door to the backyard, and in one quick motion, threw him into our little blow up pool that my mother would set up for us kids every summer. It wasn't a large pool, but it was deep enough for Tim-Tam to go in head first and spasm out just as fast. I remained standing at the door as I watched, smiling. I was the victorious one that day. Until my mother called me into the kitchen later that night to ask why the pool was leaking.

Over the years, I found that I could get away with anything. The platinum blonde hair – inherited from my mother – and large brown eyes were often the key in the hole to my getaway. I could manipulate people so well that they didn't even realize they'd been manipulated. My parents thought I was an angel. I was their only daughter, born between two rowdy and obnoxious boys.

Liam, the youngest, shares a particularly similar aesthetic to me. Both of us full heads of blonde and eerily similar facial structures. However, contrasting to my dark brown eyes, Liam inherited my father's deep shades of blue. Their eldest child, Colton, did not look like us at all, with his dark brown hair, skinny chin, and brown eyes. It was an ongoing joke between Liam and me that Colton was adopted since he didn't resemble us in any way. My father, maybe a little. The facial structure and the hair, really. But other than that, people often didn't realize he was our sibling. Anytime the three of us went anywhere, it was obvious to everybody in the room that Liam and I were brother and sister. No questions asked. Colton, on the other hand, was not as obvious to pinpoint to our family.

I often took advantage of my fortunate genetics and used my angelic face to fuel my agenda and get what I wanted. The newest My Little Pony set was only a tilted head and batted eyelashes. Renovating my room in the ninth grade; getting my own car when I was sixteen. It all came without protest or consideration. Little did they know that beneath the cute face and polite enquiries was a determined girl seeking equilibrium and vengeance.

Growing up with two brothers, I was rough-housed on the daily. Most of our fights ended in a scraped chin or a bruised cheek. While the boys took their aim through punches, and settled scores by yelling and tackling each other, I took a different approach to getting even. Before I knew better – how to get revenge, that is – I would fight dirty. I'd throw pens at their face, aiming for the eye. I'd kick them where I knew it would hurt. I'd pinch their nose so hard that I drew blood. Eventually, I graduated from rough-housing to scheming. Like the time I poured drain cleaner in Colton's drink. He must have smelt the toxic chemicals radiating from the glass because he immediately dumped it down the sink and never drank from an open cup again, always carefully eyeing me when I entered a room.

Living with boys taught me to be tough. I didn't want to be weak, allowing kids at school to push me around and have their way. When I was in high school, there was this girl named Lacy. You know the type – pretty, popular, adored by all of the boys. One morning at school, Lacy approached me to inform me that my outfit looked like that of a welfare child. While she stood there with her hand resting on her jutted out hip, a sly smirk on her face, I remained silent, my mind swirling with possibilities. Later that day during gym class, I snuck into the change-room and gathered up all of her clothes. I flushed them down the toilet, which obviously did not go down smoothly, clogging up in the center and bobbing up and down as water filled to the brims and spilled over. It's safe to say that Lacy didn't bother me again after that.

My mother was a stay-at-home mom who spent her days cooking and cleaning. A beautiful woman who I admired at most, but didn't want to be remotely similar to. If anything, her stay-at-home-mom ways inspired me to work harder in school and find a career that would support me financially, all on my own, without a husband to rely on. I was independent. I could thrive on my own. And with the toughness from my brothers, and lack of a strong-headed female role model in the home, I was well on my way to becoming everything I ever dreamed of.

After four years at university and two years in a Master's program, I officially had a Bachelors in Arts and Science, and a Masters in Computer Science, which then proceeded me to my career as IT Manager at District Systems Inc.

I oversee projects, analyze market trends, increase profitability for the company, and develop communication strategies with other networks. It's perfect for me, due to the fact that I'm a perfectionist Type-A. Extremely organized, ambitious, relish being in charge. Something I thrive in. Not to mention the pay, which is more than reasonable. Weston brings in over a hundred and eighty grand a year, and I bring in one twenty, so we're more than comfortable, financially.

Weston. We met during my first year at Northwestern. He was in the third year of his undergrad, and would ultimately move on to four more years at Marquette to receive his PhD and DMD. Though I was a mere freshman and he was a junior, we clicked instantly, and before I knew it, we were head over heels for each other. We married in 2012, just shortly after he graduated from Marquette. I was twenty-five, he was twenty-seven. Compared to my parents, twenty-five was late to be getting married. They were married and expecting Colton at the age of twenty-one. Weston opened his orthodontic practice a year later. Lucky for me, his practice is only a twenty minute drive from our home here in Davenport, so he makes it home by five o'clock for dinner every night.

It's interesting how drastic things seem to change over the years. Such as, how my parents married straight out of high school and celebrated my mother's pregnancy, looking forward to the day their first child arrived into the world. Today, sixteen-year-old's are still getting knocked up, but they either get an abortion or remain frowned upon until that child turns six and nobody really remembers how old the mother was when they were born.

Some couples wait until they're in their late twenties, early thirties – a time they are most certain and one hundred percent ready – before settling down and preparing for their first child. I turned twenty-eight in July. I would presume I'm at the prime age now; the age that most women would look at me and decide, well she's ripe and fertile, might as well make a baby!

Twenty-eight is a perfect age. Not too young and irresponsible. Not too old and dried out. Weston and I have a healthy marriage – four years next June – and a more than steady income to provide for a baby or six.

But you see, that's not my problem. Age, income, fertility – none of those are an issue for me. My issue is that I don't want children. I don't want a baby. Period. Only thing is, my belly is bursting and my due date is tomorrow.

CHAPTER THREE

A FTER Cordelia Waters Thursday May 18, 2016

It's been thirty minutes since we discovered the empty crib. The police arrived almost immediately, asking us dozens of questions, moving through our home with a fine-tooth comb. There are three officers here: two men and a woman. My husband had them convinced from the get-go that I may have had something to do with our daughter's disappearance. 'My wife suffered from severe postpartum psychosis.' 'She's not one hundred percent stable.' 'She doesn't remember what happened.' I may have had mixed feelings about Emerald in the past, but all those thoughts were diminished months ago. I'm better now. I would never harm another living being, especially my own child.

That's when they started looking at me peculiarly, walking on egg shells around me, ensuring they spoke in gentle tones. As if I'm some lunatic who might break at any moment. They can believe Weston's desperate accusations, but I know the truth. Someone came in here and took my child. But I understand. They have to do their job. Even if that includes interrogating me.

He tells me it's just standard questioning, but I know that the seed of suspicion has been planted in all of their minds. Rowan Ashby, that's the officer's name. He has dark brown eyes and looks at me like I'm a small bird. He begins by asking me to recite everything that I did today, right up until the moment that Weston came home and found the empty crib. I scan through my memory, racking my brain for all of the details. It proves more difficult than I'd like, but I don't mention this. Instead, I take deep breaths, fold my hands in my lap, and attempt to speak as clearly as I can without letting my voice falter, revealing the illusion of my confidence.

He writes everything down, nodding his head in sync with my words. Once I'm done rehearsing the events of my Thursday, he goes on to ask if I've been feeling stressed lately. I suppress the voice inside that wants to laugh and say: Stress is an understatement. Do you have children, Officer Ashby? He looks too young to have kids. He can't be more than twenty-three. Twenty-four at most. He asks me what I do for a living. How long Weston and I have been married. When did we move into this house. Do I get enough sleep at night. Do I have any ill thoughts towards my daughter. I try not to laugh.

Once he's finished his questions, he leaves me to sit on the couch alone, but not without his weary eyes trailing behind. I watch the scene unfold in front of me. A crime scene unit has been dispatched and is now analyzing the house. A man in a navy blue jacket asks me if we have a place to stay tonight. He explains that this is now a crime scene, and they need to gather evidence. I flinch at the word crime scene. My eyes wander to the front door, where another navy jacket is knelt down, fixated on the door handle, determining if it was tampered with.

Minutes that feel like hours pass, and when I blink, nothing has changed. I check the time: six-fifteen. I spot Officer Ashby standing in the corner speaking with my husband. I'm sure Weston isn't getting the third degree that Rowan Ashby kindly delivered to me.

―――――

I'm distracted, staring at the wall, a vacant look on my face, when a man in a dark grey suit approaches and asks if he can have a seat. I nod. The only thought going through my mind is the colour of the wall. It's a dark shade of green. Hideous, really. I don't know why Weston chose that colour. I don't know why I agreed to even let him choose that colour. But that's what marriage is about, compromise and acceptance.

He introduces himself as Detective Gerard Sullivan. "Would you like me to get you anything to drink? Tea? Coffee?" he speaks softly and his eyes are sympathetic. His disposition is a one-eighty from Officer Ashby. "Coffee." I say. "Coffee would be nice. Two creams, please."

He nods and takes off towards the kitchen. Navy jackets are filling the house, sealing off Emerald's room with yellow tape, searching for fingerprints and any sign of intruders. Another one is posted by the front door. He's waiting for someone to check the door handle for fingerprints. All he's going to find is mine and Weston's. Unless whoever took my daughter was stupid enough to leave obvious evidence behind, which I highly doubt. A stranger off the street didn't just stumble across our house, come inside, and take my child. This abduction was properly executed and well thought out. Diabolical.

The detective returns and places the mug in front of me on a coaster. I stare at it for a minute before picking it up, allowing the heat to warm my hands, and take a small sip. "If you're up to it, I'd like to ask you some more questions," he says, removing a small notepad from his pocket. I eye the notepad, watching the way he fumbles with it in his hands. I look up and meet his eyes. "Sure. Yes, of course. Anything." He nods and clears his throat. "Where were you when your husband realized your daughter was missing?" "I was on the couch. I had just woken up." "How long were you unconscious for?" "I'm not sure. I guess I must have dozed off around.... Two-thirty, maybe? That's when she went down for her nap." The lie comes easier than I imagined. The truth is, I don't remember what time I fell asleep. I don't remember anything. "So that leaves two and a half hours of unaccounted time," he says as he writes in his notebook. "Approximate time of disappearance can be placed anytime between three and five o'clock," he continues to write, then looks up and meets my gaze. "And you were home all day?" "Yes. I work from home on Tuesdays and Thursdays." "Can anyone verify that?" "My boss," He writes something down. "Who looks after Emerald on days when you're at the office?" "Her nanny – Marcia." Mar-See-Ah. I look up at him. "You think she had something to do with this?" "We have to gather information from everyone involved in you and your daughter's life. That includes friends, family members, babysitters... You understand, yes?" I nod my head. "Why were you asleep when your husband came home?" He revisits the topic of my unconsciousness. I stare at him, unsure how to answer without revealing how aggravated I truly am by that question. "I was tired," I say. "I've been working a lot and looking after Emerald." "My intentions are not to offend you, Mrs. Waters," he says, sensing my irritation. "We have to cover all bases. Look at the big picture." He pauses, looks down, flips another page over, writes something. He looks back up at me. "If I could continue," "Sorry," He clears his throat. "Have you been feeling stressed or under pressure lately?" I bite my tongue. I know what's coming next. Did you have a mental breakdown, Mrs. Waters? Did you snap and kill your daughter, Mrs. Waters? I stare at him, trying to remain neutral. "No more than usual. Just the usual work stuff." "And caring for Emerald?" "What about it?" "Has it been difficult for you lately? I'm sure it's hectic being a new mother," he says, but doesn't mention the postpartum. I exhale quietly. "Yes, it is difficult at times. But I can handle it. I'm a tough woman. I've always been able to handle myself, detective." He jots something else down in his notepad and I discretely try to strain my neck to see what he's writing. He looks up at me and I shift backwards. "How has your husband been lately? Under any stress from work?" "No. Not that I know of. He loves his job." I take the detective's advice and try not to be offended by his words, even though I know every question has an assumption. I know my husband wouldn't hurt our baby girl. "To your knowledge, does anyone have a grudge against you or your husband? Anyone who might want to do this to you?" "No. Not that I can think of. We're friendly people. We have barbeques in the summer with the neighbours and attend staff Christmas parties. We don't have many close friends, but the ones we do have would never do anything like this." "How about any debts? Money loans? Anything you can think of that someone perhaps might have against you?" "No. We don't owe anyone money. We pay all of our bills on time." He nods and writes something down. "Would you mind giving me the contact information for anyone who's been in or around the house in the past few months? The nanny, neighbours, family, friends; anyone you can think of. We just want to check everything out, ask some questions, and find your daughter, all right, ma'am?" "Yes, of course." I say. He flips the notepad open to a new page and hands it to me. I look up at him. "Everyone?" "Everyone you can think of."

———

Three hours later and I'm sitting on a cold hotel bed. Perhaps the bed is warm, but it's me who is cold. I need to shower – let the steam fill up the room, the scalding water run down my back. We should be able to return home in the morning, but until then, our house is a crime scene. The police have both of our cellphones tapped in the event that we get a ransom call. It's a likely possibility. Whoever did this knows we have money. Perhaps that's all they want.

Before leaving, Detective Sullivan assured me that they would do everything in their power to find Emerald as soon as possible. He promised to call me immediately if they found anything. There's something about him that makes me feel reassured, safe. Perhaps it's the way he speaks to me like

I'm an actual human being. He's giving me a chance to tell my side of the story. The other officers already have their preconceived judgements.

Weston has been pacing the suite, sporadically crying since we arrived. It's so hard for me to hear him cry and know there's nothing I can do to stop the pain he feels. But what bothers me even more is the fact that I'm in a better state than he is. I should be broken – devastated. Devoted mother, heartbroken at the bare thought of her child missing. But for some reason – a reason I don't want to think about – I'm not as distraught. I'm holding myself together fairly well. Not to say that I'm not worried, because, hell, I am. I'm so worried that whoever did this is going to kill Emerald. Maybe they already have. The thought alone makes me ill. Emerald is gone. Our six-month-old infant was abducted. There is no positive way to look at this situation.

But there's this tiny part inside of me – a part that I don't like to look at too often – that feels a sense of… relief. Is that horrible to admit? I'd be lying to myself if I said otherwise.

I love my daughter. But I can't help but feel a reprieve from her absence. As though my prayers from all those months ago have finally been answered.

CHAPTER FOUR

B EFORE Cordelia Waters November 14, 2015

It happened today: I gave birth. Right on time, just as expected.

I woke up feeling normal, no pains or aches in my stomach. I ate breakfast and even went for a walk. Weston took the day off in advance, just in case. Well, it's a good thing he did. Around two o'clock I started experiencing sharp pains. Shortly after that, my water broke. I was standing in the kitchen, bending over in the fridge and reaching for the carton of milk when the water spilt onto the floor. Weston, who was sitting at the kitchen table reading the newspaper, jumped up and ran to me. He grabbed my overnight bag that was already packed in our bedroom, and off we went to the hospital.

When the contractions began, I thought I may die. Never in my life have I experienced something so excruciating. As though all of my organs were being ripped out from inside of me. I was screaming and crying, biting towels, clenching onto Weston's hand as hard as I could. Multiple times he had to let go and shake it out just so I didn't break it.

She finally arrived at 7:24 p.m., screaming and crying, much like I was after seven hours of labour. She was pink and slimy, an alien creature. The initial emotion that flooded my body was relief. Thank God that thing is out of me!

They informed me that she was a girl. The nurse wiped her off, wrapped her in a blanket, pink, obviously, and handed her to me. I didn't extend my arms in anticipation or excitement. They simply placed her tiny body into my arms, and I accepted her, as though I didn't really have a choice. I looked down at her face, her plump little face, and my initial thought was: newborns are not attractive at all, with their red skin and scrunched up, wrinkly faces. My next thought was: what the hell do we name her?

We decided on Emerald. Prior to her birth, Weston and I had compiled a list of baby names that we liked. We chose not to know the sex of the baby – wanted it to be a surprise. It sure was! We had two columns: boy's names and girl's names. After months of deciding on one name, then changing it to another, we had finally narrowed it down to four names. For a boy, we chose Christian (Weston's grandfather) and Isaac. For a girl, we chose Lillian (after my mother, Lily), and Emerald. After Weston held her for the first time, he looked at me, tears brimming in his eyes, and said, "She's our Emerald." And that was it. That was her name. He didn't ask me if Emerald was the right name. He just stated it, as though it was a predetermined fact. I didn't argue, though. I liked Emerald. We both did. So when he said Emerald, it just stuck. And that became her name.

I'm still lying in the hospital bed. The doctors told me to rest and get some sleep tonight. Emerald is in the room next door with the other babies. Weston keeps going to visit her. Then he comes back and tells me the most arbitrary things, like: She wiggled her toes! She latched onto my pinky finger! She opened her mouth and made a funny sound! I just smile and tell him to stay in there with her. He insists on switching back and forth to see the both of us.

At one point, he brings me a cup of orange juice and I tell him to go home and get some sleep since it's almost midnight. He insists on staying here with me, but I know he won't be able to sleep comfortably in the chair. Finally, he agrees, promising to be back in a couple of hours.

Sitting alone in the hospital room, I begin to wonder what it will be like for her, growing up with a fall birthday. My birthday is mid-summer, so I've always associated my coming of age with warm, sunny days and swimming pools. All my life, my mother hosted pool parties for my birthday. We'd invite all the kids from school and of course all the kids who lived on our street. She'd bake a vanilla cake and decorate it with rainbow frosting, which was my favourite. We'd splash around in the kitty pool, taking turns jumping in one at a time. That's all I remember, really. Sunshine and swimming pools. It's great having a summer birthday. Something to look forward to once school is over. Emerald will have a fall birthday. So close to the Christmas season. I hope her birthday isn't forgotten about. November fourteenth. What zodiac sign is that? Scorpio? I think it's Scorpio.

As I'm drifting off to sleep, my mind is filled with eagerness and exhaustion. It still feels surreal to me. The fact that I just gave birth to a human being. I created a life. Who would have thought? Me, a mother. I never thought I'd see the day. And I think that's why it feels so strange. Perhaps this is just one big dream, and tomorrow morning I'll wake up and tell Weston, and he'll laugh and say, You, pregnant? I don't think so.

But this is not a dream. And I'm not going to wake up laughing. This is real life. This is my reality now. I'm a mother. I am now responsible for the life of that little creature in the other room. And that scares the hell out of me.

CHAPTER FIVE

AFTER Cordelia Waters Friday May 19, 2016

My cellphone rang at six a.m., which didn't disturb me considering I was up at five. I didn't sleep all night, tossing and turning, chest filled with fear and anxiety, worrisome thoughts consuming my brain. The police officer on the phone informed me that the preliminary investigation of the house was complete and we could return when we were ready.

I wake Weston, gather our things – which is just pajamas and our toothbrushes – and drive home. Not ten minutes of being home, Weston grabs his car keys and leaves. He has barely said four words to me since last night. Now he's going to drive the streets and search for our daughter. As though he'll simply find her, sitting on someone's front lawn, waiting for him. At least I've come to grips with this reality; Weston is in a state of denial. And blame. His mind is impartial to what he thinks happened to our daughter. He wants to believe that she's out there somewhere, and going to search for her is the hope that drives him. But then there's his other suspicion, and that would be me. And since there's nothing he can do here, he leaves.

———

After staring at the wall for another hour, then managing to scrape my clothes off and take a shower, I sit on the couch that faces the front window and wait, gripping my mug of coffee between my palms. I don't know what it is exactly that I'm waiting for. Something, anything.

A little while later, I see a police car pull in front of the house and I jump up, nearly spilling my third cup of coffee. I steady myself, carefully placing the mug on the table, then walk to the front door and swing it wide open, just as the officer is starting up the walkway. My chest tightens and I brace myself for whatever news he is here to tell me.

"Mrs. Waters," he says once he sees me standing there eagerly. "May I come in?" My heart pounds through my chest. "Did you find her? Is she alright?" "I'm sorry, ma'am, no news yet. I just need to come in and go over a few things with you." I nod my head and step backwards, opening the door so the man can come inside. My mind fixates on the word yet. "I'm Officer Matt Holden, the lead officer on this case." He extends his hand. I reach forward and give it a light shake. "I'm very sorry for what you're going through." "Thank you," I manage to say. I turn and lead him into the living room. "Would you like anything to drink? Coffee?" "I'm alright, thanks," he sits down and makes himself comfortable in the chair. I stare at him for a moment, unsure what to do with my hands, then I sit down on the couch adjacent to him. "Did Detective Sullivan check out any of the names I gave him?" I ask eagerly. "That's actually why I'm here. I just wanted to discuss the details of your personal life; your close family and friends," "Okay." He clears his throat and readjusts in his seat. "So on the list here," he pulls it out and holds the paper in front of him. "You only listen about a dozen names. Is that all of the people who have been here in the last few months?" "Well, people who matter. What did you want me to write, the mailman?" "Anyone, Mrs. Waters. At this moment, everyone is a person of interest." He pauses for a moment. "In cases of child abductions, the most common perpetrator is usually someone known by the family." I swallow, even though my mouth is dry. "Alright," I say. He taps his pen against his leg, staring at me. "Um, well, other than those few people I wrote down, not many others come by. Weston is always busy at work. He runs his own orthodontic practice, you know," "Yes, he told us." I smile flatly. "So he's usually working, and I'm either here or working. We see friends sometimes, but... not as often as we used to." "What do you mean?" "Before Emerald was born. We used to go out more often. But then afterwards..." He nods his head and writes something down. "Detective Sullivan is actually going over shortly to speak with your nanny – Mrs. Mendoza – and her husband." My heart leaps. "Why? Did something happen?" "No, ma'am. Mrs. Mendoza is a secondary care-taker for your daughter, so it's imperative that we speak with her. Perhaps she knows something that may help us in the investigation." "You may want to speak with Ainsley then as well. I wrote her on the list." I nod my head towards the paper in his hands. "She's our part-time sitter for weekends and other occasions." He jots something down. "How often does she sit for you?" "Only once in a while. If Wes and I want to go out for dinner. Or if we both get held up at work one day and Marcia needs to leave." "Alright, I'll make sure that someone speaks with her." I nod my head and he begins reading the list aloud. "Savannah, Colton, Dave, Marissa, Jonah, Lily – those are your parents, yes?" "Yes." "And, Weston's parents are..." "Madeline and Carlisle," "Why is it that you didn't write their names?" "They haven't been by in a while," "But they are primary family. You need to include everyone." He doesn't hide his annoyance. "Is there anyone else that you failed to include?" I think for a moment, trying to ignore the insolence in his tone, then shake my head. "Not that I can think of." "Who is Savannah?" "My friend. From work." "Does she come by often?" "Um, sometimes. We usually grab coffee once a week, before work. We go out on weekends occasionally, but she doesn't drop by here too often, unless she's picking me up or needs to get something." He nods and writes something in the notepad. "Can you tell me about your husband?" "What do you mean?" "Tell me about the two of you. How you met, what he's like..." "I already told you, he runs his orthodontic practice, we married four years ago, he loves Emerald. So much. She's his pride and joy. What else do you want to know?" "How did the two of you meet?" "What is the relevance?" He sighs. "I'm just trying to get an idea. See the larger picture here." I bite my lip, then nod my head, thinking back all those years ago. "We met when I was a freshman at Northwestern. He was in his third year." "What were you studying?" "I did a Bachelors of Art and Science before getting my degree in Computer Science." "And he was going for..." "His undergrad in science. He got his Masters and PhD afterwards." Officer Holden writes something down, then looks back up at me, expecting me to continue talking. "He was actually, um," I smile to myself. "He was dating another girl when we first met. Hannah, I think her name was. But Weston and I had a psychology class together – don't ask me what I was doing taking a third year psych class in first year. But," I smile again. "We became really good friends and something more grew out of it. Eventually he broke up with Hannah and we started dating." "So the two of you were involved while he was still dating her?" I'm taken back by his question. "Yes," I pause, feeling the warmth come to my cheeks. I'm embarrassed. Guilty. "I never intended to be one of those homewreckers. But... we don't choose who we love. Or when. And sometimes it's inconvenient. That's all I have to say." He writes something down and I lean in, trying to read what he's writing. He looks up at me and subtly pulls the notepad closer to his lap. "What are you writing? That I'm a homewrecker? That has absolutely no relevance to what is happening now." "Mrs. Waters, have you ever heard the saying... oh how's it go? If he will cheat with you, he will have no problem cheating on you." I stare at him, trying to analyze his words. "What are you implying?" "Has Weston ever been unfaithful? Could there possibly be another woman involved?" "No," I say without hesitation. "Weston would never cheat on me. Our marriage is perfectly fine. He loves me and he loves Emerald and he values this family. Why would you even ask such a thing?" "It's just a question, ma'am. If there are any other factors that need to be considered, we need to know." "Well there isn't. I can tell you that for certain. Weston loves me. You should focus on the neighbors. Or Weston's co-workers. Maybe they had something to do with this."

I say these words with conviction. But who am I trying to convince of this: the officer, or myself?

———

Officer Holden leaves and I can't say that I'm sad to see him go. He promises to keep me updated. He explained that they're going to talk to everyone they can: my parents, Weston's parents, our friends, coworkers, neighbours – everyone. He also informed me that they put out an Amber Alert last night, so now the public can join the search for my daughter as well.

I hope that wherever Emerald is, she's okay. Maybe this is one big misunderstanding. Maybe she's safe somewhere, in the home of a friend. Maybe someone came over and took her for a little visit to give me a break.

But that possibility seems highly unlikely. I just pray she's not in the arms of danger, locked in a room somewhere, crying for her mother.

I hope she's alive.

CHAPTER SIX

B EFORE Cordelia Waters December 5, 2015

They're calling it Postpartum Psychosis. It's the only explainable answer they have for my behaviour and feelings as of late. It all started during the first week after Emerald was born.

I knew something wasn't right from the time she was conceived. From that very moment that I held out the stick that read positive. But Weston was so ecstatic; he'd always wanted a baby. We had talked about it briefly in the past. I made it abundantly clear that I didn't want children. That my career would always come first in my life, and I planned on keeping it that way. Around the time that we found out, I had just been promoted to top ranking Project Manager, which meant higher pay and more responsibilities. The pregnancy couldn't have come at a worse time. But despite our conversations in the past, Weston never took me quite seriously. No one did. I was used to my feelings being disregarded. Oh, you're still young, you don't know what you want yet. Or, you'll change your mind. All women are meant to be mothers!

Weston felt that way as well – that I would eventually change my views on child rearing. I tried to laugh off his ignorance and politely warn him –

before he married me – that children were not in my foreseeable future. He was convinced that I'd change my mind one day. I guess he remained hopeful for that very thought.

I came out of the bathroom crying. Once I saw the pink double lines, I broke. Aware of the fact that tests can sometimes reveal false positives, I took another. And another. And they all gave me the same result: positive.

I broke down when I told Weston. But when I said the words, his eyes lit up, and I hadn't seen him look that excited since our wedding day. As I cried and expressed my protest towards the pregnancy, he reassured me that it would be okay and that he would take care of me.

You're probably wondering what happened. Most women in my situation would have gotten an abortion. Most women wouldn't have been persuaded by their husband's sweet eyes and persistent cries. But whatever strength I had on refraining from child rearing seemed to dissolve as the weeks progressed. I began feeling guilty for wanting to have an abortion. I was raised in a religious home – abortion is murder! Pro Life! – so the very thought alone, no matter how hard I tried to disregard my mother's voice in my head, just seemed wrong to me. And with that guilt, and Weston's persistence and excitement, I somehow came to the conclusion that I would keep the baby. That was my first mistake: deciding to keep an unwanted child solely for the sake of another person.

There were a number of reasons why I never wanted children. The first and foremost was that I simply had no desire. I never felt 'motherly' feelings towards anything before. I'd watched my friends gush over babies over the years, dreaming of the day they'd have their own. I'd cringe and think, God help me if I ever get knocked up. But somehow even condoms and birth control couldn't prevent my Emerald from being conceived.

Maybe I wasn't held enough as a child. My father used to tell me how much I hated being held. Said I was never much of a cuddler. Liam loved to be held, they said. Relished every minute of it. But every time they placed me on their laps or tried to hold me, I'd cry and squirm, trying to get away and be on my own.

As a teenager I despised children, though I'd never make that sentiment obvious. I babysat a lot. For neighbors, teachers, my mother's friends. I did it because I needed money. Teenagers buy a lot of things that they don't need. I'd put on a big, fake smile, get real close to the kids, tickle them, laugh with them, pick them up, anything really. Parents loved me. Said I was an angel with their children. An angel.

When the parents were out of sight, I couldn't be bothered with the children. Thank God for the television, which became the easiest escape from my duties. Sometimes I'd find myself babysitting infants who were constantly crying and needing attention. I think that was what initially put me off from the idea of having children. They were so much work. And quite frankly, I felt neutral towards their existence.

But it wasn't just infants I despised. It was any small creature, really. I'd be sitting in the backyard, lounging in the sun or playing with Colton, when one of those strays would wander in. Colton loved the cats. He'd run inside and fetch them some treats. He loved petting them and spending time with them. But I was a different story. When they'd approach me, I'd glare at them until they got the hint to leave me alone. Clearly feline intuition isn't as sharp as a humans, because they'd come over, rubbing their heads against my legs, purring.

I'm not sure why my body lacked such empathy and compassion. But regardless of that fact, I sure as hell was good at faking it. If others were around, I'd smile and pet the cats, forcing giggles each time one of their whiskers brushed against my cheek. But as soon as I was alone again, I'd push them away and head inside.

In the eleventh grade I had to take a mandatory class called Parenthood and Family Planning. That is where I witnessed my first childbirth, onscreen. It was the single most graphic and volatile thing I ever saw. After that day, I swore I would always use condoms and vowed never to get pregnant. As if it's something we can honestly control.

My friends were a bit put off by the graphic footage, especially after viewing the birth of the placenta. Yet that still didn't deter them from wanting children. My friend, Amy, would go on and on about her perfect future family and the six children she would have. Six! Who in their right mind honestly plans for six children? Some families have accidents or don't believe in contraceptives, but to actually plan for something of that capacity was downright impractical.

I specifically remember this one conversation we had where Amy was going on about the inherent need to have a baby and be a mother. To hold her baby's fresh, naked body to her chest after giving birth. I remember thinking how strange that was. I suppose she must have thought the same thing about me. I mean, what kind of woman doesn't want a baby?

The second reason I didn't want children was also simple: they were a burden, both financially and mentally. Weston and I make plenty of money, but this ideology of mine originated back when I was young and didn't know what I was going to do with my life. I knew that my parents struggled sometimes, financially, and I always pinpointed the cause of their struggles to the fact that they had three children. I vowed I would never do that to myself – put myself through that kind of financial strain for a child. I also knew from early on that I wouldn't be able to deal with a child, mentally. I witnessed first-hand the madness we brought upon our mother. She wasn't an angry person, and rarely did she raise her voice. But there were times when she would get so angry that I regretted misbehaving. She didn't deserve that.

I must admit, we were a rambunctious bunch. People would call us the Crazy Cruz Kids. But nonetheless, I knew that we weren't the only crazy children on the planet. All children are crazy. And before they are crazy, they are whiny, and smelly, and constantly needing your undivided attention. You can't leave the room without whining and tears. You can't go out for dinner without organizing a sitter. You can't live your life without worrying about another life first. I knew I wouldn't be able to do it. Right from the get-go of our marriage, I made it clear that I did not want children. But Weston didn't listen.

So now the doctors are saying I have postpartum psychosis, which is a tad bit different from postpartum depression, because I'm not just depressed – I've gone fucking mad.

It's not as simple as: 'oh this new mom thing is tough,' but rather, 'I cannot live with myself right now. I can't be a mother.'

At first it was the feeling of unease and anxiety. I felt separated from Emerald, as though I wasn't actually her mother. I kept having second thoughts, like she wasn't real, or that she wasn't mine. I would think: Did I really give birth to her? And then, I can't do this.

I question myself: why did I become a mother? How did I ever let that fucking man talk me into this? The tears fall day and night. I can't stop them, they come uncontrollably. I'll be sitting at the kitchen table eating cereal, and then I just break down, sobbing over the bowl. Because I can't fucking do this. I feel so disconnected from her. I never bonded with her like new moms are supposed to. When they cut the umbilical cord and placed her in my arms, I felt emotionless, detached. I didn't smile or cry tears of joy. I felt lost. Confused. Swimming in a sea that is constantly trying to swallow me whole.

Aside from this feeling of disconnect also comes constant feelings of aggravation and anger. I'm not a snappy person. I'm actually quite surprised how calm and patient I can be at times. But lately, all I want to do is yell and cry. A magnet falls off the fridge and I'm cursing. Someone accidentally bumps into me and my blood pressure rises. The house will be quiet, Emerald just settled down in her crib, and right before I can relax, she's screaming and crying again. And then I'm screaming and crying and ripping the hair out of my scalp. Weston has had to take the past few weeks off work so he can stay home and monitor both me and the baby.

I feel weak. I feel hopeless. The feeling that this darkness will never end. As though the light at the end of the tunnel has died out and there is no hope of it ever being lit again. That the depression and the mania have taken over my life, moved in and declared permanent residency. That's the worst part: feeling that there is no hope.

No, the worst part is that I don't even feel guilty. As though I should somehow feel bad that I'm feeling this way. That I should want my baby daughter, and be willing to do anything to get better so that I can be with her and help her.

But I can't. I don't want to. The guilt isn't there. I don't even feel bad. I couldn't care less.

Emotionless. Numb.

I don't want her. She's not my daughter. I don't want this. I never wanted this.

CHAPTER SEVEN

A FTER Cordelia Waters Friday May 19, 2016

Weston walks through the front door at 10:06 a.m. He hangs up his jacket – it's a fairly cool May morning – and walks right past me, down the hall, into our bedroom.

I follow behind him, shuffling my feet as I make my way across the floor. He stands in front of the dresser, pulling his shirt over his head. I stand there for a moment in silence, allowing my eyes to linger on his bare back. He's always been muscular. Staying in shape is a priority to Weston, even back when we first met. I remember how he'd set his alarm clock for six in the morning to go to the gym before class. The corners of my mouth curl upwards at the memory.

He looks over at me, eyes sharp as daggers, and not a moment later, turns back towards the dresser, pulls open the top drawer, and grabs a blue polo. He slips it over his head, walks to the bathroom, then shuts the door behind him. He might as well have slammed it in my face.

I'm not sure why he's so angry with me. Does he honestly believe that I did something to our daughter?

I shouldn't be surprised, really. Things haven't been the greatest with us for a while now. I'd be lying to myself if I said I wasn't to blame. He doesn't look at me the way he used to. He doesn't even touch me anymore. I can't remember the last time we had sex.

The last few months have been difficult, to say the least. But if he thinks it's been hard, he's clearly forgetting about what I've gone through. He can't continue blaming me and acting as though I'm the bad guy. I can't control what happened to me. I had a psychotic break. At least, that's what the doctors said. I honestly don't know what to think. I mean, a psychotic break makes sense. What else could explain my severe depression and excessive mood swings? I admit, I had ill feelings towards this pregnancy from the beginning. But simply not wanting a child doesn't cause extreme behavioural change... does it?

It was a psychotic break. It wasn't my fault.

I love and appreciate Weston. I know how difficult it was for him to go through all of that with me. Especially while practically raising Emerald on his own as well as taking care of me. My parents came in from Evanston and stayed in the spare room for a few weeks while things were at its worst. At least that way Weston could get some sleep and not lose his own mind while trying to help me find mine.

He was finally able to return back to work after the Christmas break in the beginning of January. That was a big deal for him, considering he owns the practice. People were continuously calling and rescheduling their appointments. But that is the sacrifice that he made for this family. I know how difficult it was for him, and he stuck by my side. For better and for worst, right? That was our worst.

But we made it past that. I got better. I began holding Emerald, feeding her – although I never could breastfeed – and spending more time with her.

With constant watchful eyes from psychologists and the support from my family, I was able to make an almost-full recovery within four months.

I've been pretty much independent these last two months. Back in the swing of things: returned to work, able to go grocery shopping and get my to-do lists accomplished. I still have to meet with Doctor Wyatt once a week. She's been helping me through the entire recovery process. Ensuring to restore my wellbeing. And she adores Emerald. I guess I'm learning to as well.

Since I'm able to work from home twice a week, I usually keep Emerald in the play pen while I work at my desk. She doesn't cry too often anymore, thank goodness. I think the crying was what drove me mad. That constant screeching sound, loud enough to break my eardrums. I don't know how most mothers handle it. We have lunch-time and play-time around noon. She likes watching cartoons. She really loves music.

Every time I look at her, I can see her resemblance to both Weston and me. Her eyes are a kaleidoscope of brown and hazel. Her hair is a light, dirty blonde. She'll be gorgeous when she grows up. A little heart-breaker in the making. I still can't believe that she's mine.

The bathroom door opens and Weston emerges, brushing right past me and heading straight for the kitchen. I follow at his feet, finally grabbing his shoulder and spinning him around. "What are you doing?" I ask, trying to hide the despair in my voice. "What do you mean what am I doing? I'm going back out there." "Why are you being so distant?" He closes his eyes and rubs his hands across his forehead. "I can't do this right now." "What did I do to make you hate me so much?" I yell. He opens his eyes and glares at me. "Do you really want me to answer that?" My throat feels tight; the feeling when a cry is coming but you have to hold it in. "Wes," I choke. "What, Cordelia? What do you want from me?" The tears form in my eyes, blurring my vision. "I'm worried about her too. I'm every bit as worried as you –" "Are you, though? Are you really? Or are you secretly relishing in this?" "How dare you!" "I'm not doing this." He turns and begins to walk away. I follow after him. "Weston!" I yell again, but he keeps walking. "You're not going to find her out there!" He stops in his tracks, then turns around slowly. "Why is that, Cordelia? Did you put her somewhere else?" "What?" I'm temporarily stunned by his question. "No, I... I just meant," I stutter. "She's not going to be out on the streets waiting for you. What is the point of continuously going out there?" "To find our daughter. At least I'm looking. That's more than you can say you're doing."

———

I sit around for an hour or two, fiddling with objects and staring out windows. I feel lost and hopeless. But worst of all, I feel betrayed by my husband. I keep going through the list of names in my head. Anyone who could be a suspect. Anyone who may know something about the whereabouts of my daughter.

This day feels surreal – like a terrible nightmare that I'm waiting to wake up from. It's the sort of thing you see in the movies. But you never think that something like that could actually happen to you. How could it?

One minute she was there, the next, she was gone. Vanished. As if into thin air. It just doesn't make any sense. None of this makes sense. Who would want to take a baby? She's innocent and has done nothing wrong. We as parents have done nothing wrong! Unless you count my psychotic break as something wrong.

Could someone be punishing me? Taking away my child because they deem me unfit? Hundreds of thoughts race through my mind, and I picture some stranger watching me from a distance, taking notes about how irresponsible and heartless I am, then sneaking into my home and taking Emerald. Could this be my fault?

The doorbell rings and breaks me from my thoughts. I feel tears on my cheeks, so I quickly wipe them away with my sleeve before heading to the front door. I turn the lock and pull the door back in one swift motion. There stands my eldest brother.

"Colton!" I nearly cry as he takes a step forward and brings me into his arms. "Hi baby sis," he breathes into my hair. "How are you holding up?" I pull away and look into his eyes. Dark brown, mirroring mine. "I'm alright," I sniffle. "Please, come in," I step back into the house and he walks in behind me. I close the door and we head to the kitchen. He takes a seat at the table and picks up the photograph of Emerald that's sitting there. The same photo I gave to the police yesterday which they photocopied by the dozens and sent to every news outlet. "Wow," he smiles at the photo. "It's been too long since I've seen her." "You don't come by enough," He looks up at me. "You're right. I'm sorry." He places the photo back down on the table. His face is somber, filled with sorrow and sympathy. "Have you spoken to mom and dad?" I ask. "They're catching the next flight back to Chicago. Should be here by tonight." I nod my head and look down at my fingers, adjusting my ring up and down. My parents go to Florida for a few months every year. Usually they go in the winter – typical snow birds –but since Emerald was due in November, they held off and decided to go later in the year. They flew out in April, once they were sure I was stable and could handle being on my own with Emerald. They haven't been gone two months and they're already having to cancel their plans and return home – always because of me. But this is out of my control. And to be quite honest, I need them now more than ever. "Have you heard from Liam?" he asks. I let my eyes linger on my hands for a moment too long. Then I look up and meet his eyes. "No." He shakes his head in annoyance. I wish my answer could have been different. "When did you speak with him last?" he asks me. I think about it. We spoke about month ago – I called him for his birthday. But I don't want Colton knowing that I've been in frequent contact with our brother who neglects to speak to him.

After the falling out a couple years ago, Liam barely speaks to either of us. He lives out in Indiana with his wife and two kids. Lianna got pregnant when she was twenty-two. They married and had a girl named Sophie. A year later she was pregnant again. A boy, Clayton. I only got to see them a couple of times before we all stopped speaking.

It's quite unfortunate, really. Siblings are supposed to be close with each other. They're supposed to see each other every Christmas and have their children grow up as best friends. It would be so nice for Emerald to see her cousins once in a while.

Colton and his wife, Jada, don't have any children. It's not something they've completely crossed off as I once did. But they said they'll consider it when the time is right. Colton is 31, the same age as Weston, and Jada is 29, so they still have some time. Perhaps if they have a baby within the next year or so, Emerald will have a best friend.

The fight was stupid. It was three years ago, when we were trying to organize my parent's estate. There are always issues when money is involved, and for some reason, Liam wasn't seeing eye-to-eye with Colton and me about the finances, our parent's inheritance, even the funeral arrangements. He was arguing with us about everything.

I didn't even want to discuss these things in the first place. But my parents had insisted, if God forbid something happened to them sooner than later, we needed to have the estate sorted out. We went into it as a family, and came out angry and fighting with one another.

It's unfortunate that Liam still hasn't moved on from this situation. He doesn't speak with us, except rarely on occasion to check in or when he needs something. Typical. He prefers to be on his own, doing his thing. He has his own family now, out there, away from all of us. And that's all he needs.

But now I need him. And regardless of our past, I wish he'd just drop everything and come be here.

"A couple of months ago," I lie as I turn around and open the fridge. "Do you want anything?" "Water is fine. Did he say how the kids are doing?" "They're good. Sophie's starting a pre-school program in the summer." I take a glass from the cupboard and pour some water in, then slide it across the counter for Colton. He grabs it and takes a sip. "He hasn't spoken to me in at least a year." He puts the glass back down. I bite my lip and tuck a stray piece of hair behind my ear. "Perhaps mom and dad will talk to him. He has to come. He should be here." Colton nods. "Yeah, well, try telling him that. He's a tough one to talk to." "Emerald is his niece. He should be here." "He hasn't even met her, Cordy. I'm sure he has other priorities." While what Colton says is true, the words still hurt. The fact that my own brother didn't even come to see me while I went through hell. It makes me realize just how fucked up our familial situation truly is. "Hey," Colton says gently when he notices that I'm on the verge of tears, yet again. "Don't let him get to you." I sniffle and shake out my head. "You're right. It's fine. Mom and dad will be here soon. And the police will find her. I know they will. They have everyone out looking for her." Colton gives me a reassuring smile. "They'll find her." He says.

At least I have one brother who cares.

CHAPTER EIGHT

AFTER Detective Gerard Sullivan Friday May 19, 2016

The child has been missing for sixteen hours. So far we have no tangible leads or any idea where the baby may be. I've dealt with a few abduction cases in my time, but not many. The crime rates are fairly low here in Davenport, which is nice considering we're only two and a half hours out from Chicago: my home and birthplace. I grew up in Hyde Park, raised by two headstrong parents, accompanied by a little sister.

I think I was inspired to become a cop due to the fact that I was immersed in a city filled with crime and deviance. My mother was a nurse and my father was an electrician, so I didn't inherit my aspirations for justice from them. I can recall being ten-years-old and playing with the kids on the street. We'd play games like Cops and Robbers. I'd insist on being the Cop so that I could chase my friends and arrest them. On all of my school assignments, when questions would arise regarding my future career, 'What do you want to be when you grow up?' I'd always write police officer. I had a knack for justice. For wanting to catch bad guys and put them away so that they couldn't hurt people anymore.

As I got older, my admiration for crime grew. I read a lot of Patterson and Doyle. It taught me about crime and mysteries. That's what I loved the most: mysteries. I enjoyed the perplexity of it all; scenarios that made me question everything, look at every angle, examine each suspect with a new mindset, see things from every perspective.

As a teenager, I was dedicated to solving crime. I'd take notes, writing down things that I found odd or conspicuous. I became obsessed with clues, following leads, and solving mysteries. I'd try to figure out which of my high school teachers were secretly dating. I'd search the neighborhood for missing dogs and cats. I became invested in putting other people's lives before my own. And that's when I knew that I had to be a detective. I wanted to solve crime and save people. Bring justice to the people who needed it.

Most crimes here in Davenport are petty things, arson and theft at most. A few times a year we get the occasional homicide or suicide, but it's not common. I've dealt with a few abductions over the years, ranging from ransom to custody disputes. Those ones piss me off the most. The fathers who don't win custody battles and the court takes their kid away from them. Then, being the geniuses they are, kidnap their own kid, have the mother worried sick, and have us putting out Amber Alerts, running around looking for them. I just don't understand how they think that will work. That everything will be okay and that everyone will just accept them as the sole guardian. It never works out that way. The father is charged or goes to prison, and the mother is reunited with her child. Men need to stop doing that.

I've seen many things in my years, but this is the first case I've worked dealing with an infant abduction. Six-months-old. I've been on the force for twenty years, as soon as I got out of college. I stayed in Chicago for a little while. There was always work needed there. But after eight tedious years of that, I needed a change, something new to occupy my time.

I transferred to Davenport in 2004. The last twelve years here have been great. No wife or kids, yet, but I'm not worried. My main focus is my job. My priorities involve bringing kids' home to their families, and making sure the citizens are safe. I think a family would have gotten in the way of that. I wouldn't have been able to fulfil my full potential of being the best dad or husband. But I've never put it out of the picture for good. Who knows, maybe I'll meet a lady sooner than later, and maybe we'll start up a family. I turn thirty-six this year, which could be seen as both old and young, depending on how you look at it. Thirty-six isn't too old to have children. I guess I'll just have find a lady who can put up with me, as well as my second marriage: my job.

I knock twice and take a step back, examining once more the photograph that Cordelia Waters gave me. Wide brown eyes stare up at me from the photograph, pleading for me to find her. She wears a pink polka dotted dress and has a tiny bow in her full head of hair. She's smiling, mid-laugh, revealing empty gums, no teeth. I try not to get attached to my cases, but it's hard not to. Staring down at this infant, my stomach twists, knowing what kind of sick people are out there.

The most common reasons for child abductions are pedophilia, sadism, and extortion. Over fifty percent of the time, the perpetrator is someone known by the victim, either a family member or relative. After that, we look to anyone close to the family – neighbors, teachers, babysitters. Rarely in these cases is it a complete stranger who abducts the child, but that does happen as well. In that case, it's usually for sexual purpose, or financial gain.

Looking at the Waters' situation, my initial thoughts were that it has to be someone close to the family. The abduction was executed too concisely for a stranger to come up with. They would have to know a lot of information about the Waters', such as Cordelia's work schedule, which is peculiar considering she was working from home yesterday. People don't usually come into homes and abduct children in broad daylight. No, this was planned.

Whoever took Emerald knows the family, knows that they have money, knows the schedule of their work and day-to-day lives. I wouldn't be surprised if this was motivated by financial gain and the perp is looking to hold the baby for ransom, perhaps get some money out of them. However, it's been sixteen hours since the abduction, so if the perp is going to make a ransom call, it's going to be soon.

Then there's the other scenario: that it could be someone close to the family who is delusional or suffers from mental illness. Perhaps they saw what kind of state Cordelia has been in over the past few months and wanted the child for themselves. People like that believe that they deserve someone else's child.

There is, of course, the incontestable third scenario: that the perp is right under our noses as we speak. The possibility that Cordelia did something to that child. And in that case, we're just running around chasing false leads. Am I foolish for believing her when she says that she's innocent?

Of course not. I've been doing this far too long to be that naïve. I'm a good detective. I check out all possibilities and narrow down what I find. I'm giving her the benefit of the doubt, and quite frankly, I don't think she did it. If she was planning on getting rid of her child, why not do it months ago when she was going through the postpartum psychosis? Why wait until now?

Going with my instinct – that it is someone close to the family – I have to start with anyone and everyone who has stepped foot in that house over the past six months. And the woman I'm starting with happens to step foot in that house quite often – three times a week, to be exact.

The door swings open to reveal a short woman, dark brown hair, olive skin, staring at me.

"Mrs. Mendoza?" I ask. She looks taken back, like she wasn't expecting me. "Yes...?" "Good morning ma'am, I'm Detective Sullivan, from the Davenport Police Department." I flash my badge. "Would you mind if I come in for a moment to ask you a few questions?" She stands there for a moment, staring at my badge, studying it. "What is this regarding?" "The disappearance of Emerald Waters." Her expression drops and she meets my eyes. "Emerald is missing?"Cordelia hasn't told her. "I'm afraid so. Would you mind if I come in?" She nods her head silently, opening the door and allowing me to enter her home. She leads me to the living room. It's a quaint little place, not much too it. Already I can ball-park their income, by the size of the house and the condition of their front lawn. The sofa is a dark red/pinkish colour, and the coffee table that sits in front looks like its falling apart. She offers me a seat on the couch, then sits down on the chair that is beside it. "I didn't even know Emerald was missing," she says quickly. She looks flushed. "When did this happen?" "She was abducted yesterday, somewhere between the hours of three and five in the evening. Do you mind if I ask you some questions?" "You think I had something to do with this? Because I can assure you –" "Ma'am," I say slowly. "You are the child's secondary caretaker – I am not accusing you of anything. I just need you to answer some questions for me. Standard protocol. Can you do that for me?" She nods, the look of concern growing on her face. I remove the notepad from my pocket. "Let's just get this out of the way first, so we can cross you off," I start. "Where were you yesterday afternoon? Between three and five p.m.?" I hold the pen steady in my hand. "Um," she thinks for a moment. "I was at the Laundromat with Steven. He can confirm this with you." "Steven is your husband?" "Yes." I write this down, then look back up at her. "Can anybody else account for you being there? Any customers come in?" "Most likely. It's always busy on Thursdays" "Alright, I'm just going to need to confirm this. Security footage or customer alibi will do." "Alibi? So you do think I'm involved!" "Mrs. Mendoza, I just need to eliminate you so that we can find the person who did this. It is crucial that we confirm everyone's whereabouts at the time of the disappearance. You understand this, don't you? Having children of your own?" She nods her head. "Yes. You're right, I'm sorry. I can get something to you as soon as possible. Although we don't currently have surveillance cameras at the shop. They broke a couple months ago." I write this down as well. I don't think the nanny is our abductor. But it's always good to ensure an alibi, which she will need. "So tell me what it's like working for the Waters'. Do you have a good relationship?" "Yes. Yes of course. I adore Cordelia and Weston. They're like family to me. And so is Emerald. Oh that poor precious baby. You've got me worried sick." Her face scrunches up and she look like she might cry. She takes in a gust of air, then continues. "I've only been employed by them for the past few months. It was shortly after, um, Cordelia's illness that they hired me to come in part time. I would come in on days when Cordelia's doctor would be there, trying to work with her and get her better. I would stay with baby Emerald. We'd play games, watch TV, sing songs. She's a beautiful child. Looks just like her mother. It was about a month or so later that Cordelia was stable enough to return to work. But she only does three days in the office, and the rest at home." "Which is where she was yesterday, yes?" "Yes. Which means I don't go over on Tuesdays and Thursdays." "What time do you usually go over?" "Eight-forty-five." "Is that what time Cordelia leaves for work?" "Yes. I always make it there a bit early, just to give her some extra time." I write this down. "Do you know if the Waters' have any enemies? Anyone who may want to hurt Emerald or the family in any way?" She shakes her head quickly. "No, no. Nobody. Cordelia and Weston are lovely people, really. They have always treated me like family. They don't have too many friends, well, at least many that I'm aware of. The last few months have been an adjustment period for their family. So I guess seeing friends and having company hasn't been one of their main priorities." I write this down as well. "So no one you can think of? No one suspicious hanging around the house or anything?" "No. I've only answered the door a handful of times while there. Usually it's the delivery man or one of Cordelia's friends or doctors dropping something off." She pauses for a moment, seeming to get lost in a thought. "Oh, now that I think of it," she pipes up. "This is probably irrelevant, but about two weeks ago a woman came to the house looking for Weston. I think her name was... Rose. Or Rosella? Something like that." "A woman? Did she say what she wanted?" "She seemed a bit surprised to see me, actually. Peeked her little head in and said she was looking for Weston. I told her he was at work. She laughed modestly, as though she'd forgotten. She thanked me then left. That was it. I never thought anything of it. I assumed she was a friend of the Waters'." "Did you ask him about this?" "Yes, I mentioned it once he got home from work. He said he had no idea." "Okay," I say, writing this down as quickly as I can. Rosella. "I'll talk to Mr. Waters about it, just to be sure. Thank you for mentioning this to me." She smiles sympathetically and nods. "Tell me about your family. How are your husband and kids?" I try to switch the focus back to her. "They're good. I have three littles, which you probably know by now. Gracie, Yovanna, and Emilio. They're very sweet, loving children. They're in school right now." "Do you and your husband make much money at the Laundromat?" Her mouth flattens into a line. "We're managing. Steven is looking for another job right now. We need some extra money for the children's schooling and such. It hasn't been easy for us." I jot down financial struggles. Possible motive for kidnap and ransom? Perhaps. But perhaps not. Do I really think the nanny took the child? No. She seems to be a genuine, sweet woman. But with financial strain, that's a possible motive. And in my career, I've learned that even the sweetest faces can have the darkest intentions.

We chat a little while longer, getting as many questions in as I can. I glance down at my watch again and see that it's a little after nine-thirty. I was planning to head back over to the Waters' and update them on the investigation, which at the moment, reveals nothing new. But nonetheless, I told Cordelia that I would keep her updated, so that is what I plan to do.

———

By the time I get back to the station, file some paper work, and talk to a few of the officers, it's nearly eleven-thirty. I shut off my computer and head for the Waters' residence.

A large Victorian bungalow, mahogany bricks, double garage with beige doors. There's a blue Honda Civic parked in the driveway. I don't recognize it from yesterday, which means someone else is here. I walk up the steps and ring the doorbell, noticing the flowers beginning to sprout in the garden. Spring time.

The door opens and Cordelia stands there eagerly, as if expecting me. I take in her appearance. She's wearing light grey track pants and a white t-shirt. Her blonde hair thrown up into a messy pony tail, her slim figure evident even through the baggy clothes she wears. Her eyes red and swollen; she's been crying.

"Any news?" she asks, hopeful at merely the sight of me. When I show up at someone's doorstep, it's either good news, bad news, or no news at all. "Nothing yet, I'm afraid. May I come in?" She opens the door wider and I step inside. There's a man sitting at the kitchen table. Our eyes meet and he stands up, walks towards me. "I'm Colton," he says once he's close enough, sticks out his hand. "Cordelia's brother," I shake it, firm grip, "Detective Sullivan." "Officer Holden was here," Cordelia says as she walks around the kitchen table and stands against the counter. "He said that someone was going to speak with Marcia?" I stand there, unsure whether to take a seat or continue standing. I decide to stand. "I was just over there, actually." "Does she know anything?" "Not really, I'm afraid. Do you or your husband know anyone by the name of Rose or Rosella?" "No, why?" "You're sure? Could Weston possibly have a co-worker by this name?" "Not that I'm aware of. Why? Who is she?" "Just something your nanny mentioned, but nothing to worry about," I say. "Anyway, Mrs. Mendoza did mention their financial troubles. Were you aware of this?" "Financial troubles?" "Yes. They've been struggling with money for a while now." "And... what does this have to do with Emerald?" "Are you and Mrs. Mendoza close?" She hesitates. "I wouldn't say close. She looks after my child. What more is there to it?" "She said you and Weston are like family," "I guess. We treat her nicely and pay her well. I appreciate her coming in and looking after Emerald." "Do you know her husband, Steven?" "No, not really. I may have met him once or twice when he was picking up Marcia. They only have one car, so when she doesn't take the bus, he drives her." "Did Steven ever meet Emerald?" She thinks for a moment. "I don't think so. I'm not really sure." "Would you say that Mr. Mendoza is, how do I put this, a determined man? He cares for his family, wants them to be safe, secure... happy?" "Well, yes, I'd assume so," she says. "Don't most fathers? I mean, I empathize for their family, I really do. I wish we could give them more. Their situation isn't the greatest." "I see," "Why are you asking me this? You think he had something to do with Emerald's abduction?" I don't want to frighten her. That's the worst thing you can do to an already-scared mother. I don't have any solid proof – just a theory, a very rudimentary theory with nothing to back me up so far. But I have to be objective. Theory goes: Steven Mendoza sees his family struggling. He knows his wife works for a well-off family with a child. Perhaps Steven believes he has a solution to their money problems after all. However, if Steven is responsible, why hasn't he made a ransom demand yet? I don't want to start pointing fingers when there is zero evidence of such a thing. For now, I will keep Cordelia in the dark while I investigate. "No need to be worried," I say. "I'm just following protocol. I will follow up on some leads I may have and I'll get back to you in a few hours." She still looks concerned, but tries to force a smile. "Alright, thank you – for everything." "Of course. I will do everything in my power to bring your daughter home."

CHAPTER NINE

B EFORE Cordelia Waters January 1, 2016

It's twenty-sixteen. The last year has flown by in a whirlwind. Except the past month, that is. It's been seeming to drag on for centuries. The constant heaviness in my chest and the weight on my shoulders makes it impossible to participate in everyday activities, let alone smile.

Doctor Wyatt came to see me today. She enjoys these visits with Emerald and me. I assume it's because she's checking on her and making sure I haven't killed myself. She told me that fifteen to twenty percent of women experience postpartum depression, which equates to approximately 600,000 women annually. Strangely, that statistic makes me feel a little bit better. Knowing that there are other women out there going through the same thing that I'm experiencing. Others who can relate to me and understand my irrational thoughts and mood swings. I'm not alone.

I take my medications every morning: Chlorpromazine and Lithium. The first is to treat the mania and psychosis, and the latter is a mood stabilizer. I'm not allowed to breast feed while taking the meds, but to be honest, I don't think I'd want to breast feed regardless. Some of the side effects of the meds consist of drowsiness, weight gain, and high blood pressure. I haven't experienced too much weight gain, but I have noticed the flabbiness that has accumulated around my stomach, even though it's only been just over a month. The one good thing about the meds is that they leave me feeling numb and emotionless. To most that would be a bad thing, feeling nothing. But when you're experiencing severe depression, anxiety, insomnia, confusion, and erratic thoughts every second of the day, simply feeling nothing is a privilege.

When I was a student at Northwestern, a girl killed herself after giving birth. I remember my friend, Margo, telling me about it one afternoon in English class. The professor was speaking loudly, going over a Shakespeare play, when Margo slipped into the seat next to me and began chirping my ear off about all the latest drama on campus. And then she stopped, I remember this very clearly, almost as if she'd seen a ghost. And then she turned to me, her face ashen. Cordy, she said, promise me you won't repeat what I am about to tell you. Promise me you won't tell anyone! I promised, of course. So she told me the story.

There was a girl on campus, whose name I can't recall because it was that long ago. Only a select few people knew she was pregnant due to how tiny she was. Skinny and small-boned. She had the baby, I guess it must have been the beginning of February, and within two weeks, she had killed herself. Overdosed on a bunch of pills. Her own mother found her lying in her bed. Just horrific.

The reason Margo even knew about this was because a friend of hers was good friends with the girl's sister, and apparently there was some speculation in the beginning that it was homicide. But the M.E ruled that out once they did a complete autopsy. It was concluded that she overdosed. They even found the suicide note a few days later, hidden under her baby's crib. I guess she couldn't handle motherhood.

Looking back now, I always thought it was so crazy that this girl killed herself because of a baby. The ignorance I once possessed. The capacity to understand something that an individual like me could never truly understand.

But it wasn't until last night, when I was lying in bed, tossing and turning as usual, that I remembered that girl and her story. And then I finally realized why she did it. I could relate to her. I know how hard it is and I know that it's even more difficult for other people to understand. They think you're just a bit upset at first. Perhaps overreacting a bit. They don't comprehend that this thing is killing you inside.

I sympathize with that poor girl who had to experience that all on her own, at such a young age. I finally understand now why she did it. And I consider that, at best, some kind of closure for her.

———

It's been a few hours since Doctor Wyatt left and Weston is asleep on the chair in the nursery after reading Emerald a story. I walk into the home office, which is just down the hall from the nursery, and slide into the computer desk. I turn on the monitor, pull up the internet browser, and begin typing 'postpartum psychosis'.

Doctor Wyatt was right about one thing: the symptoms really can range to just about anything, including delusions, hallucinations, paranoia, manic and radical behaviour. But then I scroll to the bottom of the page and see the statistic. Postpartum psychosis is very different from the regular Baby Blues or postpartum depression. It is a very severe illness, including a variety of ways in which it can begin. It occurs in about 1 in every 1000 women, which equates to 0.1% of those who have a baby.

She lied. Doctor Wyatt lied. The statistic she relayed to me was for post-partum depression, not psychosis. The familiar comfort I felt earlier in the large quantity of women who can relate to me has vanished. I feel sick and alone.

I feel even more insane than I did before.

CHAPTER TEN

B EFORE Weston Waters January 24, 2016

I've been back at work for two weeks now. It's almost as if there's been a shift in the atmosphere. A reverse metamorphosis, where rather than evolving, I'm shrinking, unbecoming the man I once was.

I've become distant from my work and my patients. I can't sit still or relax without my mind drowning in thoughts of Cordelia, how she's doing at home without me. There's a heavy guilt that weighs me down – a guilt that does not belong to me. This is not my fault. None of it is. Yet I feel guilty for what happened to her. For leaving her to return to work.

How is a man supposed to make a decision like that? Return to work – his life-long passion and what makes him happy – or stay home longer with his sick wife and child.

Doctor Wyatt assured me that she would be there as often as she could, and when she couldn't be there, another doctor would be. Cordelia would never be unattended with Emerald. Still, I fear that something may happen. That Cordelia may have another psychotic break and harm herself. Or worse.

It makes me ill worrying about her so much. She doesn't deserve to go through this. She's a great wife. And she may not be the best mother right now, but she will be. I know she will. We just have to get through this. In a few years we will look back and this will all be something of the past. She and Emerald will be inseparable, going for walks, painting each other's nails – all the things that mothers are supposed to do with their daughters.

Cordelia has always been a very headstrong woman. From the moment I met her back in school, she was always a go-getter. Chasing her dreams, pursuing what she wanted. That's what I admired most about her. If she wanted something, she made sure to get it. That's how she got me.

I was dating Hannah Turner when Cordelia and I first met. She was in her freshman year, and, for reasons unknown to me, was taking a third-year psych class. I still remember it like it were yesterday. She sat down in the seat next to me, swiftly bringing out her notebook and scribbling down what the professor was saying. She was late for class, as I'd later find out was routine for her. Her hair, a shade of vanilla pudding, was pinned in a high ponytail.

She noticed me staring. I think people can sense that – when someone's eyes are watching them. She looked up at me and I looked away, not fooling anyone to the illusion that I wasn't staring. But I could tell that she was still staring at me. Even though the professor was talking, she didn't look down and continue writing. She kept staring at me, daring me to turn my head and face her again.

Slowly, I did. She was looking at me with these big brown eyes, doe like. "Do you need something?" She asked. I stuttered, unsure what to say. I was nervous for some reason, and I didn't normally get nervous. "Do you have a spare pencil?" was the only thing I managed to say. Her eyes drifted downwards to the pencil that I was holding in my hand. I followed her gaze, then quickly jammed it into the desk, breaking the tip. I looked back up at her and shrugged. She laughed and gave me a pencil. That was how it began.

Hannah was great, but we'd only been dating for six months when I met Cordelia. It wasn't a difficult decision to do the math on that one. Some believe that it's wrong to cheat on your partner, but I didn't intend for it to happen that way. We were friends, Cordelia and I – nothing more. Until we kissed. And then I couldn't help myself. I knew I couldn't continue dating someone while seeing Cordelia, so I broke things off with Hannah. I never really thought about her again.

I graduated two years later – while Cordelia was just starting her third year – but I promised her that we would stay together, and that nothing, not even distance, would come between us.

I kept my promise. And she stayed by my side, regardless of the ups and downs we went through. I was a struggling dental student, and she was trying to learn computer science. We'd laugh at ourselves when things got too serious. Life's a journey, and nobody makes it out alive anyways. But if there was one thing I was certain of back then, it was that I wanted to spend the rest of my life with that woman. I proposed later that year, and we agreed to wait until we'd both finished school to get married.

When it came to our childhoods, Cordelia and I were polar opposites. She came from a crazy, outgoing family, sandwiched between two brothers. I grew up an only child. Her parents were wild and fun. Mine were strict and conservative. They say that only-children are spoiled, and I guess they are right, because my parents gave all of their energy and devotion to me and only me. Without any siblings, their focus was constantly on me. What does Weston need? What kind of car does he want? What school will he attend? I guess it was pretty great always having my wants and needs looked after. Their attention was only great until it wasn't, like when I tried skipping school or hanging out with a different crowd of people. They noticed everything I did, every little change in my personality or life. And they'd jump on it, trying to fix and manage every detail. I guess they shaped me into the man I became. I owe my success to them. They helped me stay on track when I was nearly falling off. It is because of them that my dreams and aspirations were able to become reality.

I grew up in Chicago and my parents still live there today. It's only two and a half hours from our place here in Davenport, but they don't come out to visit as much as I'd like. My father will be retiring soon and maybe then they can make an effort to come out and spend time with their grandchild.

They came to see us when Emerald was born. They brought presents upon presents for her. I knew immediately that she would be spoiled, just as I was. But their visits became sparse after Cordelia's illness began getting worse. My parent's – I love them dearly, but I'd be lying to myself if I said they weren't pretentious people. They'd never dealt with a daughter, let alone a mental illness, and those things combined had them heading for the hills.

It angered me and I was affected by their abandonment. I told Cordelia that they were busy and simply didn't have time to come around much. Not that she cared, really. The medication left her feeling tired and emotionless.

I can only hope that once she starts to get better, they'll come around again. God, I hope they do. My daughter needs grandparents in her life.

———

After a long day of filling moulds, checking X-rays, and tightening braces, I make the short drive home, both nervous and excited to see my family.

When I walk through the front door, the first thing I see is Marcia playing with the toys on the floor next to Emerald, who lies on her stomach, laughing. Her smile warms my heart. I've always wanted kids, or a kid, really. I liked the idea of having one child, just as my parents did. It allowed them to focus on me and help with everything I needed. I wanted to do the same for my own child. One is the perfect amount. One was all I needed. A little daughter, an angel, was more than I could have asked for.

When Cordelia first told me that she didn't want kids, I honestly thought she was joking. We were still at Northwestern at the time when we first discussed it. It wasn't a serious discussion, so should we have babies? It was more of a casual conversation, brought up arbitrarily. She told me how she hated kids and could never picture herself being a mother. I laughed, thinking she was joking. She was so sweet and kind-hearted. I didn't know what she was talking about. I thought she would be a great mother. Five years after that initial conversation, I knew I wanted her to be the mother of my child.

She was upset when she told me about the pregnancy. Upset might be an understatement. She was devastated, saying her life was over and she would have to either abort the baby or give it up for adoption. That was never going to happen. I held my wife in my arms and explained to her that this was our little miracle. I told her how much happiness a baby would bring into our lives – not that we were unhappy – but a child fills places inside of you that you didn't even know were empty.

A baby. I wanted that. I wanted a life and a future with Cordelia. And having a baby would make our lives complete. I gave her some time to herself, but every so often, I'd tell her about the benefits of having a baby and how much joy it would bring us. Finally, she agreed with me, and I think she may have even been happy about it. I knew she would be a great mother. I just knew it.

But she wasn't. She isn't.

I know that none of this is her fault, so I do not blame her. It's something beyond her control. And I will stay by her side, fighting with her until all of this has passed.

I walk over and kneel beside Marcia. I reach for my daughter, pulling her into my arms. So tiny and fragile in my large hands. She smells like strawberry soap, fresh and clean.

I tell Marcia that she can go for the night, then I stand up, still holding Emerald close to me, and head towards the bedroom to see Cordelia.

She's lying on the bed, not sleeping, but not awake. Somewhere in between. Doctor Wyatt sits in the corner, reading a book, as she usually does. Where would we be without Fiona Wyatt?

"How is she?" I ask quietly as I walk in the room, switching Emerald to my other arm. Fiona looks up at me and closes her book. "She's alright. Just a bit tired right now, that's all." I nod my head. She's always tired. "Can I get her anything?" "Perhaps some food? I can make dinner if you'd like?" Fiona offers. "No, it's fine. I can go start something." I smile at the doctor, then turn to look at my wife. Her skin is pale and her eyes are staring up towards the ceiling. "Hi honey," I whisper. Her eyes turn slightly so they're facing me. "Hi babe," she mutters. "Can I get you anything? Water? Orange juice?" "I'm good, thank you." She pauses. "What are you going to make for dinner?" "Is pasta alright?" "Sounds perfect." She strains to smile.

I walk to the nursery and place Emerald in her crib, then head into the kitchen. I grab the pot from the cupboard and fill it with water. This will all be over soon, I tell myself. This is what I tell myself every day. I know words can't do anything or help in this situation, but all I can do is pray that those words become reality.

CHAPTER ELEVEN

AFTER Detective Gerard Sullivan Friday May 19, 2016

I study her face. The elongated jawline, the curve of her nose. The way her eyelids blink attentively when she's listening. Does this woman speak the truth? Does she radiate honesty? Or is there something she's hiding? A hint of falsehoods that are suppressed behind her exterior.

As Cordelia speaks, I glance sideways at the brother – Colton – who has been staring intently and listening to our conversation. When Cordelia finishes speaking, I turn to Colton. "Mr. Cruz, before I leave, do you mind if I ask you a few questions?" He tilts his chin up, his attention focused on me now rather than his sister. "Yes, of course. Anything I can do to help." "Would you mind giving us a minute?" I say to Cordelia. "Sure. Yes," she pauses to look around. "I'm going to go have a shower." Her hair is still damp from her last one. I watch as she exists the space where we sit, disappearing down the hall. Once she's out of sight, I turn to Colton and take a seat across from him at the table. "So," I begin. "You and Cordelia... the two of you close?" "Yes. We've always got along well. We've drifted a bit over the years, but that's normal, especially since she moved away and started her life here." "Right," I flip to the next page in my notebook. "You're from Evanston?" "Yeah. We were born and raised there so it's always been home for me. My wife is from there as well, so we didn't really plan on going anywhere else." "What do you do?" "I'm a biological engineer." I jot this down, then proceed with the standards. "Does your sister have any enemies? Anyone who would want to harm Emerald or her and Weston?" "No," he says without hesitation. "Cordy's a good person. She may be quick-witted and mordant at times, but it's all in good heart. She's never really had any enemies. I don't know who would do this." I hear the distant sound of the shower coming to life. "You have another sibling, right? A brother?" "Yes, Liam. He's the youngest." "Where does he live?" "Indiana. With his wife and two kids. They don't come around much." I look up from my notepad and meet his gaze. "Why is that?" He looks hesitant, picking at his cuticles. "Just family problems." "If you don't mind my asking, what happened?" "Oh, just the typical stuff. It's trivial, really." I stare at him, waiting for him to elaborate. He looks uneasy. I've been doing this for too long to let him get away with that response. "Are you sure?" He glances down the hall towards the bedroom, ensuring his sister's presence isn't lurking, I assume. He looks down at his hands that rest on the table and sighs. "It's ridiculous, really." "Your fight?" "Yeah," "Is there something that Cordelia doesn't know?" He flattens his mouth into a line. "If I tell you," he begins. "You can't tell her. Can you promise me that?" "As long as it doesn't interfere with this case in any way." He's quiet for a moment, then sighs again. "It all started about a year after he and Lianna got married. They were newlyweds – so happy and in love. They just had their daughter, Sophie, and everything was perfect. But something happened," he pauses, rubbing his right hand over his left. "I never meant for it to happen. You have to believe me," he pauses again, then looks up at me. "We had an affair – Lianna and I. Neither one of us intended for it to happen. And we both regretted it deeply. We vowed that it would never happen again. But it did. "A few months later, we ended things for good. I wanted to tell Liam, and Jada, even. I felt so guilty. I betrayed my own brother. But Lianna made me promise not to say anything. Sophie was almost a year, and she didn't want Liam to file for a divorce and get full custody. I agreed not to say anything. Just so it wouldn't ruin their family. "But then... Liam found out. I'm still not sure how, but he was livid, as you can imagine. It was around the time we were dealing with our parent's estate. Cordelia thinks he was just angry about that. He was angry about the estate as well, we simply didn't see eye-to-eye on some things. But the reason he was angry was because of me. "He never told Cordelia or our parents, so they don't know. And I'd like to keep it that way. But he won't speak to me. And he barely speaks to Cordelia. I don't know why. It's not like she did anything. But he just cut us off. All of us. He's blaming them for my mistakes." Colton pauses again, taking a minute to gather his thoughts. "He stayed with Lianna, tried to make it work. She swore to him that nothing would ever happen again. But one night, a few months later, she called me. Told me that she was pregnant. It made sense why he chose to stay with her – they were expecting another child. I congratulated her, wished her the best. But then she told me that the baby wasn't Liam's – it was mine," he stops, resting his forehead in his palms. "God, I never wanted that. I never wanted to jeopardize his marriage and fuck everything up." "Does he know?" I ask. "That the child isn't his?" "No. He has no idea. And we'd like to keep it that way." "Have you ever met the kid?" "No. His name is Clayton. Lianna says he has my eyes. But people always say he looks like Lianna. Some days I wonder if Liam ever looks at his son and questions things. But he hasn't said anything, yet. And Lianna hasn't said anything either. So for now, I assume, that everything is normal with them. But he can never know. I can never tell him. And you have to promise not to tell Cordelia." I let out a small breath. "That's a lot of information to take in," I say. "But your issues are your issues. I have no need to say anything. Unless you think Liam had something to do with this." "No. Liam's not like that." "He wouldn't come around, looking for revenge? He can't take any child from you, so he takes your sister's?" "No!" he snaps, trying to keep his voice quiet. "I'm telling you, Liam wouldn't have done this." The shower stops and we both turn. "Please," he says. "Please don't tell her. Liam would never do that. He may have a problem with me, but he would never do anything like that to Cordy."

Looking at Colton's desperate face, I believe him. It's not like Liam is at the top of my suspect list anyway, but it's something I'll definitely need to look further into.

I look down at my notepad and circle his name. Liam Cruz. I'll give him a call soon, get this whole mess sorted out.

Nineteen hours. It's been nineteen hours. I need to find this baby.

CHAPTER TWELVE

BEFORE Cordelia Waters January 28, 2016

It's been just over two months since Emerald was born. Her tiny body seems to be growing so quickly, no longer resembling the minuscule creature that once came out of me.

I'm making progress, if you could even call it that. Doctor Wyatt has played a pivotal role in my recovery. She's always so kind and patient with me, even when I'm on the verge of insanity. I'm working on getting more involved with Emerald, small steps.

Last week we began with simply sitting in the living room watching television with Emerald in her rocker beside us. Doctor Wyatt tells me to focus on the positive things about Emerald, rather than the negatives. I told her that's a little bit difficult, considering I regret ever conceiving her. But she tells me that this is the psychosis talking, and soon enough, those thoughts will be gone.

Today we are working on holding Emerald and feeding her the formula. I'm apprehensive at first. Doctor Wyatt hands her to me and I accept my daughter into my arms. I look down and stare at her face. It feels strange, holding her. I fight the urge to put her down and run back into my bedroom, where I can hide beneath the darkness of the sheets. But these are what Doctor Wyatt calls Bad Thoughts, and any time I have even the slightest notion, I'm supposed to push them away, suppress them, rid the Bad Thoughts from my mind.

Easier said than done.

I try to focus on Emerald's face. I study the creases in her eyes, the way she latches on onto my finger with her entire hand. It hits me again – the realization that I created this tiny, odd-looking creature. It's still a wonder to me why I never took to infants. There's just something in my biological makeup that causes me to reject the concept of motherhood.

I cringe as the smell begins to waft through the air. Her little mouth turns upwards into a smile, a gurgle erupts from her mouth. I turn to Doctor Wyatt, looking petrified. She takes Emerald from me and heads into the nursery to change her diaper.

My friend, Savannah, is supposed to be coming over today. She came to the house just after Emerald was born to bring a gift. In typical Savannah manner, she brought a dress and shoes for Emerald, and a bottle of wine for Weston and me. Other than that, I haven't seen her since the beginning of November, before I left for maternity leave. I just haven't had time or been well enough to see anyone. She's been calling quite a bit, checking in on me. Doctor Wyatt said it would be alright if she came over for a short visit. Said it may be good for me to see a familiar face.

Savannah is the type of person that most women aspire to be. She's young – twenty-five – enthusiastic about everything in life, and has the type of body that makes anyone envious. She loves her job, but also loves to have fun. We met three years ago when she first got hired at District Systems. We became good friends within the office, then eventually extended our friendship to outside the office walls.

It's always fascinated me that Savannah and I became friends, because to be frank, we are polar opposites. I, the calm, self-sufficient introvert. Her, the energetic, lovable extrovert. I remember in the early days of our friendship, her begging me to accompany her on Girls Night Out in town. Sometimes I would cave and go with her, but most times, I would politely decline, preferring to stay in and watch a movie with Weston.

Regardless of our contrasting personalities, I love Savannah. She brings out another side of me that I forgot was there. She has the ability to make even the most anti-social of people become social butterflies. Not to mention the fact that she's drop-dead-gorgeous, and I often find myself sitting there staring at her, contemplating my own beauty. With her long, chocolate hair and vibrant green eyes. She's luscious, like looking at a Cover Girl model. I'm no match, with my non-voluptuous figure and thin white hair. It actually surprises me that she hasn't settled down with anyone yet. I'm sure there's no shortage of men lining up, ready to put a ring on it. But she's a heartbreaker. Can't keep a steady thing in her life.

The doorbell rings and I instantly feel nervous. I'm not sure why. It's not that I think Savannah will judge me. Or, maybe subconsciously, I do think that. I look a mess, I feel a mess, and quite frankly, I'm intimated by her right now because she has her life together and I do not.

I stand up, smoothing out my shirt that flows over my yoga pants – I put some effort into getting dressed today – and head towards the front door.

"Cordelia!" she beams upon seeing me. She takes a step forwards and flings her arms around me. "Hi, Sav!" I breathe into her thick hair. It smells like honey and cranberries. She steps back and surveys me. "Wow, you look good!" I'm unaware if she is serious or just trying to make me feel better. I haven't showered in three days, but decided to take one this morning in preparation for her arrival. I don't have any makeup on, and the insomnia makes itself evident through large, dark bags under my eyes. "Thanks," I smile faintly. "Please, come inside." We walk into the living room and take a seat on the couch. Doctor Wyatt returns, holding Emerald in her arms. Savannah's face immediately lights up. "Oh my goodness, look at the little angel!" I try to smile. "There she is," I say, a synthetic enthusiasm in my voice. "I haven't seen her since she was like, this big," she holds her fingers a few centimeters from each other. Doctor Wyatt walks closer until she's in front of Savannah. "Would you like to hold her?" "I'd love to!" Savannah reaches her arms out and takes my daughter. "Oh my, she's just so little and tiny and cute!" she squeals.Babies. They have that effect on people. Doctor Wyatt smiles, then looks over at me to check in. I glance at her, then turn my attention back to Savannah and Emerald. Savannah's holding out her finger and Emerald has it grasped in her tiny hand. "She looks just like you, Cor!" "You think? My parents say she looks like Weston." "No way. She has your eyes. And hair." "That might change," I say. "Apparently all babies' hair and eye colour are subject to change after the first year." It's quiet for a moment. Doctor Wyatt takes a seat in the chair across from us. "Do you have children?" she says to Savannah. Savannah looks up at her. "Children? No. I wish. They're just so darn cute," she says in that high pitch voice as she looks back down at my daughter. You can have that one, I think to myself, then instantly try to take it back and replace the Bad Thoughts with good ones. "You married?" Doctor Wyatt inquires. Anything to keep a conversation going. "No, I'm not. Not yet, anyway. I hope to be someday." Savannah smiles. "You're probably eager to start a family of your own, then. Become a mother," Doctor Wyatt nods towards Emerald. "Oh, I am," Savannah beams. "I almost was..." her voice fades and she closes her mouth suddenly. "What?" I turn to her. "Nothing," she smiles down at Emerald. "Never mind." "How do you almost become a mother?" I ask, curiosity and suspicion arising simultaneously. "It was a few years ago. Not that big of a deal." "What isn't a big deal? What happened?" I press. She doesn't look at me, just continues looking at Emerald. She takes in a breath. "A few years back, when I was twenty-two, my boyfriend at the time, Lucas, and I had gotten pregnant. It was a complete accident, really.

Neither of us wanted a baby. But I have this thing – everything happens for a reason – so I decided to keep it, even though we weren't in the best situation to raise a child. But we decided to, regardless. "As the months progressed and my stomach grew, Lucas became more and more excited. I did too. I was so eager to meet this little life that was growing inside of me." She pauses, twirling her fingers around Emerald's. "But unfortunately, we lost her. She was... stillborn." I stare at her, wide-eyed. "Savannah, I am so sorry. I had no idea." She looks up at me, finally. "It's okay, you didn't know. I don't really tell many people." "I can see why," I say. "It probably broke you." "It did, for a while. But like I said, it was a few years ago. I'm fine now, promise." She smiles at me. "What happened with Lucas, if you don't mind my asking?" "No, that's fine. We stayed together for a little while after the loss. But we eventually grew apart. Sometimes I think the only reason we stayed together all that time was because of the baby. But like I said, everything happens for a reason. Perhaps I wasn't ready to be a mother after all. And perhaps that short time that I was pregnant taught me some valuable lessons. I don't regret it. That, or my relationship with Lucas. Those circumstances helped contribute to who I am today." "That's good, Sav. I'm glad to hear." I smile. And I truly am. She's so strong and positive. The exact opposite of what I am. "You sound like a very wise young woman," Doctor Wyatt says. "Your parents must be proud of you." Savannah smiles. "Thank you. My mother died when I was young, but my dad is my biggest supporter. God bless him." She takes a moment. "But enough about me! For goodness sake, how are you, love? This must be so difficult for you." She readjusts in her seat, shifting her arms slightly so that Emerald fits comfortably. "I'm alright," I lie. "It's been tough lately. But I'm hanging in there. I wouldn't even be here if it wasn't for Doctor Wyatt," I turn my head to face her. "I owe it all to her." "Oh, nonsense," she says. "I may be the crutch, but you're doing all the work. I'm only doing my best to help. The rest is up to you." She's so modest. I really do appreciate everything she has done for me. "Do you know when you'll be coming back to work?" Savannah asks. "Not too sure," I say. "Hopefully within the next month or so." Wishful thinking. "That long?" "I'm still trying to get better. It's a lot harder than it may seem." "I bet. I can't imagine what you've gone through – what you're still going through. You're a real trooper, Cordelia." I smile.

If only I could believe those words myself.

―――

The remainder of the day goes better than expected. I suppose Doctor Wyatt was right when she said a visit could lighten my mood. Seeing Savannah made me realize how much I truly miss the outside world; going for runs in the morning, going to work, seeing my friends. I can't do any of those things when I'm cooped up in this house.

But that thought alone gives me the motivation I need to get better. I know I'll get there eventually. I will. I just have to keep the positive thoughts in, and the bad ones out.

I truly do believe that I can get better. The only thing I'm uncertain about is my perceptions toward Emerald. How do I suddenly start caring for something that I wish never existed?

This may be harder than I thought.

CHAPTER THIRTEEN

A FTER Detective Gerard Sullivan Friday May 19, 2016

After speaking with Colton, I wait in the living room for Cordelia to come back out. She appears suddenly, wearing the same outfit as before, hair damp.

"You're still here," she says, as though she's surprised to see me. "I just had a few more questions." "Alright," she runs her fingers through her hair and takes a seat on the couch. I clear my throat. "How close are you with Weston's parents?" "Not close at all, why?" "I haven't spoken to them yet. Thought I'd give them a call." She nods her nod. "I'm not sure they'll be any help. They don't come around much. They tend to keep to themselves." "Why is that?" She shrugs. "They're... how do I put this without sounding rude. Stuck up? Pretentious? I don't know. They only care about themselves. Weston absolutely adores them so I can never mention anything like this to him. But how can he give them such praise when they don't even come see their own granddaughter?" "Do they know that she's missing?" "That's a good question. I don't speak with them so it would be up to Weston to have said something. I have no idea whether he did or not." "When was the last time you or Weston saw them?" She thinks about this. "They only came to visit once. Right after Emerald was born. They haven't been back since." "Why's that?" "Why do you think, detective?" "The postpartum?" She nods. "Have they ever had a problem with you?" "Me? No. It's not that they necessarily have a problem with me. It's that they simply don't care." "I see." "His father is one of those people who think you can buy anything you need in life. Like love. All Weston's life, he got whatever he wanted. His parents come from old money, so Weston's needs were never an issue. And that wouldn't be a problem, really, except they don't care about his life or wellbeing. They don't ask him questions about his life, wonder how his family is, or even care what he's doing at work. His father thinks he can just buy his love. Bought him anything he wanted, as long as he didn't have to spend time with him." "But to your knowledge, they don't have an issue with you and Weston's marriage? Or any problems with Weston for that matter?" "No. As I said, they don't care much. They're too busy with their own lives." "Alright. Thank you, Cordelia." She nods her head. "Let me know if you need anything else."

I leave the Waters' house and head out to my car. I dial the phone number for Weston's parents and back out of the driveway, the dial tone echoing through the Bluetooth speaker.

I almost don't think anyone will answer, but after the fifth ring, someone picks up. "Hello?" says a woman's voice. It's mellow, smooth. "Is this Madeline Waters?" "This is. And who might this be?" She asks. Her tone gives away what kind of woman she is. Poised, dignified. Everything that Cordelia described? Possibly. "This is Detective Sullivan from the Davenport Police Department. I'm calling regarding the disappearance of your granddaughter, Emerald." I turn the steering wheel and the car moves swiftly onto the next street. "I beg your pardon? I think I may have heard you incorrectly,"

That's when I realize: Weston hasn't told them. I signal and pull over to the side of the road. "Ma'am, I'm sorry. When was the last time you spoke with your son?"

"A few weeks ago." She pauses. "What happened?

"Your granddaughter disappeared from their home yesterday evening." The line is quiet. "What do you mean disappeared?" "She's officially a missing person, ma'am. I apologize for having to tell you this way. I was sure your son had told you." "He did no such thing!" She nearly yells into the phone. "My heavens," silence again. She clears her throat, collects herself. "Apologies. Why exactly are you calling?" "I just have some questions about your son." "What kind of questions? Is he in trouble?" "No, nothing like that. I just wanted to speak with you, get a better understanding of the situation."

"Alright. Go on, then."

I clear my throat. "How is your relationship with Weston?" "Our relationship is fine. We don't see him much anymore. We hardly see him at all, actually. Since he up and left Chicago for good with that one."

"Cordelia?"

"Yes, who else?" I pause a moment. "Did that upset you? Him moving?" "Of course! He's my only baby. And he just left town and moved to Davenport," she says as though it's such a disgusting place. "It was hard on us." "So you and your husband haven't come out to see Weston and the family in a while?" "We've been busy the last couple of months." "Doing what, exactly?" "We're renovating the house. And planning a cruise for July. The Mediterranean." "I see. Does Weston know about this?" "No. He doesn't speak to us much." "And you never call him?" Silence. "Is there something you need to ask me, detective? Because quite frankly I need to call my son and ask him why the hell he didn't call his own mother when his only daughter is missing." "Apologies, Mrs. Waters. Just one last question." "What is it?" "To your knowledge, does your son have any enemies? Anybody who may want to hurt him or come after his family?" "Heavens no! Weston is a wonderful man. Owns his own orthodontic practice, you know. He's very established for himself. He's always been a very kind, well-rounded man. Always respectful of others. I couldn't imagine anyone who would want to hurt him or the baby." "What about money? He doesn't owe anyone money? Perhaps someone from the past?" "No. Money is no issue for us. Weston has no debts that I'm aware of." "Any childhood friends, neighbors, or family friends from home that could possibly do anything like this?" "Kidnap his child? Of course not. What kind of place do you think we live in?" she asks. Chicago, I think to myself. "Everyone that Weston grew up with was a good influence on him. He was never permitted to hang around with bad children. He's a good man. Whoever took my granddaughter was definitely not doing it because of Weston." She lets her words hang, insinuating something else. "So, what you're saying is, it must be because of Cordelia?" I ask. She doesn't answer and I take her silence as a yes: that's exactly what she's implying. "May I ask why you think that?" "That Cordelia... she's a lovely girl, really. But she was a troubled child. Always messing around and getting into mischief. And I tell you, some things just never change." "How do you know this?" "Oh, Weston has told me stories. He thinks it's comical. I find no amusement out of them. Quite frankly I think it's inappropriate for a young lady to be behaving that way." "What way are you referring to?" "I'm not getting into it. If you want to know about Cordelia's childhood, you should ask her." By the tone of her voice, I can tell that this conversation is over. "Alright. Well, again, I apologize for having to inform you of the news this way. Thank you for taking the time to speak with me. And... go easy on Weston. He's going through a difficult time right now. His daughter is missing and I've seen what that can do to a person." The line is silent for a moment and I almost think she's hung up. "Goodnight, detective."

The phone disconnects.

———

I head back over to the precinct before paying a visit to the babysitter, Ainsley Kain. At this time in the investigation, I need to speak with everyone who has had contact with that child, anyone who might know something and be of some assistance.

It's around one o'clock when I get to the station. Officers Matt Holden and Rowan Ashby are standing at the front desk, looking over paper work. I give a friendly nod to Rebecca, our secretary, as I come through the doors and head straight for my office.

Warm and cozy, as always. I like to keep the heat up and the door closed to trap warmth in. Despite the fact that it's May and summer is well on its way, I enjoy the warmth. The thing about me is that I've always been a cold person, can never seem get warm enough. It annoyed my parents to no end, constantly turning the heat on and buying floor-heaters. Something about the way I was built.

As I slide into my chair and turn on my computer monitor, I hear a soft knock and the door opens slightly. Rebecca peeks her head inside. "How's it going?" she gives me a friendly smile. I've always liked Rebecca. She's worked here for the past six years. This woman always has a smile on her face, even in the worst situations. She's the spiritual type, the ones that have those positive mantras plastered around their house. Her positivity increases our stamina around here, especially on days like this when I want to sink into a hole. "It's going alright," I say. I turn my chair so I'm facing her. "It's terrible, isn't it? Who would take a baby? Any leads yet?" "Not really. Well," I pause, remembering the Mendoza's. "Maybe one, but I'm not even sure you could call it a lead. Nothing solid yet," I pause, bringing my fist to my chin. "I just need to get this child back to her parents." She opens her mouth slightly, then snaps it closed again, changing her mind, deciding not to say whatever it was she was thinking. "What?" I say. "Nothing," she shakes her head modestly. "Is it about the baby?" She opens her mouth again slightly, hesitates, then, "Isn't the mother a bit of, um, what's the word I'm looking for," she pauses. "Nut job?" I give her a stern look. "Sorry, I didn't mean it like that, but –" "She suffered from postpartum psychosis," I explain. "Many women experience it." "I'm sorry. I shouldn't have said anything," It's quiet for a moment. "Who's talking?" I ask. She looks embarrassed, as though she doesn't want to reveal the source of the gossip. "It's Rowan," she says quietly. "He says he took statements from both of them last night. He was pretty convinced that the wife is guilty." "Ashby," I scoff. "He can believe whatever he wants, but at this moment, I don't have any plausible evidence to put this on the mother. Not yet, anyway." "You're right. It's probably nothing," she smiles. "Just Rowan's theory, I guess." "He can have his theories," I say. "And I have mine. I'll let you know when we catch this guy." I wink. She smiles and closes the door on her way out.

———

After typing up my notes and sorting through some files, I shut down the computer and head back into the foyer, hoping Holden and Ashby are still there. Sure enough, they're standing in the corner, talking and sipping coffee.

"Officers," I nod my head towards them as I get closer. "Sully," they say in unison. "Find anything?" "That's actually why I came to speak with you." I let my eyes hover over Rowan for a moment, deciding not to bring up his slight indiscretions around the station. "Can one of you head over to the Laundromat up on 53rd Street? Talk to the Mendozas. See if the husband knows anything. They also need alibis for their whereabouts at the time of the abduction yesterday." "You spoke to the wife, right? Marcia?" Holden asks. "Yes." "Anything?" "Not entirely. She loves the kid. Says the Waters' are like family to her." "Thoughts so far?" Ashby asks, fiddling with his coffee cup. "Possible motive? Money. They're not in the best financial situation." "So what, you think this is a kidnap-and-ransom case? Get some money from the Waters'?" Holden asks. "Maybe. That's why I need you to go over there and check it out." "Will do," Holden says. "I'll update you after we speak to the husband. Where are you headed?" "The babysitters'." "They have a nanny and a babysitter?" I stifle a small laugh. "Don't ask." "Yuppie problems."

———

As I drive downtown and pass the river, I think back to my college days when I dated a girl named Ainsley. She was a petite brunette with a bob cut. Nice girl, really. We only dated for a couple of months. She was pursuing a law degree. Was always so interested in the work I was doing. She used to say that we'd make a great pair, solving crimes and prosecuting the bad guys.

I didn't hear from her much after we broke up. Someone told me years later that she moved to LA to join some big law firm. I haven't thought about her since then. But after hearing the name Ainsley yesterday and today, I can't get her off my mind. I wonder where she is now. If she's a successful lawyer somewhere, bringing justice to the people. It makes you wonder, really, where everybody you used to know ended up. How quickly our lives pass before us, and how drastically things can change.

I pull into the parking lot of an unkempt apartment building. I double-check the address to make sure I have the right place. Cordelia mentioned that she's a student at Davenport College, studying social work or something along those lines.

As I walk towards the building, an older man sits on the ground beside the doors, a dog beside him, smoking a cigarette and holding out a hat.

"Can you spare any change?" he mumbles as I pass. I reach into my pocket to see if I have anything. I pull out a few dimes and quarters, drop them in. "Thank you, God bless." He nods his head and I give a brief smile before tugging on the door and going inside.

The lobby is brightly lit and empty. There's an intercom system on the left. Two elevators sit directly across from the front doors. I pull out my notepad and check what her number is. A34. I press the button and wait.

"Yeah?" a female voice says through the speaker. "Is this Ms. Kain?" "Who's asking?" "I'm Detective Sullivan from the Davenport Police Department. Do you mind if I come up?" The speaker is quiet for a moment. "Police? Why are the police here?" "It's regarding the disappearance of Emerald Waters." Silence again. Then, "Shit. Hold on." I hear the sound of a buzzer, and the door unlocks.

When she opens the door, she's not at all what I was expecting. Then again, Ainsley from college was still in my mind; her big brown eyes, short bob cut. The voice I heard through the intercom doesn't match the girl that stands in front of me. This girl is young, early twenties maybe, tall and skinny. She has thin hair, a shade of dirty blonde. Her face is pleasant looking, hazel eyes and a small mouth.

She leads me through the small apartment and into a living room area. There is one medium-sized couch and two chairs, a large television set in front. Next to the living room is the kitchen, which isn't big either. This is probably a small, two bedroom place that she can barely afford. Why do the Waters' have a thing for hiring people who are tight on money?

She sits down in the chair, offering me the couch. "Sorry, did I hear you correctly? You say Emerald is missing?" she asks. "Yes. She was abducted yesterday somewhere between the hours of three and five in the evening." "Holy shit," she brings her hand to her mouth. She leans back and peers around the corner. "Babe!" she yells. "Get out here!" I stare at her. She politely turns back to me and waits. For what, or who, I don't know. I hear a door open and a moment later, a tall, lanky man appears in the hallway and walks into the living room. "Dyl," she says to him. "Emerald is fucking missing!" His eyes widen, as though he was in a trance prior to hearing this information. "What? The baby?" "Yeah the baby, who else?" "Who's this?" he turns to me. Ainsley speaks, "This is Detective..." "Sullivan," "Detective Sullivan," she repeats. "He's trying to find her. Says she went missing yesterday." "Shit," he rubs the back of his neck as he walks over and takes a seat on the edge of the chair that Ainsley sits on. "Do you know who took er?" he asks me. "No, not yet. But that's why I'm here. Do you mind if I ask the two of you some questions?" "Of course, of course!" Ainsley says. "Anything we can do to help." I pull out my notepad and click the pen. "What's your name, sorry?" I look to the man. "Dylan Rollings." I write this down, then look back to Ainsley. "How long have you been babysitting for the Waters'?" "Um, only about... a month and a half? Two months? Not really sure. I only watch Emerald once in a while. Like, weekends and stuff. When the parents want to go out and have some alone time." "Do they do that often? Go out?" "Um, not really. Maybe once a week or so. Usually on Saturdays." I write this down. "How is your relationship with the family?" "Me? Oh, good. I don't know them too well or anything. But Weston is very nice. Always polite and friendly to see me." "And Cordelia?" "She's nice too. But kind of neutral. I don't know, sometimes I get the vibe that she's annoyed at me." "What makes you say that?" She shrugs. "Just the vibe I get. Can't really explain it." Vibes. Right. "Has Cordelia ever said anything unkind to you? Something that made you uncomfortable?" "No." She doesn't hesitate. "She may not like me, but like I said, she's kind of neutral. Isn't super nice, but isn't rude or anything." "How would you describe their marriage?" "What do you mean?" "Would you say that they're happy? Do they fight? Are they –" "Yeah, they're happy. At least, when I see em they are," she pauses for a moment. "Except this one time, I was over a little early because the bus was on time for once. Weston answered the door but he looked a little... upset or something. He told me to come in and wait on the couch. He went back down the hall to the bedroom. I swear I could hear crying or something. I assumed it was Cordelia. But I never said anything. Wasn't my business." "Did Cordelia seem alright after you saw them?" "Yeah, I think so. It wasn't a big deal cause like, I forgot about it. It was probably nothing." I write this down. Assuming she isn't aware of Cordelia's condition, I decide to omit elaborating on the subject. "Has anyone ever come by the house while you were there? Looking for Cordelia or Weston?" "Nope. I've never had to answer the door. Oh, except one time, yeah, actually. But it was just her friend from work dropping something off." "Do you remember her name?" "Um, Sandy... or –" "Savannah?" "Yeah! I think that's it." "What was she dropping off?" "Oh, I don't know. Some computer piece or something. Cordelia and her tech." "What do you mean?" "She loves computers and technology." "I see," I pause for a moment. "Do you know if the Waters' have any enemies? Anyone who may want to take Emerald from them?" She thinks for a moment. "Not that I can think of. Like I said, I'm not around much. But they seem like nice people. Weston is really nice. I can't imagine anyone wanting to hurt their baby. Oh God, I still can't believe that someone took her." "We'll find her soon," I try to reassure her. She nods her head. "Well," I start. "If you think of anything else –" "Babe," Dylan whispers. "Tell him about the car." Ainsley looks at him, confused almost. Then her face changes, as though she's remembered something. She turns to me. "Right, um, I totally forgot about this. Thanks for reminding me babe," she pats her boyfriend's leg. "There was this one night I was sitting for them. They were going out for dinner. I fed Emerald and put her to bed, so she was sleeping in her room, and I was just sitting on the couch watching TV. I remember at one point, I was walking by the front window and I saw a car pull up in front of the house. I thought it was them coming home early or something, but they didn't pull in the driveway, so I waited and watched for a minute. But then I realized it wasn't their car. And only one person was in the driver's seat." "Did you see who it was?" "No, it was dark and the car was on the street." "Male or female?" "I don't know. I couldn't tell. But anyways, I ignored it and thought it must have been the neighbors. Or maybe someone was lost or something. I went to the kitchen to get a snack. When I came back a few minutes later, I saw movement from the car. Like they were looking for something. I just assumed they were lost or waiting for someone. But then at one point, the landline rang. Weston told me I didn't have to answer the phone, but I did, just in case it was them calling or something. But when I picked it up, there was no one there. Almost like somebody was on the line listening. And then it went to that dial tone or whatever. Freaky. "So I finished watching the episode of Gilmore Girls, which must have been like, half an hour or so. I stood back up and walked past the window and the person was still in the car! I was so freaked out, so I shut the blinds and called Dyl right away." He nods as if to corroborate. "Do you know what kind of car it was?" I ask. "Umm, shit. My memory is so damn bad," she says. "It was, um," Dylan begins, "A Chevy Impala. I think you said. Right?" "Yeah," her face lifts. "It was a red Impala!" I jot this down on the notepad. "Thank you." "Do you think that could have anything to do with this?" she asks. "How long ago did this happen?" "Um, sometime in March, at least." "Nothing's certain, but that is a bit unusual. I'll have to look into it." "Oh God," she brings her hands to her mouth. "No need to worry. It was probably nothing." I try to reassure her. She nods her head. "What if... Oh God, what if they had taken her while I was there! I don't know how I would have lived with myself." "Babe, it's okay," Dylan touches her arm. "You're fine." She nods her head and he wraps his arm around her shoulders. "Well, thank you for taking the time to speak with me," I say. "Please, if you remember anything else that you think may be important – anything – don't hesitate to call me." I lean forward and hand her my card. She looks up at me, big hazel eyes locked on mine. "You'll catch this guy? And bring Emerald home?" "I'm trying my very best."

CHAPTER FOURTEEN

B EFORE Weston Waters February 9, 2016

When I was a kid, I would let my imagination wander, thinking about what life would be like when I grew up. Having successful parents and a well-rounded family kept me anticipative and optimistic about what my future held. I wanted to finish school, find a high paying job, get married, have kids, live in a big house in the suburbs, get a dog, maybe two or three. That was the idealistic embodiment of success. The American Dream. Happiness.

I watched my parents succeed and live the American Dream every day. I aspired to be like them. When I thought about my future, happiness was always of primary importance. But there was always that one thing that came above happiness, and that was money.

I grew up in a large house, five acres of property. I was accustomed to the lavished life, so anything below that wouldn't be adequate. It was during my first year of high school that I decided I wanted to pursue medicine, get my PhD, become a doctor. My mother was a surgeon, my father a successful orthodontist. I had to follow in his footsteps, make him proud.

I had my entire life planned out: Where I would go to school, what kind of car I would drive – Mercedes or a Bentley – how my own orthodontist practice would look. Everything, I assumed, would be impeccable. And sure enough, everything I predicted and hoped for came true.

Except the part about having a wife with postpartum psychosis. I never planned for that.

Not even in my worst nightmares would I have imagined a life where this was my reality. A life where my wife was severely depressed, crying all day long, unable to feel happiness, solely because of our own child. I didn't even know what postpartum psychosis was, let alone think that my wife could develop it.

I don't blame her, I really don't. I'm just having a difficult time coping with this situation. I know it's hard on her, of course, don't think otherwise. But it's hard on me as well. Having to stand by and see her like this. Feeling like a helpless bystander as I watch her days turn to misery and her nights become a sleepless battle of tears, tossing and turning until dawn. Nothing could have prepared me for this.

Some days I don't know what to do. I feel as though I'm on the verge of having a break down myself. But I can't. I won't let myself break down. Because I need to be strong. I need to support Cordelia and Emerald. I will be the glue that holds this family together. I am the man of the house, and it's my sole responsibility to make sure that everything is alright.

As I'm sitting in my office finishing up the final paperwork of the night, I glance at the clock. Four-fifty-eight. I sigh, letting out a breath I didn't know I was holding. What has my life come to that when my workday ends, I don't even look forward to going home?

Of course I want to see my daughter, but there is so much darkness looming around that house right now. I need somewhere to go. An escape. Even if just for a little while. Anything to evade my reality.

I end up at a bar down on Cheyenne Avenue. Finnick's Tap, it's called. I wasn't planning on stopping. I was driving home, mind wandering about going anywhere other than home, when I saw the sign.

I didn't think twice. I pulled into the parking lot and went inside. And now I'm sitting here, all by myself at the bar, wondering what the hell I'm doing here. What was I thinking, coming to a bar at dinner time when my wife and child are at home waiting for me? It's stupid, really. I should leave.

Just as I'm about to grab my car keys and stand, the bartender comes over. A petite red-head with electric green eyes. "Hi hon, what can I getcha?" she smiles, chewing some sort of bubble gum. I hesitate. I should tell her that this was a mistake and that I should be on my way home by now. But something inside of me lacks the ability to speak up at this point, so I shake out these thoughts and adjust in my seat. "Scotch," I say flatly. "No ice."

I nurse the glass between my palms. My life is a mess. Valentine's Day is next week. What the hell do I get Cordelia? It's not like she needs a Valentine's Day gift. What she needs is to get better.

I'll get her flowers. I know that for sure. Her favourites are lilacs. She loves the smell. Maybe a box of chocolates. A nice romantic gesture to remind her that I still love her.

Dammit, that's not enough. I can't just give my wife flowers and chocolate. I need to try harder. Maybe we can go somewhere special. Dinner perhaps? We could get a babysitter.

But she hasn't been out for so long. Would she even want to leave?

I'll find a sitter.

Maybe we could do lunch, the three of us. Emerald will be twelve weeks on the fourteenth. It would be nice, going out with my wife and child.

Emerald is such a happy baby. I'm glad her mother's mental state hasn't had a negative effect on her. She loves everything. I can't believe she's already three months. Growing so fast and even more beautiful every single day.

Three months old. Three months of growing and smiles. Three months of happy giggles and changing diapers.

But it's also been three months of tears and anxiety. Three months of mood swings and insomnia. Three months of screaming, crying, arguing.

Three months.

I don't know how much longer I can do this.

CHAPTER FIFTEEN

A FTER Cordelia Waters Friday May 19, 2016

I'm sitting on the couch in the living room, trying to refrain from crying, yet again. It's officially been twenty-four hours since she was taken.

I peer out the window just in time to see the sky turning a mixture of orange and pink. The days are getting longer now that it's spring. Soon enough, the sun will be out until eight o'clock.

Staring at the landscape before me reminds me of summer nights as a child, when I would yearn for the sunlight at all hours of the day. My admiration for warmth and sunshine must come from the fact that I'm a summer baby. I despise winter and the cold. Nothing irritates me more than having to hide under layers upon layers before leaving the house due to the temperature. And snow – don't even get me thinking about snow.

But then I do think about snow. And I think about winter. And then I think about November and Emerald's birth. I feel the tears fill my eyes and spill down my cheeks. I guess it took having her taken away from me to realize how much I truly needed her.

Detective Sullivan is back and I feel somewhat glad to see him. I appreciate the fact that he's been coming here periodically throughout the day, giving me updates on whatever they have, even when it's nothing at all.

The news about Marcia's husband came as a shock, but then again, it's just marijuana. At least it wasn't cocaine or methamphetamine. But none of that matters because they still haven't found my daughter.

Detective Sullivan returns to the woman detective, a petite blonde with vibrant blue eyes. I've already decided that I don't like her. She arrived this afternoon, bringing with her a whirlwind of accusations and patronising tones. I should be used to it by now, the staring and the blame. It doesn't get easier, though.

The entire day has dragged on, as if it isn't bad enough as it is. From officers coming in and out the house all day, to Weston being MIA since this morning. Our daughter is missing and you think he'd at least have the decency to be home with me. It's times like these where Weston proves to be selfish, only thinking about himself and his feelings. Times like these when I need him the most. At least Colton was able to come by, even if only for a short time. My parents' flight should have landed by now and they'll be arriving soon.

I catch them glancing at me, Detective Sullivan and the blonde. They continue to speak among themselves, eyeing me from time to time. My heart pounds in my chest. They're talking about me.

Detective Sullivan nods, pulls out his phone. I watch him carefully, trying to read his lips. The call isn't long. He slides the phone back into his pocket and begins making his way over to me.

"Cordelia Waters," he says formally. All traces of the detective I thought I knew gone, replaced by some official, doing his job. "We need to bring you down to the precinct for questioning." My throat constricts. I can't breathe. "What's going on? Why can't you ask me questions here? Everyone's been questioning me here!" "Please, Mrs. Waters, let's not make this more difficult. If you could please come with me –" "You think I did this? They convinced you that I killed my own daughter!" I scream. The blonde rushes over and restrains me. I feel metal lock around my wrists, which she holds behind my back. I bet she's loving this. "Why are you doing this to me!?" I cry. Detective Sullivan stares at me, blank expression. He doesn't answer.

———

I've never been in an interrogation room before. It's cold and I wish I'd brought a sweater. I'm offered a glass of water but I decline. A woman I don't know is setting up a video camera. Detective Sullivan walks in, sits across from me at the table.

"Gerard, please," I beg. "Let me go home." "We just need you to answer some questions for us." "Okay." I sit up straight, adjusting in the hard, metal chair. "Ask me anything." He clears his throat, states the date, time, and who is in the room. Then he begins. "Let's start from the beginning. I want you to tell me everything that happened on Thursday May eighteenth, from the moment you woke up, to the moment that Emerald went missing." I stare at him. "I've already gone over this. Multiple times." "Please." His eyes will me not to argue. "Okay," I say. I take in a breath. "I woke up at the usual time, seven-forty-five. I checked on Emerald, who was already awake and sitting up in her crib, and put her in the playpen. Weston watched her while I showered quickly, then we switched and I fed her breakfast." I pause, gathering my thoughts. "Weston left for work around eight-thirty. I made some oatmeal. I start work at nine, so I put Emerald in the playpen beside my desk and got to work. She's a good girl – hardly ever cries or fusses. She's content just playing on the floor with her toys," I smile, remembering. "I took her to watch some cartoons for a little bit around ten-thirty –" "But you didn't log out." "No, it was just for ten minutes or so.

To calm her down." "She was upset?" "She was getting fussy. Crying a little bit. So we watched Mickey Mouse for a bit, then I changed her diaper... Do I need to go into details?" "Just tell me everything that happened." I nod my head. "I went back to work, Emerald in her playpen beside me. We ate lunch around noon. I had a sandwich, and Emerald had some apple sauce and mashed-up berries –" "What time did you log out for lunch?" "Around twelve o'clock. That's what time I usually take my break." "Records show that you logged out at eleven-forty-eight." "Okay...? Twelve minutes before noon. My apologies." "Every minute counts, Mrs. Waters. Especially since you logged out and never logged back in." "What are you talking about?" "You logged out at eleven-forty-eight and there is no record of you logging back in." "Are you sure?" "Yes." "Oh," I pause, trying to collect my thoughts. "I must have forgot," "So you claim to have been working that afternoon?" "Yes. I worked until around two-thirty. Then she started getting cranky so I put her down for a nap. Or was it three?" I pause. "No, it must have been two-thirty –" "In your original statement you say two-thirty," "Yes, sorry. It was two-thirty. I was a bit tired myself. I knew that nobody needed me urgently at work, so I sat on the couch for a moment. I must have dozed off. I didn't wake until Weston got home and was calling my name." "As your initial statement goes," "Yes, because that is what happened. You think I'm lying?" "I just find it odd that you never logged back into work." "As I told you, I must have forgot. I guess I was more exhausted than I thought." "Pretty convenient, isn't it?" My eyes dart up and meet his. "What's convenient?" "That there is five hours of unaccounted time, and you just happened to be exhausted." "I beg your pardon?" "I'm going to ask you this once," he says. "Did you kill your daughter, Mrs. Waters?" My eyes widen. "No." I fight to keep my voice calm and composed, despite the fact that my body is on fire. "I did not kill my daughter. I have not seen my daughter since yesterday at two-thirty p.m., Thursday May eighteenth. And she was perfectly content, in her crib sleeping." He eyes me, unsure of how to proceed. "Am I being arrested?" I ask. "Not at this moment." "Then can I go?" He holds my gaze. "We're finished here, for now. But I don't think I have to remind you that this is far from over. We're watching you, Cordelia." His words are cold as ice. "Don't go too far, now."

So I don't. I don't go far at all. Where else would I go other than home?

———

I've not been home thirty minutes when there's a knock at the door. It's nearly seven o'clock and I dread opening the door to more officers coming in to interrogate me.

I left the police station feeling shaken up and horrified. My stomach is in knots and I have a pounding headache. It's one thing to have your daughter go missing – that's enough stress and upset for one person to handle. But being accused of murdering your only baby? I can't put into words how that feels.

I had just made myself a cup of tea to calm my nerves, settled onto the couch, when I hear the knocking. I find this very concept odd since officers have just been walking in and out of our home for the past couple of hours at their own accord.

I tilt my head sideways, wondering if I should answer it or if someone else will. A few officers are posted around my home, monitoring me. The one's I know by name: Matt Holden, the one who accused Weston of being a serial cheater. Rowan Ashby, who took my statement last night and uses an accusing tone while speaking with me. And the newest member to the clan: Detective Claire Robbins, the blonde who cuffed me and smiled. Along with her came Sergeant Olivia Sol, who has remained neutral on her assumptions about me. What a lovely little gang we have here.

My thoughts are answered when Detective Robbins struts towards my front door and opens it wide, allowing an older man to come inside. Great, as if there weren't enough people here already.

He smiles at her as he removes his jacket, revealing a dark green sweater vest. He wears small spectacles that cover his eyes, and his hair is beginning to gray slightly. He must be in his early sixties, at least. I keep my eyes focused on him, wondering who he might be since he's clearly not an officer.

As if reading my mind, he looks my way and our eyes meet. I hold his gaze. He smiles, a friendly, welcoming smile. He turns to Detective Robbins and begins to speak, although what he is saying is unknown to me. She nods and the man begins walking towards me.

"You must be Cordelia," he smiles as he stands in front of me. "May I?" he gestures to the chair. I nod. "I'm Doctor Eilsteen," he sticks out his hand. I hesitate before shaking it. "Did they invite you here?" I nod towards the officers. "They did. I'm here to chat with you, perhaps monitor you for the night, if that's alright with you." Upon watching my mouth open in protest, he begins speaking again. "Due to your history over these past few months, Detective Robbins felt it was best that you had someone here with you." "I'm sorry, what is this? Are you here to babysit me because you don't think I'm stable enough to handle things on my own? Where is Doctor Wyatt? She's my doctor. She's been here for the past six months. She'll tell you that I'm fine." "Doctor Wyatt is not at liberty to be with you right now. She's waiting to be questioned." "By the police? They think she had something to do with this?" "Easy now," he smiles. His words flow steadily through a calm and collected voice. "The police are doing every-thing they can do find your daughter, Cordelia. Doctor Wyatt worked very closely with both you and your daughter over the past six months. Of course they're going to question her. I'm not saying that she's guilty or had anything to do with Emerald's abduction at all, but we can't have people who were so involved in your life making critical decisions regarding your well-being at this stage." "Right, only you can do that." He smiles again. "May I ask you some questions?" "I just got home from being questioned, actually. In an interrogation room at the police station." I snap. He stares at me, eyes sympathetic. "But if you feel the need to ask more, then please, go right ahead." He clears his throat and cranks his neck slightly, adjusting in the seat. "I understand you suffered from a very severe postpartum psychosis. That must have been very difficult for you," "Is that a question or are you telling me?" "It was a question." "Yes. It was difficult. You can't imagine what I went through." "I've worked with many patients who have suffered from postpartum psychosis and much worse," he explains. "But I've also seen many of my patients get better. They've progressed so well with their lives that they hardly ever remember their postpartum days." "Okay." I pick at my nails, from nerves, out of habit. "How did you initially feel when your daughter was born?" I pause for a moment, considering how to answer his question. "I felt that she wasn't really mine. I didn't want her." "And after your extensive therapy with Doctor Wyatt, would you say those thoughts and feelings changed?" "Yes. Yes, of course. I was cleared to go back to work over two months ago. I'm fine now." "How do you feel about your daughter now, Mrs. Waters?" I raise my eyebrow. He's treating me like a suspect. I know my honest feelings towards Emerald: tolerated. That's how I feel about her. Whenever she's around, I simply tolerate her. I anticipate the days that Marcia comes over to watch her, and I loathe the times that I am alone with her. My head feels like it might explode every time I hear her cry. But I tolerate it. I don't snap, I don't cry. I'm much better now. I know how to deal with these thoughts. Healthy and new. My depression and anxiety are gone. So are all of the Bad Thoughts. Doctor Wyatt was very pleased with my progress. I accepted the fact that Emerald will be a part of my life for a long time. That doesn't mean I'm ecstatic about it, but I tolerate it. That's all I need to do. But I'm sure as hell not going to tell this man that. "I love my daughter," I state proudly. "I would never do anything to hurt her." "I wasn't implying..." he pauses. "But what are your feelings towards her?" "I already told you my feelings. I love her. She's my pride and joy. What else do you expect me to say?" "Well, some mothers might describe their feelings towards their child as admiration, magical, a beautiful bond, their entire life." "Yeah, she's the apple to my eye. I've had a difficult six months, I don't know what else you want me to say." He pauses for a moment, then readjusts his glasses. "Mrs. Waters," he begins. "Have you been feeling stressed or overwhelmed lately?" "No," I answer without hesitation. I know where he's going with this. "Sometimes the first few months can be hard. It's a difficult transition, switching from such an extreme lifestyle and getting back into swing of things with your old life." "I'm fine, really. Work is good. I love my job." "That's good. You're with District Systems, correct?" "Yes, I'm the IT manager. I oversee all the big projects, decision making and such." "Lots of responsibility I take it," he says. I don't respond, so he continues. "Does the job ever get to you? Is it ever too much?" "Why do you keep asking about my job? I already told you that I love my job. In fact –" I stop myself. "In fact what, Mrs. Waters?"In fact, I love my job more anything. Including my child, I think to myself but don't dare say out loud. I'm digging the hole deeper and deeper for myself. "Nothing," I say. "I really enjoy what I do." "I'm glad," he pauses again, thinking, I assume. "You think I had something to do with this. I know the police do." "Well that's why I'm here, Cordelia," he says my name again. "That's what we're going to figure out. But I just want to assure you, that if something did happen –" "I can assure you, doctor, nothing happened. I don't know how many times I have to say that. If I knew where my fucking child was, do you think I'd be sitting here listening to you lecture me?" I snap. I can't help it. The accusations, the police officers in my home – I can't take it any longer. They think I'm guilty. They think I killed Emerald. "Mrs. Waters, please," he reaches out to steady me but I pull away. He takes in a breath, then folds his hands in his lap. "I'm going to give you some time. I understand you need your space. I'll be posted here overnight, just in case you need anything," Because we believe that you're guilty. "Sergeant Olivia Sol will be stationed here overnight as well. You can speak with her and ask her any questions you may have. Is this alright with you?" he asks. "Do I have a choice?"

———

I'm distracted from my thoughts of anguish and misery when the front door opens and my parents walk in. I turn my head and watch as they step inside, looking all but confused and out of sorts as they take in the array of police officers who are standing around my house.

"Oh, Cordelia!" my mother cries as I push myself into her embrace. Besides Colton, she's the first person I've felt that I can rely on during this time of crisis. Someone who I know is on my side. Someone I can cry to. "We are so sorry we didn't get here sooner. Oh my God, my baby." She holds my face in her hands and the tears start flowing. I can't help it. I'm so overwhelmed with anger, anxiety, and now, relief. "I missed you," I smile through the tears. "Oh honey, we weren't gone that long." My father puts his hand on my shoulder. I wipe my nose with my sleeve. "It's just been... so hard," I break down again. I feel both my parents holding me tight as their only daughter sobs. I wipe my eyes, trying to calm myself down and catch a breath. "Have they found anything yet?" my father asks. "No, not yet. But everyone's looking for her. They're going to find her." "They will, honey. They will."

I spend the next little while catching up with my parents. I tell them everything that has happened in the past twenty-four hours. They ask multiple times if I'm okay, mentally. It's like everyone around me is walking on eggshells regarding the topic.

Yes, I had postpartum psychosis. This fact has nothing to do with the abduction of my daughter. Why doesn't anyone understand that? It's like they're afraid I might crumble and break. Perhaps I will if they don't start talking to me like a normal human being. Like a normal mother.

On second thought, I guess I've never been a normal mother.

After talking about Emerald and her disappearance for as long as I can stand, we smoothly gear the conversation over to their time in Florida.

They tell me about the beautiful weather and the salty beaches. They've always loved Florida; it's a second home to them.

I ask if they've heard from Liam lately, but unfortunately he stays pretty off the grid with them as well. It's unfortunate, really, how such a silly thing could cause our once rock-solid family to fall apart. We're a puzzle, my family, and we're now missing one big piece. I wish he'd talk to us, especially now. This is his niece, for God's sake. He should be here. Even for me, he should be here.

Detective Sullivan is back, and I glare at him as he approaches us. I feel betrayed by him. The only person who believed me; the only one of them that I actually trusted. And now he's taken their side, believing that I'm guilty.

It's nearing nine o'clock, and I silently wish everyone would just leave already. But he says he needs to speak with my parents. I guess he's been awaiting their arrival.

At first I feel worried, as though they're going to speak about me behind my back. Such a trivial thing to worry about. But then I remind myself of the urgency this investigation holds. We all have one common goal: to find Emerald. However, I can't be too certain who's even on my side anymore.

Gerard leads my parents down the hall to our home-office to speak. I walk over to the kitchen to make myself a cup of tea. Only seconds upon entering what used to be one of my favourite areas of the house, I notice the mess of dishes piled in the sink. I don't have time for that right now. I'll just keep using clean dishes until they're all used up. Then, maybe I'll do dishes. Maybe.

I watch as the officers' converse around my living room. Some of them speak in hushed whispers and I can't help but wonder if they're talking about me. One man, younger looking, sits at the living room table typing away into a computer. I consider leaning over to see what he's doing, but decide its best I don't interfere. I don't want to give them any more reasons to suspect me of guilt.

Just then, the front door opens, once again, and in walks my husband. My heart nearly leaps out of my chest and I'm instantly filled with an array of emotions: happiness, then anger. Where the hell has he been all day?

I place my mug back down on the counter before I can even fill it and rush over to him as he removes his jacket and hangs it on the coat hanger.

"Where have you been all day?" my attempt at being quiethas failed. He looks at me and his eyeslook dead – emotionless, almost. Not a look I would have expected from him atthis moment. "I already told you, I've beenout with the police looking for our daughter." "All day? It's after nineo'clock, Weston. Where the hell have you been looking? Under park benches andin shopping bags?" "I'm not doing this rightnow." He pushes past me and starts off towards our bedroom. I look around and see theofficers staring at us. I ignore them and follow behind him, racing into ourbedroom and shutting the door behind us. He walks to the dresser andstands there, hands on the mahogany wood, staring down at the floor below hisfeet. "Weston," I speak gently thistime as I slowly approach him. "What's the matter? Did something happen?" Hedoesn't look at me right away. I can see him breathing heavily through hisnose. "Wes," He looks up at me. "I'msorry," he says. "I shouldn't have snapped at you. I'm just... I can't do this.Our daughter is missing. Missing! I just don't know..." he fades off. I get closer, until we'reinches apart, and place my hand on his back. "I know." He closes his eyes and I watchas tears begin to spill down his cheeks. My husband, the one who's always beenso strong and resilient through everything we've been through, has finallybroke. It breaks my heart. I lean in and wrap my armsaround him. "It's going to be okay," I whisper into his neck. "They're going tofind her. I know they will." It's quiet for a moment beforehe speaks. "I'm afraid," he mumbles through his tears. "Of what?" He breathes. "Everything."

CHAPTER SIXTEEN

A FTER Detective Gerard Sullivan Friday May 19, 2016

We step into the home-office. It's a spacious room, I assume where Cordelia is stationed for work twice a week. Perhaps where Weston comes to think.

There's a large desk in the corner with a built in book shelf and a large Mac desktop computer. A single chair sits behind the desk, so it's decided that we'll stand.

Lily and Jonah Cruz look around the room nervously, their minds distracted with thoughts of their daughter and missing grandchild. "I understand you've just arrived back from Florida," I start. "How was the Sunshine State?" "It was lovely," Lily forces a smile. "We love escaping the cold for a couple of months." "I bet," I return the smile. "I'll try to make this quick, I know you want to get back to your daughter," I pause, pulling out the notebook. "I just have a few things to go over." "Of course, anything we can do to help." Jonah says. I clear my throat. "I'm aware that you've been out of state for a little while. But prior to this, did you come here often to visit your daughter and her family?" "We try to, yes," Lily smiles. "We live up in Evanston, which as you probably know, is about a three hour drive from here, but we try to come down as often as we can." I look up and meet her eyes. "Why did Cordelia decide to move out here? Away from the family and hometown?" "She just wanted a change. I think she was tired of the same-old routine, wanted to get away from Chicago. She found Davenport, out and away from everything. A smaller, quaint place. She loved it." "I'm assuming you're close with Cordelia?" "Yes, of course. She's our baby. Our only girl. We've always been very close with her." Lily explains. "And what about your sons? I understand you have two." "Liam and Colton," Jonah says. "We were closer when the kids were young, but once they grew up... everyone just grows apart, eventually." "Liam's the baby of the family." Lily takes over. "He and his wife moved out to Indiana years ago. They have two children now, Sophie and Clayton." "But he doesn't speak with us." Jonah adds. I eye him, remembering what Colton told me earlier this morning. "Is there any particular reason?" Lily smiles gently. "Liam just doesn't see eye to eye with us. It happens." "Are you close with your other son?" "Yes, fortunately," Lily says. "He and his wife, Jada, live in Evanston as well, so we're able see them often. We've been trying to come see Cordelia and Emerald since she was born. The first months are the most important." "And how did you feel about your daughters' condition after the birth of Emerald?" Lily and Jonah turn to each other, then, exchanging expressions. "It was difficult," Jonah finally speaks. "Seeing her like that. It was heartbreaking." "Were you aware that Cordelia didn't want children?" Again, a long pause. "Cordelia always made it abundantly clear that she never intended on having children," Lily explains. "But people grow up, they change their minds. I knew she would have children eventually. We were so happy when we found out about the pregnancy. A third grandchild – what more can a grandparent ask for?" "Was there any particular reason that Cordelia didn't want kids? Or was it just a phase you think she simply grew out of?" "She, um," Lily hesitates, turns to her husband again. I watch them carefully. She's seeking approval. Of what, I'm not sure. Jonah nods his head. "Tell him." Lily keeps her eyes locked on her husband, her mouth beginning to tremble slightly. Then finally, she returns her eyes to mine. "There was an incident," she says. "When Cordelia was a child. Only eleven years old." "What kind of incident?" Just like that, she begins to cry. She squeezes her eyes closed and tears stream down her cheeks. I turn around, searching the desk for a tissue box. I find one, grab it, and hand it to her. She grabs a tissue and begins dabbing her eyes, blows her nose. I wait patiently, allowing her to take her time. Something happened. And whatever it is, it's bad. After a few moments of calming herself down and Jonah rubbing her back, reassuring her, Lily is ready to speak. "When the kids were young," she begins. "There was this boy who lived on our street. He was a couple years older than Colton, so maybe fourteen or fifteen at the time?" she turns to her husband to confirm. "His name was Samuel. The kids called him Sammy. Liam didn't play with them, he was only nine at the time. But Cordelia and Colton would play with him and some of the other kids. You know, go swimming in the summer time, ride their bicycles to the park, the regular stuff. But then, something happened with him and Cordelia. We didn't find out until much later, when she began acting strange." "Strange how?" "She didn't want to leave the house or go to school. It was very odd because she was such a friendly, outgoing kid who loved seeing other people. But this sudden change – it worried us." She stops and turns to her husband, signalling him to take over. "We took her to see a child psycholo- gist," Jonah begins. "After multiple assessments, he told us that he believed Cordelia was being, or had been, sexually abused." He pauses, as if to let this information sink in. "We were shocked. Outraged. We didn't believe it at first. We wondered how such a thing could be possible and who could be doing that to our daughter. Someone at school? A teacher perhaps?" he pauses again, taking a moment to gather his thoughts. "It took a while to figure it out, but eventually we discovered that it was Samuel. Cordelia would never say his name, and we began putting together the pieces from what Colton would tell us about their play-time and what some of the other kids in the neighborhood were saying. Although Cordelia has never spoken a word to us about it to this day, she did confirm a couple of months afterwards with her psychiatrist that it was indeed Samuel. He would make her do things..." he stops, closes his eyes. "That's fine, thank you," I say to spare him from reliving the gruesome details. I look down and jot his words into point form. "The psychiatrists said she was suffering from PTSD," he continues. "This lasted a few months. We thought she was never going to be herself again. But eventually, she returned to the same old Cordelia we knew and loved. It was almost as if she forgot about the incident entirely. She pushed it so far back into her subconscious, almost viewing it from a third person perspective, as though it didn't happen to her, but rather, someone she knew, or a character she watched on television. Like I said, she never talked about it again. But," he stops. "She began suffering from minor blackouts." "Blackouts?" "Yes. She would block out certain periods of time. The teacher's noticed that she would suddenly gain a sort of consciousness and not remember where she was or what had happened in the past hour. She would have gaps in her memories, forgetting major events, like her brother's soccer tournaments, or a school test. She didn't even remember writing them. "Again, we went back to the psychiatrist and he said that, in situations such as Cordelia's, children often suppress difficult memories or experiences as a coping mechanism, to deal with the pain. She learned to subconsciously block out specific experiences, sometimes bad ones, and sometimes arbitrary ones. She most likely has gaps in her childhood that she doesn't even know are missing, because to her, they never existed in the first place." "Does Cordelia remember the abuse?" "We're not sure," Lily says. "As I said, she's never spoken about it, so we can't be certain. For all we know, she blocked it out completely. She may not remember most of that year." "Mr. and Mrs. Cruz," I start. "Does Cordelia still experience blackouts?" "No. This happened years ago. I'm sure it wouldn't have continued for this long," Lily turns to her husband. "I mean, we're not sure. We don't live with her with her anymore. But I highly doubt it." Jonah says. "And essentially, you believe that this is the reason that Cordelia didn't want children?" "Well, that's what we thought. I mean, why else would a woman not want to have kids? She experienced a traumatic event, sexual abuse," Lily pauses, closing her eyes. "It damaged her. It changed her." I nod.

This is a big piece of information. If Cordelia is indeed somehow still experiencing losses of memory, she could have done something to her daughter and suppressed it completely, not even aware that it happened in the first place. In her mind, she honestly believes that she is innocent. That would explain the unaccounted time yesterday, when she logged out of work and wasn't heard from her until her husband got home.

I wanted to believe that she had nothing to do with this, I really did. But this new information is concerning. "Thank you for your time," I smile politely at them. "We're going to get to the bottom of this. We will find your granddaughter," I hold their gaze. "Go spend some time with Cordelia. I'm sure she needs it."

The Cruz' disappear to find their daughter. I walk back into the other room and find Robbins. "She is not to leave this house under any circumstances. And I want to be informed every time she moves. Understand?" Robbins nods her head, gives me a smirk as if to say, I told you so.

————

There is only one person left that I need to talk to. One person who knows Cordelia and her mental state better than anyone. And that would be Doctor Fiona Wyatt.

I make sure that the arrangements are in place. Doctor Eilsteen will stay overnight to keep watch on Cordelia, as well as Sergeant Sol. I feel better knowing that Olivia will be there. She'll watch her like a hawk. I also confirm that one officer will be stationed out front in the squad car.

My headache is getting worse and my stomach feels empty and nauseous. I can't recall the last time I've eaten. I wanted to believe her. I really did. I didn't think she could be capable of harming her own child. But I guess you never truly know a person.

Still, there's a part of me that's trying to convince myself and everyone else that this is one big misunderstanding. I want to believe her when she says she didn't hurt her daughter. But her story isn't adding up, and after hearing about the childhood abuse, as well as the PTSD and the blackouts... well, I think I have my answer.

I'll get some more information, talk to her doctor, then decide where to go from there. We could arrest her? Charge her with first-degree? But any lawyer would plea insanity. And it's only been twenty-four hours. We've already interrogated her once today, and if she did to something to that child, she may not even remember. What we need now is solid proof, evidence.

Until we have a body, there's no crime.

———

My watch reads nine-forty-six. I'm standing in front of a large Victorian house with wide double doors. I've rang the doorbell twice and no one has answered yet, but there's a car in the driveway, so I'm assuming someone is home.

Finally, the door opens, revealing a woman in a red robe. She has shoulder length hair, a light shade of brown, and dark green eyes. She isn't as old I'd as imagined her to be. I'm not sure why I create these images of people in my head before I meet them. I guess it gives me a better understanding of who they are before we meet face-to-face. She looks to be in her late forties, early fifties. She folds her arms tight across her chest and her expression is flat. She knows why I'm here.

"Fiona Wyatt?" "Yes." She tilts her chin. "I'm Detective Sullivan from the Davenport Police Department. I need to ask you some questions regarding a patient of yours, Cordelia Waters." "Of course. Come in." She stands back and opens the door, inviting me inside. She leads me to the kitchen and offers me a drink. "I'm fine, thanks." I take out my notepad and pen, then take a seat at the kitchen table. She slides into the seat across from me. I clear my throat. "When was it brought to your attention that Emerald Waters was missing?" "Cordelia called me this morning in a frenzy. I was prepared to go over there, make sure that she was alright. But I've been so busy today with other patients and personal matters. I was going to head over first thing tomorrow morning." I nod my head, studying her body language. The way she fiddles with the mug between her palms. "So to the extent of your knowledge, someone abducted Emerald?" "Well, yes. That's what Cordelia told me." "Doctor Wyatt –" "Please, call me Fiona." "Fiona. Given the circumstances of Cordelia's mental state, and due to the fact that you are the closest person who worked with her these past six months, I think you are the best person who can help me figure out what really happened here." "Apologies, but what exactly are you insinuating, detective?" "Do you think it's possible that Cordelia could have done something to Emerald? Something she may not have any recollection of?" She stares at me, expressionless. I can't read what she's thinking. "Are you asking me if I think Cordelia killed her daughter?" "Yes." "In my professional opinion, no. I do not. You are correct, Cordelia did suffer from severe postpartum psychosis. But many of my patients have gotten better, and Cordelia is one of them. I worked with her every day. I witnessed the progress she was making. She was happy again, no longer experiencing the depression or psychosis. She was cleared by a third-party to return to work over two months ago. We still have weekly check-ups and she updates me on everything that is going on. Everything has been fine. If there was any concern, I can assure you, I would let you know." "What about loss of consciousness? To your knowledge, has Cordelia ever suffered from blackouts?" "Blackouts? No. Not recently, anyway." "But in the past, yes?" "Well, she was going through a very difficult time after the birth of Emerald. She was suffering from minor delusions and hallucinations.

There may have been a few instances where she lost consciousness and couldn't recall what had happened. But I hardly consider that a blackout, and it surely wouldn't be concerning now. As I said, she's recovered and is better. These circumstances occurred immediately after the birth. They faded, then seized completely." "Fiona, I spoke with Cordelia's parents about an hour ago, and they told me some very disturbing things regarding her history with sexual abuse and PTSD." "Cordelia was sexually abused?" "Unfortunately, yes. A boy in her neighborhood. She was eleven and he was fifteen." "Oh, my." She brings her hand to her mouth. "I had no idea." "Her parents explained that Cordelia's subconscious blocked out traumatic experiences, resulting in gaps in her memory throughout the year. Her parents stated that Cordelia has never spoken about this event, and to this day, may not even have any idea that the events took place. From your personal experience in this field, do you think that patients who have suffered from PTSD as a child could still retain the symptoms from all those years ago?" "I'm not sure." She pauses, trying to gather her thoughts. "I mean, it's possible. Dissociative amnesia, brought on by acute repetitive psychological trauma. Or perhaps transient global amnesia. I just don't see why this behaviour would continue long after the abuse ended." "Coping mechanism?" "Perhaps. But it doesn't make sense that her subconscious would continue to block out arbitrary events that had no effect on her. Traumatic abuse, yes. But blocking out completely mundane activities?" "Is there more to the story here? Do I need to re-interrogate the parents?" "No no, I don't think that's necessary. I just... I don't know what to think. I had no idea that any of this happened," she pauses again. "Poor child." She closes her eyes and holds her left hand over her right. When she opens her eyes again, she looks me straight in the eyes. "Detective, with the information you have just given me – though it is severe and disturbing – I stand on my prior notion that Cordelia did not harm Emerald. She's been doing well. She has no prior history of violence. She wouldn't do that now, after all the progress she's made. She loves Emerald. And that I am certain." "What if she had a psychotic break? That is possible, yes? And the experience could have been so traumatizing for her that she blocked out the situation entirely?" "Perhaps. The possibility of that happening is very rare. As I said, she's happy right now. Everything is falling back into place, especially with their anniversary coming up. Everything in her life is going perfectly." "Anniversary?" "Cordelia and Weston's wedding anniversary. Four years on June sixteenth." "Ah, I see," I write this down. "So they're happy?" "Yes. Happy and in love." I pause again, thinking about the logout dilemma, the unaccounted for time. "Doctor Wyatt – Fiona, sorry – Cordelia's supervisor told another detective that she logged out for lunch yesterday around noon, and never logged back in. Emerald was taken somewhere, we estimate, between three and five. But I guess it could be anywhere after twelve since that is the last that anyone heard from Cordelia." "You really think she did this, don't you?" "I don't know what to believe right now. But it's my job to find that child. I just pray that it's not too late." She closes her eyes again and shakes her head slightly. "Well, you need to continue your investigation, looking elsewhere – outside suspects and such – because from my professional opinion and personal experience with Cordelia, I honestly do not think that she did this."

CHAPTER SEVENTEEN

B EFORE Weston Waters February 24, 2016

Another day gone and passed and the feeling of dread and defeat still consumes me. I don't know what to do with myself. It's as though I can feel the emotions draining from my body each day. She is draining the life from me.

I know that's horrible to say. I know it's horrible because she's going through hell. But she's dragging me down with her.

I've been trying to stay strong and keep my head above water. Emerald is my motivation. I have to do this for her – that's what I keep reminding myself. Because if I crack and fall apart, she'll have no one. Both of her parents will be a wreck and she'll have no one to care for her. I can't let that happen. We made the decision to bring her into this world, and I'm going to do everything in my power to make this work and give her a good life. I have to.

My receptionist, Carla, has been noticing that something is off. She's a sweet girl, but her constant checking up on me isn't helping. In fact, it's probably irritating me even more. Last week she began bringing me coffee every morning. I guess that's her way of trying to help. I appreciate it, I really do. But all of the coffee in the world can't fix what's wrong. A broken home. A broken life.

Is that what my life has become? Broken? My head-space is a disaster. I can't think straight, let alone get work done. I feel as though I'm letting my patients down every time I have to fake a smile or cancel an appointment.

Some days I feel like giving up. As though the entire weight of the world is on my shoulders. Perhaps I should speak to someone. A therapist, or someone who can help me cope.

I know I should be grateful. I should be grateful that Cordelia is alive and breathing, and that we have a healthy baby girl. But so many other things are astray.

I wish I could rewind time and prevent Cordelia from developing the psychosis. I don't even know if there is a way to prevent it, but I'd dedicate my damn life to finding out how. No one should have to experience what we have gone through these past few months. It's a tragedy, really. I've lost my wife. The old Cordelia. The woman I fell in love with.

I hope she's still in there, sheltered somewhere temporarily until the storm is over. I try to think positive and hope for the best, but right now, even that is difficult to reach for. No matter what I do, life just seems to be continuously going downhill and there's nothing I can do to stop it.

———

I've been going to Finnick's Tap a few times a week after I finish work. It's become a solace for me. Somewhere I can escape temporarily and avoid my problems.

I know that's wrong, avoiding the problems. It would be much healthier and efficient to solve the problem. But you see, I can't do that right now. There is no solution to this problem. So until there is, I will come here to escape the pain, drinking away my sorrows.

I won't turn into an alcoholic, I can guarantee that. I have far too much control and autonomy over my life. I would never let it get that far. And even if I did catch myself slipping – even just the slightest – I would bring myself back. I need to be there for Emerald. I won't destroy my life like that. This is just a break. It's what I need right now.

It's quarter-past-six when I glance at the clock and decide I should probably head home. My weekly routine has consisted of coming to Finnick's, getting a couple of drinks, staying for an hour or so, then going home. Cordelia hasn't even questioned my whereabouts. Not that I'm hiding this from her, but I'd prefer if she didn't know. She'd worry – think I was giving up on her. She's already going through enough, I couldn't put her through more.

But to be honest, I think she's too caught up in her own distress to even wonder about mine, or even consider why I'm coming home an hour later than usual each night. I've been telling her its work stuff. That Diane has been asking me to cover some new patients for her. Cordelia simply shrugs my words off like it's nothing. As long as I come home at the end of the night, that's the only thing she cares about.

Doctor Wyatt has been a huge help. I can't thank her enough for all that she's done. I just wish she had an instant cure for Cordelia so that things could go back to how they were before. But these things take time. And sitting here wishing for a miracle isn't going to make one appear.

I avert my eyes from the clock and focus on my glass, lifting it to my lips and finishing off the remaining contents. I wipe my mouth with the back of my hand and the door chimes, signaling someone has entered the bar. I turn my head slightly to get a brief glimpse of the person walking in.

It's a woman who's caught my eye. She's stunning, really. Tall and slim, walks with a beat in her step. Thick hair a shade of raven black flows over her burgundy trench coat, and I wonder what she wears underneath – considering her legs are bare – accompanied by black heels. Must be a dress or skirt. A formal outfit, perhaps.

My eyes drift upwards to her face. Her eyes are straight ahead, focused. She's walking to the bar. Her skin is a smooth bronze, despite the fact that it's winter. Her eyes are piercing blue gems, and above them, thick black lashes. She's wearing red lipstick, not too dark, but just enough to accentuate the plump shape.

I shouldn't be looking at her. I never look at other women. But something about her is so striking, alluring. The way she keeps her eyes focused as she walks, eventually sitting at the bar a few seats down from me.

I won't look anymore, I decide. I can't. I feel guilty even just thinking about looking. I have a wife. I love my wife. I will not look at other women.

I continue with my plan to leave. I stand and grab my coat that hangs over the bar stool.

The bartender returns, a polite woman named Maggie who I've grown accustomed to over my past few visits here. "Where ya goin?" she says to me as she places the glasses in her hand onto the counter. "I should probably head out now." "But the game's almost over. At least wait until it's done," she protests. "Fine." The words leave my mouth before I realize what I'm saying. Then I'm sitting back down again, removing my jacket. "Another rum and coke?" Maggie asks, grabbing a glass from behind her. "Sure. Why not." I force a smile.

I turn my head, trying to sneak the slightest glance at the woman. I start at her heels, slowing making my way up her body. When my eyes finally travel towards her face, I discover that she's staring directly at me.

I snap my head forward again, pretending it never happened. As though we didn't just lock eyes for a split second. Maggie fills the glass halfway then slides it over to me.

"Thanks," I mutter, and hold the glass to my lips. This is the last one. Then I'll go.

I turn my eyes toward the screen and focus on the game. It's football. I've never been a fan, but I have nothing else to do while I finish my drink, so I watch.

"They're doing awful tonight," I hear a voice say. I turn my head to the left to see that the woman has inched her way a few seats closer to me. There's only one empty chair between us. I'm confused at first. She can't be talking to me. Her eyes are locked on the screen, so I can't tell. As if reading my thoughts, she turns and looks at me, awaiting an answer. "Who?" is the only thing I manage to say. "The Tigers. They better get their shit together or they'll get eaten alive out there."Football. She's talking about Football. "Yeah," "You a Tigers fan?" she asks, taking a sip of her drink. "No. I don't really watch sports. It's entertaining, though. Something to keep my eyes on." "Oh, shame. Football is like religion to me. My dad was a fanatic when I was growing up. We never missed a game." I smile slightly and nod my head. I'm terrible at small talk. Especially when it comes to women whom I don't normally speak to. Women who aren't my wife. My thoughts wander and I can't help but question why she is speaking with me. I'm a good looking guy. Perhaps she's bored, wants some company. A woman that striking has to be taken. So what does she want with me? "You from around here?" she says, starting up conversation once again. "Yeah, for a few years now. I grew up in Chicago." "A Chicago native, is that so?"

"Mhm," I nod. "Born and raised." "What made you decide to come out here?" "Change of scenery, I guess." "It's nice out here. Quiet and peaceful. I used to live in the city as well." "You did? Where about?" I ask. "South Shore. Near Avalon Park." "You don't say? I'm from West Town." "I had a good friend who was from there. I'm surprised we've never run into each other." I laugh slightly and take another sip from my drink. "What's your name?" she asks, staring at me with eyes of intrigue. "Weston," I say. "And you are?" She smiles, tilts her head to the side slightly. "Rosella."

CHAPTER EIGHTEEN

AFTER Cordelia Waters Saturday May 20, 2016

Day three. The second morning I've had to wake up with the weight of the world pressing down on my chest. An absence that prevents the air from entering my lungs.

Thirty-eight hours. Emerald has officially been missing for thirty-eight hours. Why haven't the police found her yet? Isn't this their job? To find missing children? And apparently the longer that she is missing, the guiltier I'm looking.

When it was solely Weston's accusations, it was difficult, yes, but I could handle it. But now with practically the entire task-force keeping their watchful eyes on me, even Gerard having his doubts, I can't help but feel scared and hopeless.

I did not kill my daughter. Innocent until proven guilty, right? Soon enough they will find whoever did this and my name will be cleared. Emerald will be back home with us and all rights will be restored. The truth will reveal itself soon enough. I just hope it's sooner than later.

My mind is still swarming with questions that don't have answers. Who took Emerald? Who would want to take her? They've officially searched all of the Mendozas' properties and have crossed them off the list. I didn't think they were responsible, anyway. They're good people, Marcia and her husband.

Whoever took Emerald must have done it for money. Why else would someone take my child? But that begs the question: if someone did take her to get money from us, why haven't we received a ransom call?

My thoughts drift to dangerous territories: perhaps it was a child pedophile. Or a sadistic psychopath who likes babies. I try not to think like that, but I can't help it. I pray for her. I pray that she is safe and will be returned home to us soon.

The doctor has been lingering since he arrived last night. He kept his distance, but watched from a close perimeter, making sure he was aware of everything I did, right until the minute I crawled into bed.

Weston slept in our bed last night. I guess he couldn't claim the couch again since the overnight officer was there, the doctor in the spare room. They're invading our home. It doesn't even feel like a home right now – more like a crime scene. But I guess that's what it is.

I tried to talk to him before bed. But after his latest conversation with Gerard, my husband is even more paranoid than he was before, thinking I did something to our daughter. No matter how many times I tell him that someone abducted our baby – that she's out there somewhere – he won't even look at me.

I yearn for the moment that they find whoever did this. Then he will look at me and tell me how sorry he is to have ever doubted me.

I need him to just look at me. To hold me. To love me.

———

I shower, throw on some clothes, and sluggishly wander into the kitchen. Sergeant Sol sits at my kitchen table, reading the newspaper. She glances up for half a second, gives me a short smile, then returns to her reading. I try to block out her presence. It's fairly early, just past seven, and Doctor Eilsteen hasn't appeared in my sights yet, thank God. The sight of him alone causes my blood pressure to skyrocket.

After sipping my coffee and checking the internet and news websites for any updates, the doorbell rings.

When I open the door, I'm not surprised to see Detective Sullivan standing there, looking as though he got three hours of sleep, tops.

"Find anything?" I ask. "I'm afraid not. May I come in?" I nod my head and he steps inside. He greets Sergeant Sol, then heads over to the living room, takes a seat on the couch. I follow behind, perching myself on the pleather chair. "Listen," I begin. "I don't really think it's necessary having all these officers here." "With all due respect, Cordelia, I don't think you're in a position to make that call." I'm taken back by the venom in his voice. Is this the same Gerard who was so kind to me the night of the abduction? But then I remember that that Gerard is gone. Replaced by someone else. "I'm telling you, you have it all wrong. I did not do anything to my daughter!" He looks over in the direction of Sergeant Sol, who has her head down as she reads, dismissing me. Dismissing my excuses. "I spoke with Doctor Wyatt last night," he turns to face me again. "And?" My heart leaps. "She seems to remain firm in her beliefs that this was an abduction. However, we're not ruling out anything just yet. I understand that you're stressed and upset, and you're going through a very difficult time right now. But you also need to understand that it is my job to find your daughter. And I will do whatever means necessary to bring that child home. And if that means keeping you in here under tight supervision, then so be it." I close my eyes, his words sending a blow to my chest. "Alright." "I'm sorry if this upsets you. But it's what needs to be done." "Fine. I understand," I meet his eyes, searching for any sign of recognition, compassion. "Just find my daughter." He nods his head, clears his throat. "How is your husband today?" "Fine, I guess. He won't talk to me. He's still sleeping. He must be exhausted, out searching for Emerald all day." "He was out looking for Emerald?" "Yeah..." I glance up at him, slightly confused. "He said he was with the police, helping them look for her." "Well, he wasn't with any of my guys. In fact, no one saw your husband at all yesterday. They assumed he was here, hiding out in his room most of the day." My heart stammers in my chest. "Weston wasn't here. I was here. All day. While he was out looking for our daughter!" "I see," he pauses. "Perhaps he was out by himself, then." "No, he told me he was with the police." "I don't know what to tell you, Mrs. Waters'. None of my men saw him." I let this information sink in once more. "I'll have to talk to him then. If he even speaks to me." "Yes. You probably should."

————

The doorbell rings around nine-o'clock and Gerard answers it. He's been going over some files at the kitchen table with Sergeant Sol. I made them scrambled eggs, adding the frying pan to the pile of dirty dishes that I don't plan on doing.

I am so certain that it's just going to be another cop at the door that when I hear her voice, I almost don't register. I turn my head and crane my neck to see: it's Savannah.

I drop my phone on the counter and rush over to her. She turns her head, eyes widened when she sees me. I fall into her and wrap my arms around her neck, and before I realize, I'm crying, yet again.

"I'm so sorry, Cordy," she grasps my hands. Gerard closes the door and lingers behind us. "I'm Detective Sullivan," he says, sticking out his hand.

"And you are?" "Savannah Valentine." She shakes his hand. "Ah, you must be from District Systems?" "Yes." She nods. "Would you mind if we chat shortly? I'll give you a few minutes." "Yes, of course. Whatever I can do to help."

Weston has showered and is making his way to the home-office to talk with Rowan Ashby. Savannah and I pass him as we walk down the hallway towards my bedroom. I nod to her, telling her to go ahead without me, then I grab hold of my husband's arm in passing. He looks at me. "Where the hell were you yesterday?" I ask in a hushed whisper. "How many times do I have to tell you this?" "Gerard said he didn't see you. None of them did." He stares at me defiantly, Officer Ashby waiting to our left. "Doesn't matter what they saw," he says. "I was out there looking for our daughter." We hold eye contact for a moment. "I have to go," he breaks from my grasp and heads into the office, closing the door behind them.

I make my way to my bedroom and close the door behind me, relieved to finally get some privacy away from the watchful eyes in my home.

"How are you holding up?" Savannah asks once we've sat at the edge of my bed, her sympathetic eyes lingering over mine. "I'm alright. It's just... it's so hard." My throat feels raw and the tears begin to spill over again. I can't hold it in. "Oh, sweetie." She brings me close and hugs me tight. I sniffle, leaning into her neck as I cry. Once she lets go, I reach over to the nightstand and grab a tissue to dab my eyes. "Do they have any leads?" "Not really. Well, they have one person they're pretty set on." "Who?" "Me." "You? Are they crazy?" "No, but apparently I am." "Oh, that's ridiculous. You didn't do a thing to your daughter. That's fucking –" "I know, I know. That's what I keep telling them. But they don't believe me. They think I had a psychotic break or something." "Well, are they still looking for her?" "Yes, simultaneously holding me here and searching for her elsewhere." "God, I can't imagine what you're going through. This must be horrible." "It is. It really is. And what's even worse? Weston won't speak to me. He blames me as well." "No..." "Yeah." "He's your husband! He's supposed to stand by your side." "Yeah, well I guess it's a little hard when I've been so scattered the past few months." "Honey, none of that was your fault. And besides, you're all better now. The psychiatrists cleared you a while back now. You're fine! How can they even think that?" "I guess crazy people don't instantly get cured." "You're not crazy." I take in a deep breath. "Yeah, well, tell them that." "I will. That cop wants to speak with me." "He's a detective." She gives me a look. "Same shit." "But please, tell them. Anything. I need them to believe me." "I will, Cordelia. Don't worry. We'll figure this out."

CHAPTER NINETEEN

A FTER Detective Gerard Sullivan Saturday May 20, 2016

I wait in the living room for Cordelia and her friend to finish talking. Then I will need to talk to the friend myself.

While I wait, I take out my notepad and scan through the list of names. Liam Cruz. I need to call the brother. I check my watch. It's almost eleven. I find the phone number and dial it into my phone.

"Hello?" he answers. "Yes, hello, is this Liam Cruz?" "This is. Who's asking?" "Detective Sullivan from the Davenport Police Department. Do you mind if I ask you some questions about your sister, Cordelia Waters, regarding the disappearance of her daughter, Emerald?" The line is silent and I almost think he's hung up. "Um, yeah. Of course." "You are aware of her disappearance, yes?" "Yes, my parents called yesterday morning." "You live in Indiana, correct? Were you planning on coming out here?" "Yes. Well, I don't know. My family's not close. We don't really talk much." "Is that so? Because just yesterday I spoke to your entire family in one house." Silence again. "Everyone's there?" "They are. Probably wondering where you are. Aren't you the least bit concerned about what is happening with your niece?" "I am." He pauses. "Shit, you probably think I'm a horrible person. It's not like that. My wife and I were trying to find someone to watch the kids so we could drive out this weekend." "Is that so?" "Yes." "Why not bring the kids with you?" "I don't want them to have to deal with this. It will upset them." "So in that case, are you still planning on coming out here?" "Yes. I mean, we're trying." "Trying. Alright." I debate whether he's telling the truth, or if this is just a lie he made up on the spot. "You said you have some questions?" he asks. "Yes. I know you say you're not close with your family, but do you happen to know anyone who may have anything against your sister or her husband? Anyone who may want money? Someone looking for revenge from the past, perhaps?" "No, not that I can think of. They're good people. Cordelia's never really had any enemies. Then again, she's never really had that many friends either." "So I've heard." "She's kind of quiet. Introverted really. Likes to keep to herself." "So you can't think of anyone who might want to hurt her?" "No. Not one person." "Are you aware of her blackouts? From childhood, that is." The line is quiet for a moment. "Not really. I was only a kid when she started getting them. My parents told me about it years later. They said not to bring it up around her. I guess it's a touchy subject." "So you don't remember much from that year? She was eleven, you must have been, what, nine?" "Eight. Yeah, I was young. Like I said, I don't remember much." "Do you remember a boy from your neighborhood? Samuel?" "Barely. There were lots of kids we used to hang out with." "So you haven't heard from anyone over the years?" "No. After college I moved out of town. Didn't really keep in touch with anyone." "When was the last time you saw your sister?" "Um, it must have been three years ago. Just after Clayton was born. She and West came down to see him." "But other than that, you don't talk?" "No, not really." "But to your knowledge, she and Weston seemed happy? No enemies or financial problems? Nothing out of the ordinary?" He pauses again and I can hear the sound of his nails scratching the stubble on his face. "No. Nothing out of the ordinary. Except... I guess, one thing worth mentioning. I talked to Cordelia about a month ago. She called for my birthday," another pause. "She said things weren't going too well with her and West. Seemed like things were going downhill." "Downhill? What do you mean?" "I don't know, really. She was crying, saying she felt like things were over between them. Like he changed or something. After her postpartum." Odd. Everyone else I spoke to seemed to say only good things about the Happy Couple. Could there have been trouble in paradise? "Did she say anything else?" I ask. "Not really. She was crying. Said she missed me and wished I called more." "So you think things weren't going well for them?" "Didn't sound like it." "Alright." I glance at my watch. "Thank you for your time, Mr. Cruz. I will call you if I have any other questions."

I hang up the phone, a string of disordered thoughts roaming around my mind. Why didn't Cordelia mention this before? She made it seem like everything was fine between them. And no one else that I spoke to seemed to have anything negative to say. Only positive things. They are so happy. So in love. Picture-Perfect.

It's possible that no one knew. It's also possible that they sorted things out. Liam said he spoke with Cordelia a month ago. Could they have sorted out whatever problems they were facing by then?

———

We walk into the office just as Ashby and Weston are leaving. Savannah Valentine follows behind me, looks around for a chair, then decides to stand-lean against the desk. I stand adjacent to her and bring out my notepad.

"Ms. Valentine," I begin. "Were you born with that surname?" "No," a coy smile appears. "I was born a Howard. But that name brings back terrible memories. My parents were not good people. I had it legally changed when I was eighteen." "What made you choose Valentine?" "I've always thought it was a lovely word." "It is indeed," I break momentarily. "How long have you known Cordelia?" "A couple of years now," "So you've been with District Systems long?" "Three years. I met her when I first started." "I see. How do you like working there?" "I love it. I'm really happy there. My job is pretty awesome, so," "Does Cordelia have many other friends at work?" "Um, sort of. I mean, there's work-friends, and then there's friends-you-see-at-work. Cordelia and I are friends both inside the office walls, and outside. We have a closer friendship. But then there's the work-friends, who you are friendly with, but your relationship doesn't extend beyond the office." "Is she close with many other of your co-workers, besides you?" "Our one friend, Tessa. But she's always busy with her family and doesn't come out too much anymore. Other than that, I don't think Cordy is close with many others. She's very reserved – likes to keep to herself and such." "Were you aware of her postpartum psychosis?" "Yes. I came to visit her a few times. I know how difficult it was for her." "So you're familiar with Emerald and the family?" "Yes, somewhat. Emerald is a darling. Looks just like Cordy." She stops for a moment, looking down at her feet. "I can't believe this is happening." She meets my eyes. "Who would do such a thing?" "That's what I'm here to find out. Are you close with her husband?" "I wouldn't say close. He's a nice guy. But when Cordy and I get together, he's usually not around, or she's trying to escape the household, if you know what I mean." "No, I don't." She pauses and smiles. "You know... all marriages need a break sometimes. So we like to go out and just have fun." "Define fun?" "Go out, have a few drinks, see a movie maybe. Cordelia likes going to the movies." "Do you do this often?" "No, not really. But like I said, sometimes a wife just needs to get away and let loose sometimes." This comment strikes me as odd. Cordelia doesn't seem like the type to go out and let loose. She's conservative, likes her privacy. From what I can tell, at least. "Oher than the times you say she needs to let loose, how would you describe their marriage?" "Healthy. Honest. I'm not around that much to be a good judge of that, but from what I can see on the occasion that I do, they seem fine. Happy." "Do they seem happy?" "Yes. From what I can tell." "Does Cordelia ever talk about her marriage? Or Emerald?" "Not really. As I said, we try to escape from our personal lives." "So Cordelia has never mentioned anything negative about her marriage? Wanting to escape it? Mentioned anything that made her upset?" "No. Nothing. She and Weston are fine. What I meant by escaping was just, you know, girl time. Every woman needs it." "Are you married?" "Heavens no." "You say that like marriage is a bad thing." She laughs, her white teeth exposed through pink lips. "Not necessarily a bad thing. Just not for me. I don't like to be tied down." "I see. So you steer clear from all relationships?" "I didn't say that. I have boyfriends. Monthly, annually, whatever. They don't usually stick around long." "Why is that?" She shrugs. "I'm just not big on commitment." "Alright, and do you know if Cordelia or Weston have any enemies? Someone who might want to do something like this?" "God no. They're both good people. I can't even imagine why someone would take a child. A baby. It's horrible." "One last question, Ms. Valentine. Why did it take you a day and a half to come over here? I mean, I'd assumed since you and Cordelia are close, you would have come over yesterday. Or the night Emerald went missing, even." She stares at me for a moment. "She didn't call me until yesterday, and I was out of town at a business meeting." "Business meeting? Whereabouts?" "Oh, I guess I should have mentioned this before. I'm a wedding planner, on the side. I was meeting with a couple yesterday out in Chicago." She explains. I write this down, and wonder why exactly she didn't mention it before. "So the earliest I could come was today. I came as soon as I could."

———

This investigation is going absolutely nowhere. No evidence. No solid leads. Nothing. All I have is a successful drug-bust, a mysterious car, and a desperate-to-prove-her-innocence mother. So, nothing.

I need to get back to my office, get some caffeine, and figure this out. The first forty-eight hours are almost up and the clock is ticking. We're running out of time.

I tell Cordelia that I'll keep her updated, then I give Ashby a wave before I head out. I'm walking to the car, which is parked on the street, when I see the man next door knelt down in his garden. Looks like he's digging up weeds. This must be the neighbor Cordelia mentioned before. Dave, I think it was. Ashby and Holden did preliminary statements with all of the neighbors yesterday, but I should speak with him, get a feel for myself.

"Good morning," I say, standing over him. He squints up at me, hand above his eyes to block the sun. "Oh, hi there!" He stands up quickly. "You must be investigating the disappearance of the Waters' girl." "I am. I'm Detective Sullivan. Do you mind if I ask you a few questions?" "Of course! I'm Dave. Dave Harvey," he sticks out his hand, then realizes instantaneously that his glove is filled with dirt from gardening. He rips it off his hand, laughs slightly, and sticks his hand back out. I give it a firm shake. "How well do you know the Waters?" I ask. "Just about as well as you can know a neighbor. I mean, we're not super close or anything. But we're friendly. They come over to our place in the summertime for barbecues. My wife and Cordelia get along well. They love their soap operas." "What is your wife's name?" "Gillian." I write this down. "Would you say that Mr. and Mrs. Waters get along well?" "Oh yes, lovely couple they are. Always very cheerful and upbeat. Like one of those picture-perfect families you see on TV. They have the good-paying jobs, a big fancy house, the white picket fence, one little girl. They're living the dream." "So they don't argue or fight?" "Not that I know of. Every time they've been to my place they're always cuddled up in each other's arms." "Do you and your wife ever go to their place?" "Erm, not really. Been there once for a Christmas get-together. Nice place. They had renovations done about two years ago. Real nice kitchen," he pauses. "I actually haven't seen em around as often as before. I saw the baby a few times, whenever Weston would bring her out. But I haven't seen Cordelia. Weston said she was sick recently?" "Yes. She wasn't well for a few months." "Oh, is she alright now?" "I believe so." "Do you know what she was sick with?" "I'm not really at liberty to say. I just have one last question, then I'll let you go." "Sure, what is it?" "Do you happen to know anyone that owns a red Impala? Or have you seen one in this area before?" "Hmmm, red Impala? Not that I can recall." "What about on Thursday afternoon? Could you recall if you saw any unfamiliar vehicles on the street?" He thinks about this. "Uhh, nope. Nothing out of the ordinary." He glances out towards their driveway. "Just those two cars that are in the driveway now." I follow his gaze and spot Cordelia's BMW as well as the white Ford Explorer that Savannah pulled up in. "Those two vehicles there?" I ask. "Are you sure? Mr. Waters drives a Mercedes." "I'm fairly certain, because my wife wants one of those Explorers in white. I haven't seen it around lately, assumed it was new." "What time did you see the vehicle there?" "It musta been around noon, because I was taking my daughter back to school from her lunch break." "Twelve o'clock? On Thursday? You're certain?" "Yes. Why what –"

I turn away from Dave and dart back across the lawn, up the steps, and into the house. Savannah lied to me. If what Dave said is true, then that means she was at the house Thursday morning. Fifteen minutes after Cordelia logged out of work for the day and never logged back in.

CHAPTER TWENTY

B EFORE Weston Waters March 14, 2016

Emerald turns four months today. Cordelia was officially cleared to go back to work last week. Upon completing a number of tests and speaking with two different psychologists to assess her current state of mind, she was given the green light.

Doctor Wyatt says that her progress has been phenomenal. Only four short months since the birth and the doctors are saying she's safe to immerse herself back into society and her old ways of life. I don't believe it's that easy, not even for a second. Sure, I've watched her progress over the past few months, but still, I have my doubts. How could I not? She told me she wished Emerald was never born – multiple times. The amount of nights I stayed up and held her as she cried and told me she wished death upon herself – as if that was somehow better than living. It was a nightmare. Blood, sweat, and tears. And now suddenly, just like that, she's better.

It's surreal, that's what it is. As though the past four months have been a bad dream. We've both been drowning for so long, and now here we are, heads above the water, just trying to stay afloat. But somehow even the simple act of trying to breathe is enough to exhaust me.

I thought it would be different. For four desolate months I sat at my office desk dreaming of this day. Praying for a miracle that would turn our lives around and make everything better again. But even when I prayed for a miracle, there was still a part of me that had lost all hope and doubted that she could ever get better. I thought she would stay damaged and broken forever.

I don't understand. This is what I wanted. This is what I've been hoping for. So why do I feel so strange about this quick transition back to our so-called normal life? I became so accustomed to the darkness that grew around our lives that I almost took comfort in it; allowed myself to wallow in it, breathing in its toxic fumes. The darkness became my life. A never-ending hell that I couldn't quite escape.

And then eventually, things got better. Days got brighter. She began smiling a little bit, then, a lot. She began holding Emerald, feeding her, taking her for walks in the stroller. I'd try to read her facial expression; see if she was still broken inside. But it seemed genuine – all of it. I'm not sure if she miraculously started loving Emerald or if she put on a fake smile in front of the doctors, but quite frankly, I don't care. I have my wife back, at least for now, and she can finally be a mother to my daughter. That's all that matters.

But that's not true, and I'd be lying to myself if I said that everything was fine. Because everything has changed. Feelings that were once there are now difficult to find. And the woman that I once loved has been altered into someone else. Or perhaps I'm the one who's been altered. It's me who's changed now, not her. Cordelia was able to revert to her old self. Her loving, caring self. But in those months that I spent waiting for her, it was me who changed the most. And it didn't take a psychosis or mental break for it to happen. All I had to do was bear witness to those things. To live through them, every single day, until finally I couldn't take it any longer.

I had to do something. I had to get out. I had to find an escape, even if it was just a temporary one.

I guess you could consider her temporary. I'm not even sure what to call it right now. But I do know one thing: I'm happy. I know that's wrong – believe me, I know. But it's the truth. I never thought I'd become that man: the man that cheats on his wife with another woman. A man who succumbs to such weakness. But I also never thought my wife would go through a severe psychosis.

I have to accept that not everything in my life can be planned and easily controlled. I never intended for it to turn out this way, believe me. I tried time and time again to stop myself. But there was something there. A spark, a bit of magic, chemistry. Undeniable chemistry. I wasn't even sure if women still looked at me anymore. I'm thirty-one-years old and a father. I assumed I was off the market for good. But everything changed when I met Rosella.

She's charming in a subtle way and knows exactly what to say and when to say it. Her eyes have the ability to welcome me, make me feel like I belong somewhere. As though if I stare into them long enough, the rest of the world will disappear and it will only be the two of us. It's like a new high being with her. And every cell in my body feels alive. I haven't felt that way in a long time, long before Emerald was born.

God, I love Emerald. So much. And I never want to do anything to hurt her or compromise my marriage. I still love Cordelia. Of course I do. I don't think I could ever stop loving her. But there comes a point where that love just fades into something less than it was before and there's nothing you can do to stop it. It wasn't Cordelia's fault. But it's not my fault either. And I shouldn't be subject to remaining the same person my entire life. I'm not the same man I was when Cordelia and I met. And I think things with Cordelia had begun going downhill long before Emerald's birth, but we were both too blind to see it. Perhaps the postpartum was an opportunity for my eyes to open. To finally see what has been right in front of me for a while now: the truth. And the truth is, it's just not working.

I can't leave her. I know that for a fact. Especially after everything she's gone through. She would never forgive me. She'd divorce me, file for full custody of Emerald. And I know how a jury would look at a cheating husband, especially when the wife just went through the most difficult time of her life.

That's why she can never find out. I won't leave her. I swear I will stay with her for the rest of our lives. Or, at least until Emerald is eighteen and can make decisions for herself.

Eighteen years. I can do that. It won't be difficult. I can stay with Cordelia. I do love her. But I need something more. Something new, dangerous, exciting. I think the thrill and risk of being with Rosella is what I crave the most. It's exhilarating. As though I could get caught at any moment. Like when you reach the top of a roller coaster and just before it drops, your seat tilts slowly over the edge, and you can see the entire world in front of you. Then all at once, you fall, fast, and you get that rush that fills your entire body.

Do I think it will last? I don't know. I honestly don't. It could just be a temporary thing. A perfect little escape to have fun for a while. I'm not counting on her sticking around forever. She may get tired of me sooner than later. And I think I'm okay with that. I think we are perfect together now, but things may change and that's okay. Because Rosella was exactly what I needed to find. Not only to escape my current life, but to rediscover myself and understand who I am, what I truly need. I needed Rosella to discover those things. So if it doesn't last, at least I got something else out of it.

CHAPTER TWENTY-ONE

A FTERDetective Gerard Sullivan   Saturday May 20, 2016

I rush into the house, down the hallway, straight for the bedroom. I swing open the door to see Cordelia and Savannah sitting adjacent from each other, mid-conversation. Their heads turn to me, startled.

"You were here on Thursday morning," I say quickly, out of breath. "Why did you lie?" They both stare at me for a moment. Savannah doesn't take her eyes off of me. Cordelia turns to her friend, then to me. "What are you talking about?" Cordelia says. "Savannah was here, twelve o'clock, right before our approximated time of abduction. So why were you here, and why did you lie about being in Chicago?" "Chicago?" Cordelia turns to Savannah, "What is he talking about?" Savannah stands, keeping her eyes locked on mine. "Can we speak in private, detective?" "Great idea. Why don't we head on down to the precinct and I can question you there." "What is happening?" Cordelia echoes in the background. Savannah turns to her. "I'll be back, okay? Don't worry. Just stay here." She smiles at her friend, and Cordelia, worry consuming her face, sits back down on the bed.

I leave the room with Savannah, escaping to the sovereignty of the hallway. "Anything you want to say?" She turns to me. "I'll wait."

And she does. All the way to the station.

———

Back at the station, Savannah sits quietly in the interrogation room, hands clasped in front of her.

After setting up the recorder, stating the date, time, as well as her name, I begin. "You lied," I state, matter-of-factly. She doesn't answer straight away, chewing the inside of her cheek, carefully crafting the next words that will come out of her mouth. "Why do you say that?" "We have an eyewitness who can place your vehicle at the Waters' home at twelve noon on Thursday. So would you like to stick with your story that you were in Chicago?" It's quiet for a moment. "You're right," she finally speaks. "I lied. But I did not take Emerald and I have nothing to do with her disappearance. That is the truth." "So why don't you start off by explaining what exactly you were doing with Cordelia at noon on Thursday?" She picks at her finger nails. "It's stupid, really. You're going to think I'm an idiot for even lying about something so trivial." She says. I stare at her, waiting for her to continue. She breathes again. "We had a fight, okay? A stupid fight." "When, Thursday?" "No, Wednesday night. She called me and we were talking about work and stuff. She brought up her new position. I was jealous – I am jealous – I admit that. But I took it out on her, in the wrong way I guess. We had an argument and left things on bad terms. I knew she wouldn't be in the office on Thursday, so I went over the next morning on my lunch break to clear the air and apologize." "And you couldn't have just called?" "I wanted to see her." "Why is that?" "Are you honestly questioning me for going to my friend's house? How was I supposed to know that her daughter was going to be abducted only a few hours after that?" She brings her hands to her forehead and closes her eyes.

"This is why I didn't say anything earlier. Because now you're accusing me of something I didn't do." "Can anyone verify your whereabouts during the time of the abduction? A reliable alibi, say, your boss?" "Yes. Yes, he can. After I left Cordelia's I went back to the office. You can check the log-in. And my boss was there. He saw me. We have security cameras. Go look." "I will." I stare at her and she stares back. "Until I can confirm your alibi, we'll need to keep you here, do you understand?" "Do what you must. I have nothing to do with Emerald's abduction. You'll see soon enough."

————

My mind is racing. Just when I thought that we might be getting somewhere, I'm thrown another curve-ball. Is Savannah telling the truth? Why lie about something so trivial?

In Cordelia's initial statement, she never mentioned Savannah coming over that morning. In fact, she never even mentioned that they had a fight. Could she have been covering for her friend? Or could Savannah be in cohorts with Cordelia? Perhaps they planned the abduction together. And in that case, our approximated time of abduction has now been extended to twelve noon. Either way, both of them are hiding something.

Before heading to District Systems to check out Savannah's alibi, I return to the Waters' place to speak with Cordelia once again.

"Mrs. Waters," I say. She looks alarmed. Out of her element. "What is happening? Where's Savannah?" "Why did you fail to mention your fight with Ms. Valentine on Wednesday evening?" She blinks, wide eyed. "Fight? What fight?" "Ms. Valentine claims that the two of you spoke on the phone Wednesday evening and had an argument. She said she came over here the next morning to sort things out." "What are you talking about? Savannah was never here." "Do you honestly expect me to believe that? What were the two of you planning?" Her mouth falls open. "Gerard," she uses my first name. "I honestly have no idea what you're talking about. If that's what

Savannah told you, then she's lying. We never had a fight and she was never here. I swear to you."

I leave Cordelia under the supervision of Robbins with strict instructions not to let her out of sight. This is a mess. Women. Lies. A missing baby. None of this is making sense. One of them is lying, and I need to figure out which one that is.

I drive far above the speed limit, feeling slightly guilty for using my official status to get where I need to be. Then again, this is an emergency, of sorts. The baby is still missing and we're getting nowhere.

I walk through the doors of District Systems, directly approaching the front desk. I ask for the man in charge, William Kittner, and wait as the receptionist calls him. By her wary eyes, I can tell that he's busy. But after flashing my badge, she ensures that he knows it's urgent.

A few moments later, he arrives in the lobby: a tall man, a bit thicker around the waist. He has jet black hair and a rigid jaw. He walks to the desk and stands in front of me.

"What's going on?" he asks. "Mr. Kittner, I'm Detective Sullivan from the Davenport Police Department. You're aware of the disappearance of Emerald Waters, the daughter of your employee Cordelia Waters?" "Yes, I spoke to the police yesterday. Have they found her?" "No. We haven't. I'd like to ask you some questions regarding another employee of yours, Savannah Valentine." "What about her?" "She may be a person of interest in the investigation, so I need you to be very honest with me." "Savannah? What happened?" "Can you verify that she was here on Thursday from noon to five?" "I can get the log-in files. If you'd like to come up to my office?" "That would be great."

We take the elevator up to the eighteenth floor, then step out into a long hallway, lined with dark green carpet. I follow him straight to the end of the hall where we finally reach his office.

He leans over the desk, typing a password into the computer. As he looks for the files, I examine the office. Certificates hang from the walls, a filing cabinet sits against the far corner. The desk holds two picture frames. One of his family, I'm assuming, and one of a young girl, a graduation photo.

"You have kids?" I ask. "Yeah," he follows my gaze down to the picture frame. "That's Lucy. She's in university now." "What school?" "St. Ambrose, for nursing." He says. I nod my head and he returns his gaze to the screen. "Here it is," he stands back to allow me to see. "Savannah logged out for her lunch break at eleven-fifty. She didn't log back in until one-thirteen, then logged out at the end of the day at exactly at five o'clock." "Does she normally come back from lunch late?" "Not usually. But sometimes she meets a friend or someone for lunch. I let it slide as long as it doesn't become a common occurrence." "So you didn't ask where she was during that time?" "I think she mentioned that she was out with a friend. I wasn't really focused on her whereabouts." "Do you have security footage?" "We do. You need to see it?" "That would help me, yes." "Of course. Anything I can do. I just don't understand what this is about. Do you think Savannah had something to do with the baby's disappearance?" "It's unclear as of this moment. But seeing the security footage will help me a great deal."

He pulls up the security footage from Thursday and shows me Savannah entering the building just minutes before her log in, and exiting the building just shortly after she logged out. Everything seems fine, there. But with Savannah being at Cordelia's place at noon, and not returning to work until after one, perhaps the baby could have been taken between then?

But that still begs the question: why is Cordelia lying? She claims to have put Emerald down for her nap at two-thirty? Could she have been mistaken? Is she covering for Savannah, who took her baby somewhere? But if they're working together, why lie and say she was never there?

None of this makes sense.

CHAPTER TWENTY-TWO

BEFORE Cordelia Waters April 6, 2016

I'm finally getting back into the swing of things at work. Everyone accepted my return as though no time had passed. This is exactly what I've needed. My career is my life, and being away for four months has been so difficult. I'm the woman who, if asked if she'd rather choose to have children or pursue her career, would choose the latter. I tried to do that. But clearly that didn't work out too well.

Things are getting better at home. I'm managing, and even though I'm not my absolute best yet, I will get there eventually. It's surreal to see how much Emerald has grown already. The thought keeps circulating through my mind: I created that thing. She came from inside of me! Before I know it, she'll be walking and talking, going to school, making friends, getting married, having children. And then she'll become me.

Will my daughter resent me for having not wanted to create her?

I find myself wandering into her room and simply staring at her as she sleeps. I'm not admiring her, blown away by my grand fascination of her.

It's more like I'm studying her. I want to know how she acts and why she moves a certain way. I need to know what her cries mean; why her arms move the way they do; the faces she makes and their purpose. A mother shouldn't have to study her own child, but I do. As if there's going to be an exam at the end and I'm scrambling with all of my notes trying to remember everything I've learned. And there's always that paranoia that I'll fail the exam and have to retake the course all over again. Or worse – they'll kick me out for good. And in that case, they'll take her away from me. Would that be the worst thing?

Sometimes I imagine what life would be like without Emerald. It was so pleasant and peaceful before she came along. I was a business woman at the pinnacle of my career; in love with my gorgeous husband; happily living, just the two of us, in our wonderful home.

Sometimes I blame Emerald for what happened to me. I know I shouldn't, but I can't help it. Essentially, it's her fault. Well, actually, if we're playing the blame game, it's mine and Weston's fault. But the crying is not my fault. The constant screaming and late night's waking up every hour to check on her isn't my fault. No, that's her fault. This is what babies do. I knew this before getting myself into this mess.

This is why I never wanted children.

I'm glad Doctor Wyatt can't read my thoughts, because if she did, she'd surely place me back under twenty-four-hour care and have Emerald taken away. Not that I'd ever hurt Emerald. It's just that sometimes my thoughts wander.

I've always had an overzealous imagination. As a child I would imagine all the ways that I could potentially die. Not in a fantasizing way, more of a paranoia. If we were riding the school bus, I'd have this constant fear that the bus would drive off a bridge and we would all die. Or whenever I'd be near large bodies of water, I'd imagine myself or someone I love drowning.

I couldn't help it. My mind always went to the worst possible scenario. I guess you could call that paranoia. So is that what these thoughts are? Paranoia? I picture myself carrying Emerald in my arms, walking down the stairs. Then I slip and fall, and we go tumbling down. My sporadic thoughts continue to wander to a thousand accidents that could occur in our home, all resulting in death and dismay.

I want to want her. I really do. And I consider myself ninety-seven percent better as of today. I'm getting there. I'm improving. And I'm so proud of myself. Doctor Wyatt tells me I have a right to be proud, that I've accomplished so much. What I went through wasn't easy, and it's quite miraculous that I survived and made it out alive. I smile to myself.

I'm working on my feelings. Slowly, day by day. I will love her eventually. I know I will. It's like learning to ride a bike. You start out slow and fearful, scared of falling off or hurting yourself. Doubtful that accomplishing the goal will ever happen. That you'll ever be good enough. But you keep at it and you try harder and harder each day. And then eventually, before you've even realized, you're riding that bike.

———

Today is April sixth: Liam's twenty-sixth birthday. It seems like just yesterday he was turning six on the sixth. I remember those days like they were only a short time ago. Running around the backyard playing hide and seek. Spying on our parents when we were supposed to be in bed. The days we thought would last forever, but hoped would pass all too fast. Oh how I wish I could go back in time and tell myself to make it last. To not dream away the days wishing I was somebody else. To not take for granted being a kid. Because once you become an adult, your entire world changes.

I decide to call Liam. We haven't spoken in a few months, but what better time to call then the day of his birth. The phone rings four times before he answers.

"Hello?" I hear his familiar voice. "Happy Birthday, baby bro!" I smile into the phone. I don't realize how much I've missed the sound of his voice until he speaks. "Cordelia," I can almost hear the smile behind his words. "Thank you for calling." "Of course. How's it feel? Twenty-six – wow. Do you feel old yet?" He laughs. "Funny. I never really notice a change on my birthday. It's not until I look back a couple years later and think, how the hell did I get this old?" I laugh too, knowing all too well what he means. I'll be twenty-nine in July. One year away from the big thirty. "So how are things?" I ask. "Everything's good. Nothing too exciting. How are things with you? How's the baby and Wes?" "Baby's good. Wes is good. Working a lot, that's for sure." "And how have you been? With..." "Good. I'm fine now. Don't worry." "Okay, I just didn't know." "That's okay. I'm doing much better." "Is Weston helping? Doing his fair-share with the baby, I mean?" "Yes, he's basically her primary care taker. He's amazing with her. And he loves her so much." "That's good to hear." "How are Sophie and Clayton?" "They're good. Sophie's starting a pre-school program this summer to prep her for kindergarten. Clayton is well... Clayton. Being a typical boy for his age." "He's four now, right?" "Yes ma'am," "How the time flies. I swear last year he was still in diapers." "They grow up too fast." It's quiet for a moment. Dozens of memories swirl through my mind. Liam. Our Childhood. Emerald. What she's done to me. I feel the tightness in my throat and I try to hold it in. But the tears come anyway. "Cordelia? Is something wrong?" I sniffle and wipe the tears that have gathered at my chin. "I'm fine," I try to laugh it off. "Sorry, it's..." more silent sobs. "What happened?" I try to gather myself before speaking. "I'm sorry. I just miss talking to you. Why don't you call anymore? Why don't you ever come by?" He's silent for a moment. "I'm sorry, Cordelia. It's not you. Please don't take it personally. I just... I can't come back there." "But why? What happened that's so bad?" "You know." "Bullshit. What aren't you telling me?" "It's nothing. I mean, it's something. But it's my own personal problems. Not yours. I'm sorry, I just don't want to drag you into it." "I'm your sister. You're supposed to be able to tell me anything.

You're supposed to be there for me. I needed you! All those months. It was torture. And where were you?" He's quiet again. "I'm sorry. Our family has issues. There's no other way to put it." "Our family doesn't have issues," I say. "You do." Silence again. "Okay Cordelia. I'm sorry." I sniffle and wipe my eyes again. "Alright." "I better get going. Lianna wants to take me out for lunch. Tell Weston I send my best." "You can tell him yourself." "Pardon?" "Sorry. I didn't mean it like that." I pause. "It's just... I meant that it would be more efficient to tell him yourself. He barely speaks to me these days." "What are you talking about? I thought you said everything was fine?" "I lied." "What happened?" "I don't know," I feel the tightness in my throat again. "Things changed during my depression. I changed. He changed." "Everyone changes. That's just a part of life." "Yeah, well, it's not always for the better. We've grown apart, Liam. He doesn't look at me the same anymore. I just... I don't know what to do." "I'm sorry, Cordelia. I don't know what to tell you. Maybe try talking to him." "Talking to him? You don't think I've tried that?" "I don't know. Maybe things will get better. Maybe – what? Yeah, hold on." He's talking to someone else. "Sorry, Lianna's wondering what I'm doing. I really have to go." "It's okay. You go have fun and enjoy your day." "Thanks. Talk soon."

CHAPTER TWENTY-THREE

A FTER Detective Gerard Sullivan Saturday May 20, 2016

After leaving District Systems, I head back over to the station, hoping to end this now, get a confession, perhaps? I didn't understand at first. Why would one of Cordelia's friends want to take and potentially harm Emerald? And that got me thinking: what if she didn't want to harm Emerald at all?

Before I left William Kittner's office, I asked if he had Savannah's file and medical record. As he handed me the files and I flipped through the pages, everything looked fine. No criminal record, not even a speeding ticket. I flipped through the medical file. All was well, healthy as can be.

As I was nearing the end of the file, I came across a hospitalization record from three and a half years ago detailing her stay at St. Augustine's General Hospital, admitted for two days. I flipped to the last page and discovered the reason: she gave birth to a stillborn.

I walk into the interrogation room where just last night, Cordelia sat, being questioned. The same room that, earlier that day, we held and questioned Steven Mendoza. The thought crosses my mind that perhaps I'm wrong about Savannah as well – that there's some bigger story here. I push it aside and remind myself what's at stake: the baby.

I take a seat across from her, resting my hands on the table. Her eyes are hollow. She doesn't look thrilled to see me. I'm hoping for a quick confession, anything to get me out of this room and closer to the whereabouts of the baby. "Ms. Valentine," I start. "I just came from District Systems. I had a nice chat with Mr. Kittner." "Then I'm sure you've seen the log-in files and security footage by now. I was at work during the time of the abduction. You've got this whole thing wrong." "He did show me both of those things indeed. However, you were late coming back from lunch, which isn't usual for you, seeing as though you are always on time. And it still doesn't explain why you were at the Waters' residence in the first place." "I told you, I went over to talk with Cordelia." "Cordelia claims that you were never at her home on Thursday, and that the two of you never had a fight." Her eyes widen, her face contorts into that of utter confusion and shock. "What are you talking about?" "Cordelia doesn't recall speaking with you at all the last few days. In fact, she told me that whatever you say is a lie." "You've got to be fucking kidding me!" she turns in her chair and brings a fist to her mouth. "What the fuck is going on?" "I was hoping you could tell me." "Listen, detective, I understand where you're coming from. I want Emerald found just as much as you do. But you've got the wrong person. This is just one big misunderstanding. Go check my apartment. Go check anywhere! I don't have her and you'll see that. Why would I take Cordelia's child? That's insane!" I study her, trying to determine whether her emotions are genuine or fabricated. "Why didn't you tell me about the baby you lost?" Her eyes widen once again and she slowly leans back in her chair. She can't lie her way out of this one. She knows that I know. "It wasn't relevant," she says matter-of-factly. "Not relevant? You lost a baby, and then your friend's baby goes missing. How is that not relevant?" "I know it looks bad. God, it looks so bad right now. But I swear to you, I would never take Emerald or do anything to hurt her. Why would I do that to Cordelia? She's my friend!" "Perhaps you weren't doing it to hurt Cordelia. You just felt that the baby would be better off in your hands?" "No. No, you've got it all wrong." "Ms. Valentine, we're running out of options here. We need to find that baby. And I'm going to do everything in my power to make sure you tell us what really happened that morning." "I already told you what happened! Cordelia and I had a stupid fight. Then I went over to her place to talk about it. We hugged it out, had coffee, and then I went back to work. I guess I lost track of the time. We were chatting for a while. But I can assure you, I didn't bash her over the head, steal Emerald, and then go into work as though nothing happened." "We're getting a search warrant from the judge now to search your home. An eyewitness can place your vehicle at the scene of the crime Thursday around noon. We will go from there." "I want my lawyer." "That's fine. That is your legal right. But just know, I will be back. And if we don't have the baby by the time I return, I'm not going to play nice."

I leave the interrogation room and wander outside to get some air. I'm conflicted, internally. Nothing is adding up. She loses her baby three and a half years ago. What makes her suddenly decide to take Emerald? Where is the motive? Did she want the child for herself? Or did she think that Cordelia wasn't being a good enough mother?

Okay, makes sense. But why go back to work afterwards? If she did just kidnap a child, she would have planned it properly; called in sick or taken the day off work. It doesn't make sense that she'd go back there after all of that. And leave the baby where, exactly? In her apartment? Does she have another location that we don't know about? Or maybe she has an accomplice?

My mind is spinning with possibilities. But if she is innocent, how do I explain what Cordelia said? That she doesn't remember a fight. She was certain that it never happened. She was even certain that Savannah was lying. Could Cordelia have been lying? Does she think that Savannah took Emerald, and lied to point me back in her direction? They have both lied to me and I'm honestly not sure what to believe anymore.

CHAPTER TWENTY-FOUR

B EFORE Cordelia Waters April 10, 2016

These past few weeks have been cold and rainy, a reminder of how our winter has been. But today the sun has come out, and with it an eagerness for spring; a time of regrowth and solstice. How my body longs for the days that I can sit outside in nothing but a summer dress, feeling the sun bathe down on my skin, absorbing all of the warmth. I crave that feeling, the warmth that my body requires.

This spring could be the start of something new. With the past in the past, I can finally begin to move forward, have a fresh start. Spring is a time of hope, new beginnings. This thought excites me and I drive all the way to work with the windows down, the stereo blasting encouraging, upbeat tunes.

After sorting through some files and sending a mass email to the team, I make my way over to Savannah's desk to catch up. She's eager to tell me about a new guy she's been seeing. I listen to her go on about how different he is. How he's not like the rest. I find it comical that she says this every time. I nod my head, smiling as the words flow from her mouth, a river going upstream. She's unstoppable now. There's no point in trying to but in. So instead, I direct my thoughts somewhere else. Thoughts of summer, being outdoors.

I work straight through until noon, then head out for my lunch break. With these thoughts in my mind, I knew I couldn't simply stay here and grab something from the cafeteria downstairs as I usually do. I decide to go for a drive until I find something that catches my eye. I pass a strip mall that has an Italian restaurant. Lucenzo's is the name.

The moment I walk through the doors, the aroma of fresh tomatoes and garlic bread fills the air. I close my eyes as I take it all in. I walk to the take-out bar where an older man with grey hair and a salt n pepper moustache takes my order. I decide on the marinara mushroom pasta with a side of garlic bread. I never pass on the garlic bread.

I grab a seat by the window and eat my meal, staring out into the distance, observing anything that passes by. I often let my mind wander to places that I didn't even know existed. Sitting here, watching the cars go by, I feel a sense of calm and relief. Its times like these that I miss being by myself. I need to do that more often. I'm sure Weston would understand. He and Emerald could go on play dates at the park while I have a little mommy get-away.

I've always appreciated my alone-time. Growing up as an introverted kid, I never liked going out much or socializing with large groups. People often get introversion confused with shyness. They are not the same. I am confident and happy to talk with strangers; I do it every single day at work. But introversion requires down time. Time for yourself, to recharge. When I can cuddle up in bed with a good book or turn on a movie. I love being alone with Weston, curled up beside him. I miss those days, when it was just the two of us. Is that wrong of me to say? I'm sure mother's wish for that all of the time. Surely I can't be the only one. Especially mothers who have two and three children. Oh, what a nightmare that must be. I can't even imagine.

I push the thought of children away. I will stare out the window, gazing into the open nothingness, enjoying my time alone while it lasts.

Before I leave Lucenzo's, I decide to grab something for Weston and drop it off at his work. I'm in a good mood today, and I suddenly have the urge to bring happiness to everyone around me, including my husband. This little surprise will be good for him. It's been so long since I dropped by the practice to visit him. I'll get him one of his favourites: pizza. Maybe if I continue with the random acts of kindness and surprise visits at work, he'll look at me more. Notice me. Remember that I am his wife and that we're in this together. He's been so distant lately and I can't help but blame myself. I know it's because of my depression. I just wish it didn't affect him as much as it has. I can only attempt to win back his love.

I don't have long before I have to return to work so I drive a little faster to make it there in time. I park the car, grab the box from the passenger seat, and stride up towards the front doors of the practice.

Once inside, I immediately smell fluoride, a smell I despise. It reminds me of being at the dentist, having my mouth probed. Your gums are bleeding because you're not flossing enough.

I approach the receptionist desk and see the woman – Carly, is her name? – typing away into the computer. She's new to the practice, only been here about six months now.

"Good afternoon," I beam as I step towards the counter. She looks up and recognizes me immediately. "Mrs. Waters, hello! What a pleasant surprise." "I just thought I'd drop by and surprise Weston with lunch. Is he in his office or with a patient right now?" Her face alters, looking puzzled. "Oh, um. I thought he was with you?" "With me? What do you mean?" "He left work about an hour ago. Said he was taking the day off. I assumed the two of you had plans today." She tucks a stray piece of hair behind her ear. Weston left work? An hour ago? Why wouldn't he tell me? And better yet, where did he go? "Oh, um," I turn and look at the clock. "So he won't be back at the office today?" I ask holding up the box of pizza. She eyes it. "No, I don't think so. I can call him if you'd like?" "No no, that's fine. I have to get back to work now. I'll talk to him later," I force a smile and turn to leave. "Have yourself a good day now, Carly!" "You too, Mrs. Waters. And it's Carla!" I hear her call just as I push out the front door.

Where the hell is my husband?

______

I rush around the kitchen trying to prepare something nice for dinner. I quickly glance at Emerald who is sitting in her high chair smearing baby food over the tray in front of her. Why do babies do this? It's almost as though they enjoy the uncleanliness.

Upon arriving home from work, I put Weston's surprise pizza in the fridge. He can have it tomorrow. Tonight, I'm making us dinner. We can have a special family night – spend some time together.

I rush over to Emerald, grab some wipes, and begin cleaning up her mess. Its quarter past five, which means Weston should be home any minute. The mashed potatoes are finished and sitting on the table. The roast beef should be done momentarily. I scramble back to the stove to stir the veggies which are cooking in the pan.

Just then, I hear the oven beep, indicating that the roast is finished. I open the door and step back, allowing the heat and steam to exit, then I grab the oven mitts and pull out the large pot.

I'm leaning over the table cutting the beef when I hear the front door open. I glance at the clock – five-forty-two. Why has he been coming home so late recently? I hear the sound of the keys being hung on the rack, shoes being removed, then subtle footsteps as he enters the kitchen. He tries to hide the surprise on his face upon seeing me in the kitchen.

"You cooked dinner?" "I did!" I smile and walk over to him. "I thought we could have a special family night." He places one hand on my waist as I lean in and kiss him, then removes it and steps back. "Smells good. What's cooking?" he walks over to see Emerald. "Hello my beautiful girl," he leans in and swoops her up out of her highchair. "Roast beef, potatoes, vegetables…. Emerald made quite a mess, as usual," I laugh it off. But he's not listening to me. He's bouncing her up and down in his arms, laughing while she giggles. "How was work?" I speak up. He looks at me, then, as he hoists her into his arms. "It was good. How was your day?" "Good. Here, have a seat," I pull out the chair for him to sit down. He takes a seat and I gently take Emerald from his arms and place her back in the high chair. I walk over to the oven, bring over the vegetables, and place them on the table. Then I sit down at the opposing end. We pass around the pots, scraping out mashed potatoes and layering on loads of beef and vegetables. Finally, I pour us both a glass of zinfandel and slide his over. He takes a sip, then looks up at me. "You didn't have to do all of this," "I know. I wanted to. We haven't had a nice family dinner in a while." He smiles flatly, then turns to Emerald. "She already ate?" "Yes. I fed her while I was cooking." "What a good girl," he says in what can only be described as the "baby voice", and reaches his hand out to her cheek. "So," I begin as I stab my fork into the roast. "Work was good?" "Mhm," he takes another sip of wine before cutting into his meat. "I stopped by," I say. "I went over to Lucenzo's for lunch. Grabbed you a pizza and went to drop it off. But Carly said you took the day off?" I say, then nonchalantly take a forkful of vegetables into my mouth. "Oh, yes, some of the guys and I went out for lunch." "Work guys?" "Yeah." I nod my head and take another bite. "Carly said she thought you were with me." He hesitates, holding the fork halfway to his mouth. He brings it back down. "It's Carla. And that's odd. She must have been mistaken." "Hmm," I nod. "She seems like a bright girl. I would have thought she'd notice if a few of you left together." "It was only three of us. Me, Simon, and Greg. And we had interfering schedules, so we left separately. " I nod my head again and smile. "Well, I guess you have lunch for tomorrow."

CHAPTER TWENTY-FIVE

FTER Detective Gerard Sullivan Saturday May 20, 2016

I'm sitting in my office going over my notes. Holden and Ashby have left to obtain the search warrant for Savannah's place. But until they get that, I'm stuck here, idling.

I flip open my notepad and begin reading over the notes from the beginning. Weston's initial statement, Cordelia's list of potential suspects, eyewitness accounts from neighbors, statements from the nanny and babysitter.

I'm flipping through the section with Mrs. Mendoza when I see that name again – Rosella. It could be nothing, just a friend dropping by. But something isn't sitting right with me.

I continue flipping through the pages, reading over Ainsley's statement about the red Impala sitting outside the house. This, too, struck me as odd. A case of stalking, perhaps? Could someone have been targeting the Waters? Scoping out the house to see when people were home and when they were gone? But then again, if someone did do that, why take the child when her mother was home with her? Why not wait until a more opportune time to strike?

Scenario A: This "stalker" stakes out the house, plans to abduct Emerald. Comes in on Thursday afternoon and takes her.

But that doesn't explain the fact that Cordelia was home during the abduction. Could she have already been asleep when the perp came in? Or did something else happen – a confrontation, perhaps? – But Cordelia may have been in a dissociative state and forgot completely.

Was Cordelia Waters even home during the time of the abduction?

Scenario B: Cordelia Waters has a psychotic break, kills Emerald, disposes of the body, goes to sleep, and forgets any of it happened. In either scenario, we have an unreliable witness who has no idea what really happened.

That's when it clicks in my brain, puzzle pieces fitting together into place. I stand up quickly, rushing down the hall to see our tech analyst, Meredith Younger. Her door is open, but I knock twice and stick my head in. She's on her computer, typing away.

"Ger, good morning," she smiles as she spins in her chair to face me. "Hey, I have a favour to ask," I walk over and stand beside her desk. "What's up?" "Can you pull up a search for me? Red Impala's in the greater Davenport area." "Okay," she nods, pulls up another screen, types into the search. Twenty-six matches come up. "Can you be more specific? Partial licence plate, maybe?" she asks. I look at her. "Even better than a licence plate. I have a name. Can you cross reference the car with ownership?" "Sure, what's the name?" "Rosella." I say, my heart beating through my chest. I pray that I'm right about this. She clicks her mouse, presses a button, types in the name and we wait for something to come up.One result."You're in luck," Younger turns to me. "There's a 2012 Chevy Impala registered to a Rosella Collins. I'm guessing you want her address?" "Yes please."

———

I get the address for Rosella Collins and head out to her place, trying to wrap my head around this situation. The woman who came by the house two weeks ago is the same person who was lurking outside back in March. Who is this woman?

I arrive in Suburbia. It's a nice neighborhood with large, ornamented homes, nuclear families galore. A place where parents move to raise their children. Elementary school just around the corner, two parks within a two mile perimeter. Upper-middle class people who work all day, then come home to a well-prepared dinner at night. Cookie-cutter perfection.

I pull up in front of the house, which was confirmed to be Rosella's when I saw the red Impala in the driveway. I silently chastise myself for not connecting the dots sooner.

It's a fairly large house, stained mahogany double doors, fully bloomed garden out front. As I walk up the pathway to the front steps, I try to peer through the curtains to see if anyone's home. Surely she's here. If her car is here, she must be as well.

I ring the doorbell and wait patiently, thousands of thoughts filling my mind. Where to begin? How do you know the Waters'? Why were you lurking outside of their house? And do you know anything about the disappearance of Emerald Waters? I ring the doorbell again and wait. Hearing the sound of the kids playing outside, I turn and observe. Across the street are two children, bouncing a basketball and playing with a skipping rope.

I turn back and face the door. I knock loudly three times, "Ms. Collins, this is Detective Sullivan from the Davenport Police Department. Please open up."

I knock a few more times, getting aggravated that she's not answering. I don't think she'd be that senseless to ignore the door when there's a cop there. Perhaps she's not home. Does she own more than one vehicle? Is she married? Out with a friend?

I need answers to these questions, but I'm not going to get them standing here pounding on her door. I'll get a warrant to search the premise if I have to.

I hustle back down the steps and head across the street to where the children are playing. "Hi there," I smile as I approach. "Is your mom or dad home?" The kids don't answer me. In fact, they look quite frightened. The little girl in the orange t-shirt points towards the house. I smile, nod, then head up to the front steps. A man opens the door, taking in my appearance as I take in his. He's about equivalent to my height, has a head full of dark hair, and looks to be in his late forties, early fifties. "Good afternoon. I'm Detective Sullivan." I stick out my hand. He shakes it firmly. "Christopher McKinnon. What can I do for you today, detective?" "Do you mind if I ask you a few questions about your neighbor, Rosella Collins?" I nod towards her house. His eyes follow, then return to mine. "Rosella? Is she in some sort of trouble?" "Nothing to be concerned about." He nods his head. "Would you like to come inside?" I turn to look at the children. "They're fine." He says. "They'll be in shortly for lunch." "Sure." I step in the house and we walk towards the kitchen. I imagine that this is what Rosella's home must look like as well. Large brick fireplace to the left, laminate tiles, marble counter tops. "So, what do you want to know?" he says as he takes a seat at the table. He gestures for me to sit, so I pull out the chair and sit across from him. "Are the two of you close?" I ask. "We're neighborly. Everyone around here is. Her daughter, Clementine, is friends with my son." "She has a daughter?" "Yeah, she's about ten or eleven, I believe. Nice kid." "Is Ms. Collins married?" "Don't believe so," I jot this down. "How long has Ms. Collins and her daughter lived in the neighborhood?" "A couple of years now," "Three, four, five...?" "Maybe four. I'm not too sure. My wife would know better than I would," he laughs. "I know you said you're not close, but can you tell me anything else that may come to mind?" He thinks for a moment. "She's a nice lady, really. Always baking cookies for Clementine to bring to school. She's involved in a lot of community stuff. Bakes cupcakes for fundraisers and such. I don't really know much else. Real nice lady, though." "Alright," I say, jotting this down. "Do you happen to know if she's home today? I knocked on her door but there was no answer." "Hmm, I'm not too sure. I haven't seen her outside or anything the past couple of days. But that's not too unusual. She's usually out and about doing things. Works at the hospital, so her shifts are very sporadic." He stops, thinking. "Actually, now that I think about it, I haven't seen Clementine this weekend either. Perhaps they had a little mother-daughter get-away." "When exactly was the last time you saw either of them?" "Thursday, maybe. No, Friday. Yeah, it must have been yesterday because my son, Logan, delivers papers on our street and we saw them coming home from the grocery store yesterday afternoon." I write this down, then stand. "Thank you for your time, Mr. McKinnon. If I have any other questions, I will contact you." He stands, awkwardly dropping his hands to his side, then bringing them in front of him. "Is everything okay with Rosella? I mean, if you don't mind my asking, why are you asking?" I stare at him. "Like I said, it's nothing to be worried about. Just some questions I had until I reach her myself." He nods his head, accepting that I'm not going to elaborate.

Until I can either get in contact with Rosella Collins or get a search warrant for her place – with very little to go on, I might add – I need to focus on any and all other options. And the first on my list of priorities is Savannah Valentine.

CHAPTER TWENTY-SIX

B EFORE Weston Waters April 10, 2016

I ditched work and took the day off. I wanted to spend time with Rosella. It's Wednesday, which means that Cordelia will be at the office all day, possibly even later. She loves her job so much. Sometimes I think she loves it more than her family. But I'm happy for her. I truly am happy that she's doing well and is back in her old environment, doing the thing that she loves the most.

I left work around eleven, joking to Carla that since I'm in charge, I can leave whenever I want. She laughed and waved as I left.

I snuck home to see Emerald before my day out. Marcia had Winnie the Pooh on and was singing to Emerald as she sat on the floor clapping her hands. She's already so big, growing up so fast. Everything is new and pure in her eyes. Soon enough she'll be crawling, and then walking. The day seems so far away, but I know it's approaching.

I change out of my work clothes and throw on something casual. I walk back out, give Emerald a big kiss on the cheek, then tell Marcia I'm heading to a work-lunch. She smiles and waves as I walk backwards out the door, smiling as I watch Emerald attempt to wave back.

We're having a picnic by the river, Rosella, Clementine and me. Clementine is Rosella's eleven-year-old niece. Her parents – Rosella's sister – died in a car accident when she was only a baby, so Rosella took her on as her own. She's a cute kid. Dark blonde hair, light blue eyes, and a cheeky little smile. Rosella says she has her mother's eyes and it reminds her of her sister every time she looks at them.

I steal a sideways glance at Rosella. She's effortlessly beautiful. Her eyes are focused on Clementine. The three of us are sitting on a picnic blanket, snacking on fruit and sandwiches. Rosella let Clementine play hooky today, deciding that it was too lovely of a day to be in a classroom. When she told me that, I decided to play hooky as well. I enjoy spending time with Rose and Clem.

In the beginning, I never even knew about Clementine. Things were simple and uncomplicated. There was no need to bring in personal details about ourselves. But things evolved. Rosella thought that to truly know her, I would need to know Clementine, the most important thing in her life.

When I first met Rosella, I never mentioned that I was married or had a child. It felt wrong. If I admitted the truth to her, it would all become real. Me cheating. Me abandoning my family. I didn't want it to be real. So as long as she didn't know, everything was fine. I thought it was going to be a one-time thing, so of course I never mentioned it. But then it happened again. And again. And again. Soon enough I found myself going to Finnick's every night just so we could meet up in the bathroom. This soon became routine. We didn't care about each other's personal lives or what our hobbies were – it was just sex. That kept things simple. I needed simple. But of course, everything that's simple doesn't stay that way for long.

Thoughts of Rosella would consume my mind, whether I was at work or at home with my wife and daughter. The thoughts left me feeling guilty. My mind was infected for thinking of such things when I was around my family. I was living a secret double life that no one else knew about. I was two different people at once.

At home, I would try to be the best husband and father I could be. Even if that meant putting on fake smiles and suppressing how I really felt. And when I was with Rosella, I was someone else entirely. Someone new.

I liked this version of myself. He was daring and exciting and felt so alive. I couldn't get her out of my mind. Her lips. The smell of her neck. The feel of her small hands gripped onto my shoulders. It felt so wrong and so right. I found myself wanting to spend more time with her. It was more than just sex. I was developing feelings for this woman. The one thing I vowed never to do, and here I was, doing that very thing.

There came a point when I realized I couldn't keep suppressing my feelings. I couldn't keep living my life the way I was – living a lie within my own skin. I had to find an escape. So I caved. I allowed it to become something more. And that's when I had to tell her the truth.

I was expecting a slap in the face. For her to leave and never talk to me again. But she didn't. She seemed to be fine with the fact that we were having an affair – I, the married man with a baby daughter. Her, the alluring mistress. The thought almost excited her.

Sometimes when we're together, she expresses feelings of inner guilt. That she is somehow responsible for my infidelity. But it's not her fault. I wouldn't even say that what we have is something to be considered faulty. She's helping me. I couldn't continue living my life the way I was. I was drowning and she saved me. Even if just for a little while. A bit of air is better than none.

CHAPTER TWENTY-SEVEN

AFTER Detective Gerard Sullivan Saturday May 20, 2016

We got the search warrant. We're running up the stairwell to Savannah's condo. Her place is on the eighth floor – we're almost there. So many thoughts are racing through my mind. Is this it? Are we about to find the child? I hope we are. But there's a small grain of doubt in my mind that I can't quite seem to shake. Something about her story still isn't adding up, and regardless of my feelings towards Savannah or how guilty I think she is, there's a part of me that believes we still don't have the right person.

Ashby kicks the door in and we all move in behind him. Immediately everyone disperses, searching the medium-sized apartment for the child. I rush through the apartment as fast as I can, searching for anything. And then the voices start: "Clear!" "Clear!" "All clear in here!"

Dammit! She's not here. She's not fucking here.

Holden said he checked out every single detail of Savannah Valentine's life. There are no other homes or buildings registered in her name. She makes no other payments other than to this building. If she was holding Emerald anywhere, this is where she would be. But she's not.

All of the hope that was in my body previously seems to dissolve, and I feel anger bubbling up inside, ready to replace it. I tried to work the accomplice angle, but it doesn't add up either. We traced her phone records and she has no incoming or outgoing calls to conspicuous numbers. Just the same few people: work, boyfriend's cell, mother's cell. I don't know what to think. But one thing is for certain: the child isn't here.

I get a call from the station. It's Robbins telling me that Savannah's lawyer is having her released. There's no plausible cause to keep her there any longer, and without evidence at the apartment, we have to let her go.

She's smart enough to not go far. I'm not taking my eyes off her until this thing is solved and the child is back home, safe and sound. She may be innocent for now, but I still need to determine who was lying about the so-called fight that occurred on Wednesday night. One of them better give me a straight answer soon.

And then there's the newest part of this equation: Rosella Collins. Who is she and what was she doing around the Waters' house in the past? Something doesn't sit well with me about this situation, but until I can get a hold of her, there's nothing else I can do there. I could put out an APB, but that might be jumping the gun. I'll return to her place later tonight and hope that she's there this time. Rosella is on my radar, yes, but what's even more pressing as of now is the lack of honesty going on in the Waters' household. Why can't I seem to get a straight story from anyone? The only thing left to do is go back to where it all started.

———

Cordelia opens the door, a look of concern growing on her face. She was hoping for good news. Weren't we all?

I explain to her that we searched Savannah's apartment and found no evidence that she was holding Emerald. I remind her that she's not in the clear, either. This frightens her, I can tell. I ask her again about the alleged argument that occurred on Wednesday evening, but she insists it never happened. I don't have to worry too much about her – she's not going anywhere. I'll come back to her shortly. But right now, there's someone more imperative I need to speak with, and that's Weston.

She tells me that he's sequestered himself in the home-office all morning, won't come out or speak to anyone.

I knock twice, then try the handle. It's open. I push the door forward, revealing Weston sitting at the desk, typing something into the keyboard. He looks up and meets my eyes. "Can I come in?" I ask as I step inside and close the door behind me. He watches me closely. "Guess I don't have much of a choice." He leans back in his chair. "Of course you have a choice. I'd just prefer if we spoke now." "About what?" "Your daughter is missing, Mr. Waters." He looks down and shuts off the computer monitor. "Okay. Let's talk." I take a few steps forwards, stand in front of his desk. "First off, do you know a woman by the name of Rosella Collins?" He stares at me for a moment, pondering this question. "The name doesn't ring a bell." "You sure? She's not a friend of yours or your wife's?" "Not that I'm aware of." "You're positive?" "If I knew who the woman was, don't you think I would tell you?" I'm quiet for a moment. "So there would be no reason for a woman by that name to be coming by your house?" He stares at me. "No. We don't know any Rosellas." I don't know what to think. Could this woman be a stalker of some sorts? "Fair enough." I clear my throat. "To your knowledge, has your wife ever experienced a blackout, any unaccounted for periods of time?" "What do you mean?" he looks confused. "It's a pretty straight-forward question, Mr. Waters. Has Cordelia ever done something of importance and forgotten?" "No, not that I know of. She's very organized and diligent. What is the relevance?"

"You were home on Wednesday evening, correct?" "Yes." "Do you recall your wife calling anybody? Perhaps getting into an argument?" I'll need to check her phone records to verify this anyway, but if he could tell me, it would save me some trouble. "No. Not that I can remember. But then again, she may have been in another room or something," "You weren't together?" I recall my earlier conversation with Liam. Trouble in paradise? Perhaps I can get it out of him in one easy conversation. He raises an eyebrow. "We don't stay attached at the hip all day and night." "But surely you would be around each other, yes? Close enough to hear if she was fighting with someone." "I guess my answer is no, then. She wasn't on the phone. I never heard anything." I nod my head slowly. "Mr. Waters, where were you all day yesterday?" "What do you mean?" "Yesterday. Your wife says you were gone all day." "Well if my wife already talked to you then surely you'd know." I stare at him, trying to make it clear that I'm not here to play games. He challenges me, holding me gaze for a moment longer. Finally, he sighs, giving in. "I was out looking for my daughter, okay? What is this, an interrogation?" "Why did you tell your wife you were out with the police when you and I both know that's not true?" He hesitates and studies me before he answers. "I'd say anything to get her off my back. I don't know, I wasn't really thinking. I just thought if I said I was helping the police, she'd back off and stop questioning me." "Why were you trying to get her off your back?" "Because. I didn't feel like speaking with her." "Are the two of you having problems?" He tilts his head and looks up at me. "Do you have kids, detective?" "No. I don't." "Then you have no idea what I've been going through these past few days. It's fucking hell. And now you're over here questioning me. I just don't understand what we're doing right now." "I understand, Mr. Waters. And no, I can't imagine the great deal of pain and anguish you are going through right now. But I can tell you one thing. Finding your daughter is my top priority. I'm not blaming you for anything. We're just having a conversation. Man to man." I watch and study his reaction. "Now, I need you to be honest with me. Were you and your wife having problems within the days or the months leading up to Emerald's disappearance?" He eyes me and I'm not sure what he's going to say this time. "No. No, my wife and I aren't having problems. Everything is fine. Okay? It's just... the months before, with her depression and everything else. It's been hard. And I thought we had moved past it all. I thought she was better. But when I came home from work on Thursday and saw that empty crib, I don't know, I panicked. I thought she..." he pauses. "I thought she killed her. I thought she killed our baby girl. I was so distraught that I wasn't thinking clearly. I'm still not. God, I don't know how to do this. How do you deal with the fact that your six-month-old child is missing?" he places his face in his hands, shaking his head. "I don't know what to think. Honestly. And I know I shouldn't take it out on her, but I can't help it. I just can't stop myself from thinking that this is somehow all her fault." "So you truly and honestly believe that your wife is responsible for your child's disappearance?" "She told me that she wished Emerald was never born." "But she's better now, yes?" "So we're told." "But you don't believe that?" "Honestly, detective, I don't know what to believe. And that scares me."

———

As of this moment, there's nothing more I can go on. I feel like a sitting duck. I debate whether I should make another round back to all of the witness' houses, see if I can find any information that might have been overlooked.

I can't say that I feel reassured after my conversation with Weston. He seems as though he's being honest, yet I can't shake the feeling that there's more to the story that he's not telling me. He gets so offended when I ask him the simplest of questions. Perhaps this is just his demeanor, how he is. But there is still more that I need to find out. Could his wife really have done this? He seems to believe so.

And what about what Liam said over the phone about their marriage going downhill? Both Weston and Cordelia have told me that everything is fine between them. Everyone else seems to backup this notion. It is only Liam who has stated otherwise, yet I can't help but feel there's more weight to his words. Are Cordelia and Weston lying? Perhaps there was problems in the past, but they sorted things out and are fine now.

Now that I think about it, everybody has lied about something or other. Savannah lied. Cordelia lied or is lying. Even Weston lied to his wife when he said he was out with the police. I guess lying has simply become the norm these days.

There are too many factors to consider. Perhaps Liam was right about their marital issues. However, Cordelia and Weston could have worked things out since then. Either that, or both of them are lying and there's more to the story that they're not telling me. But why would someone lie and say that they're marriage is fine when it's not? Perhaps because a down-hill marriage in the midst of a child's disappearance is the most conspicuous of things.

I make my way around the living room, giving updates to a few of the men who are posted around the house. The Waters' probably aren't ecstatic about the fact that so many officers have been in and out of their home for the past forty-eight hours. But they are slowly dispersing. Only three remain – Sergeant Sol, Ashby, and Maverick – spread out around the house, and Doctor Eilsteen sits on the couch reading a book.

I look around for Cordelia. I need to speak with her once more before I head out. I ask Doctor Eilsteen where she is and he points to the bedroom. Their house is large, but it's somewhat easy to keep track of everyone's whereabouts.

I knock gently on the bedroom door, waiting for her to answer. When I don't hear a response, I knock again, louder this time. Finally, after a few knocks, I push open the door and peer inside. Nobody's there. Odd. Doctor Eilsteen said that she was in here.

I walk down the hall and back to the office, even though I just came from there. I knock and push open the door. Weston's still sitting at the desk. "Where's Cordelia?" I ask. He gives me an odd look, then says. "I thought she was with you?" I turn from him and rush down the hall, opening every door on my way. Nothing. Finally, I reach the living room again and the remaining faces turn to look at me. "What's wrong, Sully?" Olivia asks when she sees my face. "Where is Cordelia?" I look around, surveying the room. They turn and look at each other, puzzled.

She's not here. She's gone.

CHAPTER TWENTY-EIGHT

AFTER Cordelia Waters Saturday May 20, 2016

I drive down Division Street until I reach Hickory Grove. I'm speeding, going far over the limit, but that doesn't seem to bother me. I need to get there, fast. Much like my driving, my mind is erratic, flooded with thoughts of panic, doubt, and confusion. What has Savannah done? Why did she lie to the police? What could she possibly want with my daughter?

I heard the officers in my living room conversing; they had to release her from police custody due to unverified claims and lack of evidence. I grabbed my keys and took off, sneaking out the back door without a trace. They're too distracted to even pay attention to me, anyway. If not for Gerard, I could have gone unnoticed for hours. But since he showed up to the house shortly before my departure, I can count on him being hot on my trail. If I can just find Emerald and prove that Savannah did this, then they'll believe me. They have to know that I didn't do this. I'm innocent.

I accelerate, my foot pressing hard on the gas, passing residential homes, then eventually, reaching the condominiums. The look of Savannah's posh building reminds me of the apartment I lived in when I turned twenty. After living on residence for a year at Northwestern, I got my own place just off campus. It was a homey, quaint little place. Not much, but enough. I only stayed there for about a year before moving on again. The places I lived were always temporary, waiting for something better to come along. That was until Weston and I decided to move in together after I graduated. He was going to Marquette then, and we wanted a place for ourselves. However, nothing can compare to the home we live in now. The architecture, the homeliness of it, the memories that took place here. It will forever be known and remembered as the home we lived in together, where we got married, raised Emerald.

I pull into a parking spot, slam the gear into park, and march hastily towards the building. I wait impatiently as the elevator takes its time coming down, the concierge staring at me.

It dings, opening its doors for me, and I step inside, hitting the number eight with my knuckle.

Once the elevator reaches her floor, I dart down the hall and straight to her place. My fist connects with the door, banging continuously until she answers.

The door swings open almost immediately. Savannah stands there, astonishment on her face. "Cordelia," her voice falters. "What are you doing here?" I push past her, pacing the apartment. "Where is she!?" I yell. She closes the door and turns to me. "Who?" "Don't play stupid. Where is my daughter?" "What are you talking about? What did the police say to you?" "Enough. I know you have her. Where the hell is she?" I stop pacing and stare at her, panting. I bring my arms up and cross them over my chest, waiting. She takes a step forward, slowly, as if approaching a wild animal.

"Cordelia, you need to calm down. The police were mistaken. I have nothing to do with Emerald's disappearance. Why do you think they released me?" "Oh bullshit!" I yell. "You're lying! You're always lying!" "What are you talking about?" "You lied about being at my place. First you say you weren't there, then you were. Which is it?" Her facial expression alters and she looks scared, confused. "Cordy, you honestly don't remember, do you?" "Stop. I know what you're trying to do." "Honey, if you're getting sick again –" she reaches her arm out towards me. "Don't!" I yell and pull back from her. "No, don't you dare play the 'crazy' card on me. I'm not crazy. Not anymore." "Cordelia," she says in a soft voice now. "I was at your place on Thursday morning. So was Weston. You don't remember?" "Stop doing that! Stop lying!" "I'm not lying," "I think I would know if you were at my place." "Unless you had a mental break. Sometimes that can happen with people who suffer from postpartum psychosis. They have delusions, hallucinations, black outs. Especially after incidents of trauma." "What are you talking about?" "And those meds you were on. They probably made your mind so much worse. That's why I see a naturopath –" "Have you lost your mind?" She stares at me, wide eyed, insulted to have been cut off. "Have I lost my mind? Cordelia, you're the only one who sounds crazy right now. You're delusional!" "I'm calling the police," I reach into my pocket and grab my phone. She lurches forward and snatches it out of my hands. "What are you doing?" I bark. "You have this all wrong, Cordelia. We're going to get you help, okay?" I reach for the phone, attempting to grab it from her hands, but she's too quick and pulls away before I have the chance. She takes a step backwards, away from me. "Why are you doing this!?" I yell. "Why did you take my daughter?" I stare at her, breathing heavily. Then it hits me. "It's because of your baby, isn't it? You lost yours so you think you can just take mine?" "Cordelia!" she yells, finally. "Stop!" So I do. I don't speak. I just stare at her. "I need to find Emerald. They think I did this." "Well, did you?" Silence. "Are you kidding me? You too? You think I did this?" "Honestly, Cordy, I don't know what to believe. You come here yelling and acting crazy. And after Thursday morning... Who knows what you could have done. I'm assuming you don't remember what happened Wednesday, either?" "Wednesday? What are you talking about?" She shakes her head. "You really are having a psychotic break." "Fuck you!" I spit. "I'm not crazy. I didn't kill my daughter." "Are you sure about that?"

At the sound of those five words, the floodgates are open and it is impossible for my body to withstand the brimming rage any longer. I lurch forwards and dive on Savannah, ripping the phone from her hands and throwing it across the floor. It skids and bounces off the wall.

An animalistic cry escapes my throat as I pin her down with one hand, and slap her face with the free one. She's strong, though, more than I gave her credit for. She's holding me back, resisting my push, holding me as far away from her face as possible. For her, this act isn't difficult. For me, it's taking all of my strength not to be pushed off.

She digs her long nails into my arm and I falter. She uses this opportunity to roll us over. She has the advantage now, and is on top of me. She crosses my arms over my chest and holds them there, preventing me from moving.

I use all the strength I have left in me to jerk forward and knock her off of me, leaving her tumbling to the side. I sit up, but she recovers quickly and dives on me once again. I bring my leg up to kick her, and use my arms to push her sideways. I jump on top of her once again and pin down her arms.

It's then that the door swings open and I hear footsteps and yelling. People are here. Lots of them. But I can't focus on them. Not now. My vision is blurry and there's a deep pounding in my head.

Eventually, once I can hold on no longer, I release my grip. She uses this opportunity to knock me off of her with full force.

I feel the hands wrap around my arms, my body, yanking me up. I'm being dragged. There's yelling. The pounding is getting deeper. I open my mouth to say something, but all I hear is a loud ringing in my ears before my vision goes black.

———

I slowly fade into consciousness. There's a pounding in my head and I'm unsure of the source. I open my eyes, adjusting to the dim light, and take in my surroundings. I'm in my bedroom, lying in my bed. Once I see her sitting in her usual spot in the corner, I jolt upwards, wondering what the hell is going on.

"What are you doing here?" I gape. Doctor Wyatt closes the book she was reading and places it in her lap. "How are you feeling, Cordelia?" "Why am I in bed? What happened?" "You don't remember?" I don't respond. I stare at her, waiting for an answer. "What is the last thing you remember?" She stands slowly and walks over to sit at the edge of my bed. "Um," I rack my brain, trying to remember. Fuck. Why is my head aching? Why do I feel as though whatever answer I give is going to be the wrong one? "I was in the living room. Speaking with Detective Sullivan." She keeps her expression neutral, but I can tell that something's changed. She tried to hide it, but I saw it. Fear. She clears her throat. "What were the two of you speaking about?" I lick my lips, wondering why they're so dry. I need water. "I think... I think he was asking me about Savannah. A fight, maybe?" "And that's the last thing you remember?" "I think so. Did something happen? Why am I in bed?" "Cordelia," she says softly. She often does that when approaching a sensitive topic. "How often has this been happening?" "Has what been happening?" "Blackouts. Gaps of your memory, missing," I stare at her, perplexed. "What are you talking about?" She sighs, adjusts the glasses that rest on her nose. "I wanted to believe you, Cordelia. I really did. I had no idea this was happening to you." "What are you talking about? What is happening to me?" She returns her eyes to mine and I can tell this is difficult for her. "They found you at Savannah's place. You were hysterical," she says. Her words reach my chest first, causing my heart to accelerate, knocking the wind right out of my lungs. "You don't remember any of this?" her eyes hold more sympathy than they are capable of. I'm speechless, unable to form the words I need to say. "No," I finally speak. "I couldn't have. I've been here the whole time. How could I have left the house, driven to Savannah's, and not even remember?" "The blackouts, love. Dissociative amnesia. I'm assuming you've been experiencing them for the past few months. They can occur when you experience a traumatic event, a stressful situation, even. Rather than dealing with what has happened, your subconscious blocks it out." "No," is all I manage to say. "They can be brought on for a number of reasons. Say, a missing child," I look up and meet her eyes. "You're not saying..." "I don't know, Cordelia. The only person who was home that day was you. Only you know what could have happened to Emerald." "But... you don't think I hurt her, do you?" "I want to believe that you had nothing to do with it. I really do. But if these blackouts have been happening for a while now, I'm not entirely sure what to believe anymore." "Doctor Wyatt," I pause. "Fiona. I didn't hurt my daughter. I swear to you. Someone came in here and took her, and now I'm the scapegoat. Because of my mind." "Cordelia, even if you believe that entirely, it doesn't mean that there aren't other factors to consider. Something could have happened and your subconscious would have blocked it out. To the extent of your knowledge, you had nothing to do with Emerald's disappearance. But that may not be the case." I shake my head, squeezing my eyes closed as the hot tears fall down my face. I whisper, "I'm not crazy." "Oh, Cordelia." She reaches out and places her hand over mine. Soft, gentle hands with the sole purpose of healing. "It will all be over soon." I look up at her, meeting her deep green eyes. Even in the dim room I can see the very outline, the way the hazel specks form around the iris. "What do you mean?" She tilts her head down, her eyes traveling the length of my body, stopping at my feet bulged under the blanket. She pulls back the covers and that's when I see it. It's black, strapped tightly around my ankle. There's a tiny red light flashing intermittently. "What is that?"

Her eyes hover over my ankle, then eventually find their way back to mine. "It's for your own safety, Cordelia. We can't have you leaving again."

CHAPTER TWENTY-NINE

A FTER Detective Gerard Sullivan Saturday May 20, 2016

She sits in bed, propped up against the headboard, fiddling with a photograph of her daughter. I'm standing in the doorway, surveying the room. The walls are a light shade of beige. The king-size bed sits symmetrically center in the room, the wall behind. There's a dresser on the left side of the room and a vanity with a mirror above it on the right. There's a few photos on the wall: wedding photos, vacations, Emerald as a newborn. I return my gaze to Cordelia. She's still staring at the photo.

I walk over and sit in the chair that is posed in the corner. Doctor Wyatt's chair. It's been silent since I entered the room five minutes ago. I told her that we needed to talk. My mind has been on red alert since we arrived at Savannah's place to find Cordelia straddling her, clawing at her face. The theory of them being in on this together has quickly departed my mind.

My suspicions about Savannah are slowly diminishing, and replacing it are questions regarding Cordelia. I should feel rage when I look at her. I can't seem to get a straight answer from her. But right now, as I stare at her, sitting in her bed holding the photo of her missing daughter, I can't help but feel empathy. But the question remains: did she kill her own daughter?

She looks up at me, then, and smiles slightly. "Do you know what Memento Mori is?" I meet her eyes. "I don't." She looks at the photo again, then returns her gaze to me. "In the Victorian ages, people didn't have their photo taken until they were dead. The process was too long and complicated to endure while they were alive, so no one was photographed. But when somebody died, it was tradition that they would be photographed. As a memento of their life. Memento Mori. That translates to 'remember you will die.'" She pauses, looks back down at the photograph of her daughter. "Once they were dead, the families would open the eyes, apply make-up, prop them up to a sitting position. The family would pose with the deceased as the photographer took the photos. If you look back at the images, you can hardly tell which family member is dead. They all look the same. There were a lot of dead infants and children that they photographed. Often times, children would die early on. So they'd dress them up and take a family photo." She looks up at me again. "So most of the photographs that we see from that time period are of dead people." "How comforting." She places the photo on the nightstand beside the bed. "It's unsettling, really. Look up the photos when you get a chance." I nod my head and think about where to begin. "Why don't we go back to that day – Thursday? Tell me everything that happened." "We've already been over this," she protests. "I know. I have the file. Shower, breakfast, cartoons, nap, missing Emerald. But we're clearly missing something. I need you to think back and try to remember. Was there anything that seemed out of place? How were you feeling that day? Physically and emotionally?" "This is ridiculous!" she cries. "I felt fine! I didn't have a breakdown. I didn't kill my own child and forget it ever happened!" I take a deep breath and stare at her. "Please, just go over everything again." She presses her lips together and holds my gaze. She sighs, giving in, and recites everything that happened on Thursday, once again.

"So you're claiming that the last time you saw your daughter was at two-thirty p.m.?" I ask, looking down at my notes. "Claiming?" she sounds offended. "Sure. Yes, that was the last time I saw her." "And you remain firm in your testimony that you never saw Savannah that morning?" "Yes." "And you didn't wake up until Weston was home?" "Yes." "Why didn't you go to your bedroom to lie down? Why did you stay in the living room?" "I don't know, detective." She's getting aggravated. "I wasn't planning on falling asleep. I walked over to sit down for a few minutes and I dozed off. Is that a crime?" I look to my notepad again, then meet her eyes. "I apologize for all of the questions, Mrs. Waters, but you surely know how this must look. You suffered a severe psychosis, you've been suffering from dissociative amnesia and having blackouts for God knows how long, and you were sleeping during the time of the disappearance. What am I supposed to think?"

Her lip begins to tremble and I watch as she brings her hands to her face. She composes herself, and looks at me. "It looks so bad, I know that. If I were you, I'd probably think I was guilty as well. But I'm not. I didn't do this. You have to believe me. I would never hurt my baby."

"Well if not you, then who? Who would want to do this to Emerald or your family?" Tears well in her eyes once again. "I don't know."

———

I'm running out of options. It's almost five o'clock and soon enough, this day will be gone, just as the one before.

I'm conflicted. Until we find a body, we can't prove that Cordelia did anything. For now, this is still a missing-persons case. The child could be out there, somewhere, with a stranger, or perhaps, an acquaintance.

But what if she's not? What if her decaying body is floating down the river, or buried in the woods?

I decide to drive back to Savannah's and give her one last chance to tell me the truth. She knows something, yet she refuses to tell me. She was most certainly at the Waters' place on Thursday morning. The neighbor confirmed that. Robbins got back to me with the phone records and confirmed that there was indeed a call that took place between the two of them Wednesday evening. So what am I missing here? Cordelia had a blackout and didn't remember her visit? It must have been something pretty bad for Cordelia to block out and forget completely. Savannah said they were just talking. But that wouldn't cause Cordelia's dissociation. Something else happened that morning. And I need to find out what.

Cordelia is under temporary house arrest until we can figure this out. I was prepared to haul her into the station and lock her up after the little stunt she pulled at Savannah's. But Doctor Wyatt pleaded for her to be kept at home. She says her mind is fragile and she doesn't remember even being at Savannah's. For some reason, the Chief Lieutenant bought it and agreed to keep her at her home with an ankle monitor. She won't be leaving again anytime soon. Besides, all we can do now is two things: look for a body, and look for any other leads or suspects.

When I get to Savannah's place, she looks exhausted and petrified all at once. The fear of being taken away and interrogated yet again is evident on her face. But regardless of her ill feelings towards me, she invites me in and we walk over to the couch.

As we sit, I eye her carefully. She's not fidgeting or presenting any signs of nervousness. No fumbling with her hands or glancing sideways. The only thing I can sense from her right now is that she's annoyed. And she has every right to be. As do I.

"Listen, Ms. Valentine," I begin. "This little game that we're playing is getting quite old. And to be frank, I could care less about your feelings right now. There is a missing child out there. And if you know something that is of any importance, you should tell me. This is not me asking."

She presses her lips together, looks down at her hands, then sits up straight. "Okay."

"That easy, huh?"

She glares at me. "Do you want to know what happened or not?"

"The truth, or another lie?"

She continues to glare. "If you don't believe me, it's not my problem."

"Please, Ms. Valentine. Let's get this over with."

She nods her head, then begins. "I was telling you the truth before. Cordelia and I did have a fight over the phone on Wednesday night, and I did go over to see her on Thursday morning. If she doesn't remember, that's not my problem. But anyway, I may have spared some details." She looks at me, gauging my reaction. "Okay, so it all started Wednesday morning at work. I was eating lunch at my desk – a Greek salad – when I chipped my tooth on an olive seed. It hurt like a bitch. The first thought that came to my mind was Weston. He has his orthodontic practice, so I figured he could help. I didn't even think about going anywhere else because, well, he's my friend's husband and his practice is fairly close by. So I drove over there. "He took a look at my tooth and said it would be no problem to fix." She pauses and folds her hands in her lap. "So I don't know the full story here, you'll have to ask Weston about this part, but essentially, he went home that night, somehow the conversation came up about me being at the practice, and Cordelia freaked out. Went absolutely ballistic. I guess she'd been paranoid for a while that he was have an affair or something, and I guess she had this idea that it was with me!" She stops again and shakes her head. "Please. Yes, there's no denying that Weston is an attractive man. But there are boundaries, you know. Boundaries that I would never cross. Cordelia is my friend. I would never have an affair with her husband. And for her to think that of me?" She shakes her head again. "Insulting. But anyways, he tried to explain to her that it was nothing, but she wasn't having it. Called him a liar and was freaking out on him. So then I get a call from her and she starts yelling at me. She wouldn't listen to us, I'm telling you. We could not calm her down or talk her out of it. She hung up on me and I was mortified for being accused of something like that. But I felt even worse for her because she's clearly going through a hard time. So the next morning, I left work at lunch and decided to go over to her place to see how she was and to make sure everything was okay with us."

"Why didn't you go over on Wednesday night?"

"You didn't hear her, detective. I didn't even consider going over there. It wasn't until I was at work the next day that I was thinking about it and decided she'd probably have had plenty of time to cool down by then. So I went over."

"Around twelve, correct?"

"Yeah, it must have been around there. When I got there, she was not happy to see me. Starts going off about how we've been sneaking around behind her back and she never even suspected it. Crazy talk. Just going on and on. Eventually I had to call Weston and tell him to come over to help sort things out. I didn't want to drag him back into it, but I knew he could talk her down and clear things up."

"Wait a minute. Weston was there that morning?"

"Well, yes. But only for a little bit."

"What time?"

"Was he there?"

"Yes."

"Um, I think he got there around twelve-thirty, maybe? He was gone by quarter to. So was I."

"He went back to work?"

"Yes."

"Why was this not brought up before? Do you know how bad this looks on all of you?"

She looks down. "I'm sorry. I know, it's so stupid. I would have said something earlier, but..."

"But what?"

She looks up at me, ashamed. "Weston told me not to."

"He told you not to tell anyone that he was there?"

"Not that, necessarily. He just said not to tell anyone about the fight and Cordelia's behaviour. I thought she was just stressed and overwhelmed. I had no idea about the blackouts. But now I guess it makes sense why she doesn't remember the fight. She was in another state of mind or something."

"What happened when Weston came?"

"He talked to her, managed to calm her down. She was still yelling at me, though. Told me to get out. Weston told me to wait outside. I guess he managed to calm her down. Then he came out front and told me that she's just going through a hard time right now. He said not to mention it to anyone. He promised me that it wasn't a big deal. So I agreed and promised that I wouldn't say anything. Then we both left."

"You saw him drive away?"

"Yeah. I was checking my phone before I left and I watched his car pull out and leave. I waited around a few more minutes. I was so shaken up. And then I went back to work. That's why I was late."

"Ms. Valentine, you are aware that you lied to multiple police officers. Multiple times. That's an offence in its own. Interfering with an investigation. Do you know how much trouble you could be in?"

"I'm sorry. I know I shouldn't have lied. But I honestly didn't think this information was relevant. I truly believed that someone abducted Emerald, and so what relevance would Cordelia yelling at me have? I figured you guys were out there chasing some child-abductor. I didn't even know she was experiencing the dissociative amnesia. You have to understand where I'm coming from, detective."

"I do. But regardless, it was still wrong, and you will face consequences for your actions." I let out a deep breath. "Before you left, did you see anyone else around? Any cars? Anyone that might have looked suspicious?"

She shakes her head. "No. It was pretty empty at that time. And I wasn't exactly paying attention to my surroundings,"

"Did you see Emerald at all during your visit?"

She thinks about this for a moment. "No. I didn't, actually. I guess I was a little preoccupied, having Cordelia screaming at me and everything. Perhaps Weston checked on her. But then again, I'm not too sure he was even thinking of his daughter during Cordelia's episode."

I nod, taking in this bit of information. "Do you think there's any reality to Cordelia's claims?"

"What, that her husband was having an affair with me?"

"Not you specifically – an affair in general."

"No. Not at all. I just assumed she was being paranoid. I don't know Weston well, but I know that he and Cordelia have a healthy marriage. They're happy together. I don't think he'd ever do that to her. Or Emerald."

"I hope for everyone's sake that you're right."

She wipes her eye where a tear was beginning to fall, then looks back up at me. "Do you think she did it? Do you think she killed Emerald?"

I hesitate before answering. "Honestly, I don't know what to believe anymore."

One thing is clear, however: Savannah wasn't the only one who lied about Thursday. I need to find Weston.

CHAPTER THIRTY

A FTER Cordelia Waters Saturday May 20, 2016

I have no appetite, but I manage to scrape together something to eat anyways. The pile of dishes continues to grow and I know I'm going to run out of plates and silverware soon. And then someone will have to wash them.

I stir the bowl of soup and walk over to the kitchen table. I glance down at my ankle bracelet and debate whether I could saw it off with a knife. Doctor Eilsteen is sitting on the couch in the living room speaking with Doctor Wyatt. They've been sitting there for what feels like hours, subtly lurking from corners and watching me every chance that they get. I don't know what they think staring at me is going to do – I'm not going anywhere. I can't leave the house with this thing on.

Aside from the doctors, two officers wander around the house, keeping an eye on things. Weston went out, yet again. I swear he'll make up any excuse just to leave this house. Other than that, there's no one else here. Just the five of us. I'm getting pretty restless.

I must admit, there was a moment – just a brief one – where I doubted myself. But I quickly recovered from those thoughts, reassuring myself that they are wrong. I didn't do this, even if my mind is a bit unsteady right now. I'm not crazy. I know I'm not. There's no way I could have hurt Emerald. Even in my craziest state of mind I wouldn't do that. It's just not me – not anymore, at least. I've changed. I've improved so much. We were doing so well, Emerald and me. I was even starting to get used to her cries. And now my world is being tipped upside down and shaken consistently. I didn't do anything to her. I couldn't have. I'd remember that. Wouldn't I?

When I hear the doorbell ring, I immediately stand up, wondering who else could be here. Gerard again, perhaps? Doctor Wyatt motions for me to sit back down as she strides towards the front door.

When she pulls it open, my heart nearly leaps out of my chest when I see my parents standing there. I know they were only here yesterday, but yesterday feels like a lifetime ago. They drove back home to Evanston to drop their things off last night, which is reasonable considering they came to my place straight from the airport, and said they'd try to be back as soon as possible. I had completely forgotten, with everything else going on. I jump up and make my way towards the door to greet them.

Having my parents here makes everything feel so much better. A feeling of invincibility. They can't arrest me if my parents are here to protect me. It reminds me of being a child. How you know everything will be okay as long as your parents are there and on your side. They will protect you and make sure nothing bad happens.

Except now I'm not sure that they can protect me anymore. This situation has gone so far beyond my control and now, even my parents are concerned for me. They keep assuring me that everything will be fine. That they'll find the person responsible for taking Emerald. But no matter how convincing they try to be, I can still see the flicker of doubt in their eyes.

CHAPTER THIRTY-ONE

AFTER Detective Gerard Sullivan Saturday May 20, 2016

I signal left then turn onto the Waters' street. Just as I'm approaching the house, I see that we have company. Multiple cars and vans congregate in front of the house, news anchors and camera crews waiting outside like a starving pack of wolves.

I park on the side of the road and brace myself for the storm. As soon as I open my door, lenses and microphones are shoved into my face. "Excuse me, detective, can you give us an update on the Waters' case?" "Detective! Over here! Have you located the body of the missing child yet?" "Is it true that the mother is the main person of interest in the Emerald Waters' case?" "Can you give us an update on the status of Mr. Waters?" "Do you know where the child is?" "Can you give a word on Savannah Valentine?"

I walk forward, keeping my face neutral as I repeat the words "no comment." How did they already find out about the Savannah lead? Someone must have leaked information. Fuck. Now we have a PR problem on our hands.

I rush into the house and close the door tightly behind me. Holden notices me and comes over. He gives me a quick update, letting me know that the parents arrived a couple of hours ago and are in the other room watching television. But now for the real reason I'm here: the search warrant.

After leaving Savannah's place, I got a judge to grant me a warrant for any and all property, possessions, and belongings owned by Weston Waters. If he is indeed hiding something, it won't be long before I find it. "Where's Weston?" I say to Holden. "No idea." "He's not here?" "Don't believe so. The wife said he was out grabbing dinner." "Great." I say.

Holden finds Cordelia and vacates her from the premise while I begin my search. They can't go far due to the ankle bracelet and the zoo of paparazzi out front, so he takes her to the back porch. She protests at first, telling me that I have no right to search their home. But she eventually accepts this fate and willingly vacates, knowing all too well the consequences of arguing with me.

I begin with the living room, going through drawers and cabinets, not sure exactly what I'm looking for. I go through the kitchen, seeing if I can spot anything out of the ordinary. Any kind of clue or piece of evidence that can point me to something.

Next, I move to Weston and Cordelia's bedroom. If he's hiding something, surely it will be in here. Anything that can explain why he lied, and continues to lie, to both me and the police department. Something isn't adding up here.

That's when I spot it – the laptop sitting on his night stand. I walk over and perch myself at the edge of the bed, grabbing the laptop. I open it and am brought to the lock screen. Fuck. There's a password.

My moment of disappointment is only temporary as I soon remember Meredith Younger. She'll have no problem getting into this thing and finding anything of value.

————

I show up at the station, Weston's laptop in hand. I head directly to Younger's office and take a seat next to her desk. She's been awaiting my arrival.

"Let's have a look, shall we?" she says, taking the laptop from my hands.

She puts it on her desk and opens it. Within seconds, she's through the firewall and into his system.

"That easy, huh?" I say to her. "It's easier on a PC than it is a Mac." "Remind me never to leave you alone with my personal belongings," I joke. She laughs. I slide my chair closer to her and lean in to get a better look.

"Anything in particular that you're looking for?" she asks. "No idea. All I know is that he's continued to be dishonest with me from the beginning. I don't know what it is exactly that he's lying about, so we have a wide base to cover." She nods and gets to work.

The screen opens to reveal a mundane screensaver. Files and documents lined perfectly down the side of the desktop. She begins clicking through each of the files, looking for anything that stands out. It's mostly work files, we soon learn. Patient files, x-ray scans, receipts and tax information. There's a folder titled Emerald filled with hundreds upon hundreds of photos. We quickly scan through them even though they all look the same to me. Then again, I'm not a parent.

"Here, let me see," I say, taking the laptop from her and placing it in front of me. I want to navigate it myself. "I'm going to get a coffee," she stands.

"Want anything?" "I'm good, thanks." "Let me know if you need me to get through anything else." "Will do."

Younger leaves her office and I continue going through the folders on the desktop. When that proves fruitless, I open up the internet browser. Emails. That would be the ideal place to check.

Upon entering his email account, which he leaves logged in, I scan through the inbox. There's nothing too interesting that stands out, mostly just back-and-forth emails with clients and employees at the practice. Other than that, his emails don't extend much beyond subscriptions and emails to Cordelia. Is Weston Waters' life truly that uninteresting? What does the man do for fun? Who does he associate himself with? These questions remain a mystery.

The mouse hovers over the trash folder. Perhaps I'll have better luck in there. I click the button and the screen fills with multiple emails, most of them junk. But there are two emails that stand out amongst the rest, solely because they are from the same sender: Rhoden Lakes. The most recent email is dated from five days ago. I open it and see that it's only one sentence:

It would be respectful if you'd at least take my calls.

So perhaps this is not junk-mail after all? Although I wouldn't consider it a formal email either. No, "Dear Mr. Waters" or "Yours Truly." It's very straight to the point. Could it have possibly been sent by mistake? But then I remember there's another email from the same sender. I click back to the junk folder and find it, dated from just over a week ago on May ninth.

Finnick's? Regular time.

That's it – another one liner. What does this mean and what is Finnick's? I pull up another tab and Google it. Ah, it's that bar down on Cheyanne Avenue. I've passed by there a few times.

I can conclude two things from these emails. The first is that they are not junk-mail. Whoever this Rhoden Lakes person is must know Weston personally. The second thing I can gauge from these emails is that Weston is clearly hiding something – or someone. Why else would they be asking him to meet, and why else would he delete the emails?

Could this be the golden ticket I've been searching for?

I grab my phone and dial his number. "Mr. Waters, where are you?" I ask once he answers. "I'm just out grabbing dinner. Why?" "I need to speak with you immediately. Can you come down to the station?" "Is everything alright? Have you found her?" "No, I'm afraid we haven't." "Then what is this regarding?" "You and I need to have a little chat." It's quiet for a moment. The finally, he speaks. "Sure. I'm not too far from there, actually. I can be there in ten minutes."

―――――

Fifteen minutes after our phone call, Rebecca notifies me that Weston has entered the lobby. I meet him there, then together, we walk to my office. I close the door behind us, motioning for him to take a seat.

I walk around my desk, pull out the chair, and sit across from him. He's staring at the files I have spread out. He looks exhausted, as though he hasn't slept for days. I can imagine why.

"So, what did you need to talk about?" he asks, finally looking up at me. Where to begin? "You lied," I say. "Pardon me?"

"Your wife seems to think you spent the entirety of Friday with the police. I know you weren't at home, so where were you?"

"I was out looking for my daughter!"

"So why did you tell her that you were with us?"

He shrugs. "I don't know, anything to get her off my back. Make her realize that I'm actually trying to do something, not just sitting around idly."

I nod, accepting his answer. "But that's not all you lied about, Weston."

He stares at me, awaiting for me to elaborate. "You were home on Thursday morning." "What gave you that idea?" I glare at him. He should know by now not to play this game. "It isn't in your best interest to continue this lie, Mr. Waters." He glares right back, then decides that I'm right. He looks away for a moment, staring at the wall. Then he turns back to me. "Savannah told you, didn't she?" he laughs slightly and shakes his head. "This is why we didn't say anything. Because you think we had something to do with it." "Not at all. I wouldn't have thought that. In fact, considering your wife is the main person of interest in this case, my first thought would be that you were somehow protecting her." He flattens his mouth into a straight line, then massages his left hand. "It's not like that." "Well please, explain to me. I'm all ears." "She was having a bad week, okay? She was stressed and anxious. I guess she had a little melt down on Wednesday. But she was talking pure nonsense. Saying I was having an affair with Savannah." "Well were you?" "Of course not." "Then why would your wife think that?" "I told you, she wasn't in a good state of mine. She would have said anything." "I don't believe that." "Oh yeah? Why not?" "There's something else you're not telling me." "Like what?" I tilt my head slightly. "Are you having an affair, Mr. Waters? Not with Ms. Valentine. There's someone else."

His facial expression doesn't alter. He continues to stare at me, but it's as though he's frozen in time. "Mr. Waters," I say again. "No. No, I'm not having an affair," he spits like it's such a filthy word. "Why would you even ask me that?" "Would you like to tell me about Rhoden Lakes?" I ask, and watch as he tries to hide his reaction.

"I don't know what you're talking about." "Mr. Waters, there's no point in lying any longer. I found the emails on your computer. So you can either tell me the truth, or I'll have someone trace them."

He leans forward in one fast motion so our faces our inches apart. He doesn't say anything. Just keeps his face close enough that I can hear him breathing heavily through his nostrils.

"You're looking awfully guilty of something right now, Weston." He pulls away from me and sits back in his chair, avoiding eye-contact. I let him sit like this for a moment, wallowing in the silence. Finally, he readjusts in his chair and sits up straight. "Okay," he says. "Okay, what? You ready to talk?" He nods his head somberly. "On one condition,"

"You're not really in a position to be negotiating. But I'll hear what you have to say." He looks angered by this, but knows that I'm right. He doesn't have many options. "I'll tell you everything. But please don't tell Cordelia, alright? You can do anything you want, tell everyone at the station if you have to. But could we try to keep this from her?" "What are you hiding?" He takes in a deep breath and looks down at his shoes. "You were right. I'm having an affair. Was having an affair." He stops, almost to let the words sink in, then he looks back up at me. "This has nothing to do with what's going on. I guess this all came at a bad time." "What did, your affair?" He nods.

"How long?" I ask. "Only a couple of months. I never meant to.... I didn't intend for things to turn out like this. But, I guess no one really plans to have an affair. They just do." "Who is she?" "Do I have to say?"

I stare at him, letting him know through visual cues that, yes, you do. He sighs again. "It's the woman you asked me about earlier. Rosella. Rhoden Lakes is a pseudonym she made up. You know, just to be safe." "Rosella?" I say, caught off guard. I grab my phone and check the time. It's nearly ten o'clock. "What is it?" he asks, clearly catching on that something isn't right. "You should have told me this when I asked you the first time," I dial Robbins number and put the phone to my ear. "Why? What is it?" I turn to him, aggravation and annoyance flooding my body. If he would have just been honest with me earlier, I could have put together the pieces and put out an APB. "We have reason to believe that this woman was lurking outside your home back in March," I say. Robbins phone goes to voicemail and I hang up. "Your nanny also mentioned that she came by the house about two weeks ago. Now tell me, Mr. Waters, what your mistress was doing lurking outside your home at night and coming to your house in the middle of the day? "I had no idea about that," he says, and genuinely looks taken back. "What makes you say she was lurking outside?" "Your babysitter saw someone sitting outside in a red Impala back in March. Said that your landline rang but no one was on the other line. It freaked her out." "God dammit," he brings his hand to his forehead. "And what about two weeks ago?" I say. "Why did she come by then?" He opens his eyes and looks at me. "I told her not to. But she needed to see me." "Why?" "She just wanted to. I don't know," he turns and pushes his hand through his hair. "This whole situation has gotten far out of control. It was never meant to be like this." "Like what?" "This serious. It was just a fling. Temporary. But it evolved to something more. And now, with Emerald missing... God, I just can't focus on that right now. I need to focus on finding my daughter." "So you don't find it odd that the woman you are having an affair with has been stalking you and your family? That doesn't strike you as suspicious?"

"What are you implying? That Rose had something to do with Emerald's disappearance?" "That's how it looks, yes." "No, that's insane. Rose would never do something like that. And besides –" "Besides what?" "Nothing." I shake my head. "You're digging the whole deeper and deeper, Weston." He stares at me.

"Give me a number I can reach her at," I say and pull out my phone again. "Who, Rosella?" "Yes, who else?" He sighs and recites the number. "When was the last time you had contact with this woman?" I ask him. "About a week ago. We met for coffee. That was the last I saw of her." "You're sure, now?" "Yes." I dial Robbins number and try her again. I turn to Weston. "I hope you're telling me the truth this time. And if you're not, don't think I won't hesitate to drag your ass down to the station to get the answers I need. Understood?" He nods. "And please, try not to go running off again. It looks bad."

CHAPTER THIRTY-TWO

B EFORE Weston Waters May 3, 2016

The sound of chirping birds fills my ears as I walk to my car. It's five o'clock and the sun is still prominent in the sky, casting shadows across everything in its path.

As I drive home from work, my mind wanders to Rosella; a story she told me the other day about something that happened in Clementine's classroom. Apparently her teacher is very strict about note passing, but for some reason, Clem and her friend were passing notes back and forth to each other about boys they liked. The teacher ended up catching them mid note-pass and decided to hang it up at the front of the classroom, just above the chalkboard, for everybody to see. Clementine was so embarrassed, so during recess when no one was around, she snuck back inside the classroom, tore down the note, ripped it into tiny pieces, and put the scraps in her bag. I couldn't help but laugh as Rosella recited the story, reminiscing on how I used to act when I was just a clueless fifth grader.

Just as I'm pulling into the driveway, I notice Marcia's car parked beside Cordelia's. Her husband must be off work today in order for her to have the car. When I walk through the front door, Marcia is sitting on the couch holding Emerald, singing a song that I can't quite identify. I smile as I drop my briefcase and walk over to greet them.

"Hello princess!" I beam as I sit on the couch beside them, taking Emerald into my arms. She's wearing a light blue dress, a matching headband in her little patch of hair. She's almost six months now and already her hair is getting long. Soon enough it will be down to her shoulders, beautiful blonde locks, just like her mother. "Where's Cor?" I turn to Marcia. "She's taking a quick shower. Should be out soon." She smiles and watches as I bounce Emerald up and down on my lap. "It's a beautiful day." I remark. "It is." "I see you have the car today," "Yes, a friend was meeting with Steve this morning so he was able to get a ride." I nod. "Any plans with the kids tonight?" "Just going home to make dinner." She smiles. We both turn our heads to Emerald as she makes some sort of sound between a squeak and a giggle. "Oh, Mr. Waters, I forgot to mention," she turns to me again. "Somebody came by looking for you earlier. A woman." I furrow my eyebrows. "Did she leave a name?" "Um, I believe she said her name was Rosella. I told her you were at work." My heart plummets in my chest. I can feel the blood rushing to my ears as she speaks. I remain composed and clear my throat. "Oh, that's odd. Did she say what she needed?" "No. Just said she was looking for you." "Hmm, no idea," I say. "I'm sure she'll contact me if it's important." I force a smile and try to brush off the sense of unease. I should be relieved, really. She could have said anything to Marcia. But she didn't. I hear the bedroom door open and a moment later, Cordelia walks into the living room wearing her blue robe, rustling a towel through her damp hair. "Oh, you're home early," she says as though she wasn't expecting to see me. "Yeah. There weren't many patients this afternoon." She nods her head and holds the towel at her side. "Feel free to go whenever you'd like, Marcia," Cordelia smiles. "I better get going now, actually. The kids will be wondering where dinner is." She laughs as she lifts herself up off the couch. I hoist Emerald onto my hip and follow her to the door. "Thanks Marcia. We'll see you Wednesday." "Goodbye, Mr. Waters. Goodbye, little one." She gives Emerald a little poke on the nose, leaving my daughter smiling and giggling.

———

The next morning on my way to work, I make a detour to Rosella's. What the hell was she thinking coming by my house? I've told her before that my place is off limits. The only reason she even knows my address is because she saw it on a mailing envelope in my car. I have no problem meeting her if she needs to see me – anywhere but my house. Cordelia could have been there. I can only imagine what would have happened if she came today instead, a Thursday, when Cordelia is working from home. Disastrous, that's what.

Cordelia has already been on edge lately, I can tell. I know she's been wondering about my frequent absences as of late, but she hasn't said a word. She feels like this is her fault; that she is the reason we're falling apart. But she's been trying to make it up to me lately. Cooking elaborate dinners, wanting to go to the amusement park, making sure to spend more time with Emerald when I'm around. I'm glad she's making an effort. I really am. But what's done is done, and nothing can change that. I can't control my feelings. I wish I could – but I can't. The feelings I used to have towards my wife simply aren't as strong as they once were, and instead, all of my thoughts and attention are directed towards Rosella.

We've been so careful. Nobody would be able to link us together in any way. Except Clementine. But Rosella has explained to her the importance of keeping this whole thing a secret. Should we ever have involved her? Sometimes I don't know. Rosella seemed so keen on me meeting her. And she is a lovely girl. I guess she didn't want to keep her a secret from me. I told her about my family, and she told me about Clementine. It has worked out fine so far. Until yesterday.

Fortunately her car is in the driveway, meaning she hasn't left for work yet. I called into the office on my way and told Carla I was stuck in traffic and would be a few minutes late. No problem, is what she always tells me. Of course it's no problem – I own the place.

I hustle up the front steps and ring the doorbell, then proceed to knock consistently. A moment later, I hear footsteps rushing to the door and it swings open, revealing a stunning-as-always Rosella, dark hair clipped up, wearing jeans and a t-shirt, holding her scrubs.

"What's going on? Did something happen?" She looks utterly shocked to see me. When I don't answer right away, she leans her head out the door, surveying if anyone else is there, then yanks me inside by the arm and shuts the door behind us. "What the hell were you thinking?" I ask once I'm inside. "I beg your pardon?" "Coming to my house yesterday! The nanny had to tell me that some woman came by looking for me." "Oh," her face drops. "Oh? What is oh? Why did you come by?" She looks up at me, those vibrant blue eyes striking me again as they always do. "I'm so sorry, Wes. I needed to see you." "Why? Did something happen with Clem?" my anger fades and is replaced with concern. "No, it's not that," "Then what is it?" She doesn't answer me. She stares down at the floor. "What would you have done if Cordelia was there? Imagine what could have happened," I say. Her lips part as though she's going to speak, then she closes them again. "What's going on?" I say. "What could possibly be so important that it couldn't wait?" She looks up at me, then, and I see something in her eyes: fear. "I'm pregnant." The words leave her mouth, but I don't hear them. "What did you just say?" "I'm pregnant, Wes." "Are you sure? How do you know?" I feel as though I've been punched in the gut, the air knocked out of my lungs, my heart sinking further into my chest. "I didn't get my period on time. At first I didn't think anything of it. But the more I thought about it, the more unusual it was. I have a very regular cycle. So I took a pregnancy test. It was positive." "Well did you take another? Sometimes it can give a false reading." "I don't know, Wes! I don't know what to do!" Her voice gets higher suddenly and I watch her eyes fill with tears. "Fuck," I mutter and turn sideways, placing my fist over my mouth. "What do we do?" she cries. I turn back to her. "It could be wrong. The test could be wrong." "So what should I do!?" "We'll make a doctor's appointment. You can get checked there. They'll tell you if you're really pregnant or not." She nods her head, wiping the tears from her eyes. I'm so overwhelmed with emotions, rendered speechless. Anger, fear, guilt, fear, anxiety, anger, guilt, fear – playing through a loop in my brain. So many questions. What if she is pregnant? How will I hide this from Cordelia? What if I have to tell Cordelia? What about Emerald? What about Clementine? Fuck. Fuck. I turn to her, suddenly realizing that I'm being selfish. The potential life we created is in her stomach, not mine. "I'm sorry for overreacting," I say. "About coming to the house. You were probably scared. Fuck, I can't imagine how scared you are. I'm sorry, Rose." I reach forward and bring her into my arms. She cries into my chest. "It's okay," she says. "We'll figure this out." She pulls back and looks up at me, her blue eyes glassy with tears. "We will. We'll figure it out." I repeat.

CHAPTER
THIRTY-THREE

A FTER Detective Gerard Sullivan Saturday May 20, 2016

Weston leaves the station and heads home. I pace back and forth in my office, thinking. This case keeps getting more unnerving as the hours pass. Not only did he lie about having an affair, but his affair might be the very reason his child is missing. This woman is evidently stalking him and his family. What else is she hiding?

I take out my phone and call the number that Weston gave me. It rings six times before going straight to voicemail. "You've reached Rosella. Sorry I missed your call, please leave a message and I'll get back to you as soon as I can. Thank you and have a great day." Pause. Beep. "This is Detective Sullivan from the Davenport Police Department." I say quickly, unprepared to leave a message. "I have a few questions that I think you could help me with. If you could please give me a call back as soon as you're able, it would be greatly appreciated." I recite my number, then hang up.

A voice message isn't enough. I need to go over there again, talk to her in person. But what if she's not home? What if I can't find her? Then I'll put out the APB. I have enough for that now. This woman is critically needed in a missing person's investigation. Anyone who has any information on her will be of some assistance. The clock continues to tick and I can't help but feel as though we're running out of time.

———

It's nearly eleven by the time I hit the road and make my way down to Rosella's neighborhood once again. But unlike my previous visit earlier in the day, everything is quiet. No people walking their dogs, no children playing on the street. The suburban homes line the streets, not a soul in site.

I pull up in front of her house and park on the street. Nothing has changed since the last time I was here, the Impala still parked in the driveway. I make my way up the steps to her front door and ring the doorbell. Peering through side window, I can see that the house in dark, no lights on at all. I knock this time – loudly – then step back and wait. Still nothing. I backtrack down the steps and try to see if there are any lights on upstairs, if there is any trace of human life inside of this house, but I can't see anything that would prove so. The house is completely dark. Empty.

I debate getting a search warrant. Although, no judge would be around to approve it at this time of night. The soonest I could get one would be by morning. Do I have that long? What if the child is in there?

I walk back up to the door and knock once more. Then I put my fingers on the door-handle and twist. It's open.

I quickly turn my head and survey my surroundings. No one is out, but someone could be peering through their windows, watching. Then again, I'm not the guilty one here. I'm the law. But still, I'm aware that what I'm doing is illegal. I shouldn't enter the premises without a warrant or probable cause. But I just can't shake the feeling that something isn't right here.

I turn the handle and push the door open, quickly walking inside and closing it tightly behind me.

"Ms. Collins," I say aloud into the vacant house. "Are you in here?" No response.

I walk forwards, quietly and slowly, trying not to make a sound. If she isn't here, then where is she? And if she isn't here, then what am I doing in here? Do I expect to just find the child sitting in a crib all alone?

What if I'm wrong? What if this Rosella woman has nothing at all to do with Emerald's disappearance and I just broke so many rules coming in here. She could have been stalking him, yes. But that doesn't necessarily mean she's a child abductor. Did I jump to conclusions too quickly?

I continue walking through her house, curiosity getting the best of me. Perhaps if I find something – anything at all – it can give me a better sense of who this woman is, what she's like. If I can just find a clue, some piece of evidence at all. I turn left from the main hallway and enter the kitchen. And that's when I see it – see her – lying on the floor, a pool of blood beside her head.

CHAPTER THIRTY-FOUR

AFTER Cordelia Waters Saturday May 20, 2016

As I lie in bed, the darkness of the room surrounding me, I listen to the rain pouring down outside of my window, praying that I'll fall asleep soon. It's loud and violent, and I can't help but think that the sky is crying with me. I wonder again what I could have possibly done to deserve this. Is this my punishment for being a bad mother? Why does this sort of thing happen? Is there a reason for it all? Is this finally my prayers being answered? All those months of wishing I never had her, wishing she'd just disappear.

Did I do this? Am I truly responsible for my own daughter's disappearance? The mere thought makes me ill.

I hear the door creek open and I turn my head. The light from the hallway illuminates through the opening and I can see Weston's face as he enters the room. He remains quiet and moves slowly as he pulls out the covers and crawls into bed, not saying a word. At least he's not sleeping on the couch.

I lie there, debating what I should say. Finally, I build up the courage. "Weston," I say as I lie flat on my back, staring at the ceiling. He turns his head and looks at me, not saying a word. "Are they going to find our baby?" I ask through a hushed whisper. I hear him take in a deep breath. "I hope so." I turn to face him. "You know I didn't do this, right? You have to believe me." "It's been a long day, Cor. Let's just sleep. We'll talk in the morning."

I nod my head and roll over so I'm facing the window again. I pull the blankets up to my chin and wipe away the single tear that falls down my cheek.

CHAPTER THIRTY-FIVE

A FTER Detective Gerard Sullivan Saturday May 20, 2016

I stand back and observe the scene in front of me. Red and blue flashing lights line the street; families huddled on front lawns and sidewalks, trying to get a look at what's happening; a coroner stands over the body; analysts dusting everywhere for finger prints, shoe prints, anything.

It all happened so quickly. One moment I was a silent intruder in this woman's home, trying to locate her as a suspect. The next, she is the victim.

I raced over to where she lay on the floor, not thinking about disrupting the scene in any way. The only thought going through my head was to check for a pulse. And when I did, I realized all too soon that I was far too late. By the look of it, she had been dead for hours, the pool of blood dark and dried.

The forensics team has arrived now. There's a blood splat analyst photographing the body, the walls, the counter. It's eerie how everything in the home remains so intact despite the traumatic demise that occurred here. A few dishes sit in the sink, a scrap book lies open on the dining room table, a bag of groceries sit on the floor beside the counter, unpacked. The question haunting my mind: was she lying here, dead, when I came by the house earlier? Was there anything I could have done to prevent this?

Robbins appears at the corner of my eye and I turn to her. "We need to bring Weston in for questioning. Stat." I tell her. "Will do," she nods and looks down at the body. Rosella's long black hair flows effortlessly beside her, down onto the floor. There's a large gouge in her forehead where the blood leaked out. Her eyes are wide open, face pale. We both stand there, frozen, staring at her. "What do you think we're dealing with here?" Robbins asks. "They were having an affair," I say. "That's all I can gather thus far. Where the baby is and how Rosella ended up dead is beyond me." "But you think it's him?" "I'm hoping he can give me some answers."

———

Holden and Ashby go to the Waters' residence to retrieve Weston, yet again. By the time I get to the interrogation room, he's already seated inside, hands folded neatly on the table. From what I heard, he caused quite a scene as they hauled him out of bed and into the squad car, Cordelia echoing similar sentiments as she stood behind and watched the suspicion transfer from her to her husband. Why does everything seem to lead back to him?

"Evening," I say as I enter the room. He looks up. "It's morning now." I check my watch. He's right. It's after one a.m. I pull out the chair across from him and take a seat. "Why am I here?" he asks. "Nobody has told me anything. And for you to come to my house unannounced in the middle of the night, waking up my wife and I," he pauses. "It's unacceptable." "Why don't I tell you what's unacceptable, Mr. Waters? Lying multiple times in what is now to be considered a homicide investigation." His eyes widen. "What? You found Emerald?" "No, I'm afraid we haven't. Your mistress, on the other hand," He stares at me. "What are you talking about?" "Rosella

Collins. She was found dead in her home this evening." His face contorts. "What?" "When was the last time you had contact with Ms. Collins?" "I already told you, I haven't seen her since last Wednesday!" "Do you have an alibi? Anyone who might have seen the two of you together?" "I don't know, we were in a coffee shop!" He's getting worked up. "When did you first begin your relationship with Ms. Collins?" "Back in March, I think." "You don't know?" "It was March." "Did you have any reason to suspect Ms. Collins of kidnapping your daughter, Mr. Waters?" "No. No, of course not." "So you didn't find it suspicious that a week after you broke off your relationship with this woman, your infant daughter goes missing?" "No, not at all." "Hmm, interesting. And you don't find it a bit strange that tonight, two days after your daughter's disappearance, Ms. Collins turns up dead?" He stares at me. "I don't know what you want me to say. I haven't spoken to, nor seen Rosella, in over a week. I don't know what could have happened to her." "You don't seem all that broken up about it," "How dare you?" he spits. "I am devastated inside. I may not be sobbing on the floor, but the fact that Rose is dead crushes me. I loved her. I really did." The room is silent, neither one of us saying a word. "Am I being arrested?" he finally asks. "No," I say. "Not yet, anyways." "Then if you're not going to charge me with anything, am I free to go?" I stare at him, analyzing every part of him. "You may go," I say. "But this isn't over. We will find out what happened to her." "Good," he says. "I truly hope you do. And I hope you and the other cops in this place actually do your God damn job and find my daughter."

CHAPTER THIRTY-SIX

AFTER Cordelia Waters Sunday May 21, 2016

I open my eyes and check the clock beside my bed. It's eight-thirty. I've barely slept at all and can feel the heaviness of my eyes. I want to go back to sleep, but I know that no sleep will come. Especially after the night we had.

The police showed up here after midnight, reading off constitutional rights and taking my husband away in the back of a cop car. It was excruciating. But part of me couldn't understand how one minute, all eyes were on me, and the next, they're on my husband. What the hell happened? What did they find? And why is Weston being questioned by the police in regards to the disappearance of our daughter? Weston would never hurt Emerald. This is all one big misunderstanding.

Today is the third morning I've had to wake up to this nightmare. The third morning I've had to wake up without her here. Every day the sun continues to come up, and I'm still here, but she is not. I sit up in bed and look at Weston who is sound asleep. He didn't say a word once he got home. I didn't press him, either. I know what it's like to be accused of something you didn't do. I'll get on with my day and let him rest. He needs it. But hopefully I will know all the details from the night before soon. Perhaps he'll be ready to talk about it later.

I thought they would have found her by now. Come rushing through the doors with good news. She should be safe and sound, sleeping in her crib. The police are supposed to be doing their job. I can only imagine the worst. That some man has her locked in a room somewhere, and she's crying, wanting Weston or me to come and hold her. But no one's there. No one's coming for her. She doesn't know what's going on. She doesn't know that worlds are falling apart because of her absence. She has no idea.

Having your child go missing is a mother's worst nightmare. But being blamed and accused for such a thing, I can't even put into words how that feels. These thoughts are driving me mad. I'm locked in this damn house and I can't do a thing about it. All I have is my mind, hoping it will keep me sane, but I feel abandoned from even myself.

How did I not know about the blackouts? How could I allow myself to forget things that have happened? I feel so stupid. As though there's something inherently wrong with me. Doctor Wyatt tried to reassure me that none of this is my fault. That it's simply in my brain, beyond my control. But I can't help but feel responsible.

Regardless of these blackouts, I know one thing for certain: I didn't do anything to my daughter. I know this. It's a fact. I have this feeling deep down – a mother's intuition – that someone took my baby. I have to believe that's true. Because if I don't – if I let my mind slip, even just the slightest – I'll be sucked into a vortex of blame and confusion that I didn't know was possible. And if I somehow did do something to my own daughter, then God only knows what else I am capable of.

It's nine a.m. when I wander aimlessly down the hall, debating if I should eat something or not. What a pleasant surprise. Detective Robbins is back, sitting in the corner of the living room, eyeing me like I'm some sort of criminal. I try to ignore her as I walk past and into the kitchen.

When I glance in the sink, expecting to see that giant pile yet again, all of the dirty dishes are gone. Mom. She must have cleaned them last night. I smile to myself, knowing that she's here and always watching out for me.

I pour myself a double serving of coffee, then walk over to the living room and turn on the TV. Perhaps there's an update on Emerald.

I sit back in the chair and flip through the channels until I find the news. I wait a couple of minutes, watching the weather updates, news about Syrian refugees, and a car accident on the freeway this morning. But then I see her face – that same photograph I gave to the police the night she went missing – and I sit up straight. I turn up the volume and listen to what they're saying. "Police continue to investigate the disappearance of six-month-old Emerald Waters who went missing from her home Thursday evening. The Davenport Police Department released a statement early this morning stating that they still do not have any solid leads on the case. They are asking anyone who may have any information to contact the police at the phone number listed at the bottom of the screen."

After a few minutes, the screen changes and a blonde woman appears to talk about the presidential elections. I turn my head and stare at Detective Robbins. A laptop rests on her legs, she's typing something. "Did you stay awake all night?" I ask her. She lifts her head and meets my eyes. "Another officer and I took shifts. I've only been here a few hours." I nod my head. "Any updates?" "No, sorry." She says.

An hour later the doorbell rings and I jump from my seat, thinking its Gerard with an update. I do admit, I'm still angered by his accusations yesterday. Though, I can't completely blame him. It is partially my fault that they had to restrain me here. Nonetheless, I still feel the slightest sense of abandonment from him. Perhaps it was because he was the only one who showed me an ounce of compassion the night she was taken. And now I feel as though everyone has turned on me. He was my last hope, and now not even he believes me.

I walk to the door in six big strides. When I unlock the door and pull it open, I'm completely taken back to see who's standing there.

It's my brother, Liam. Lianna, Sophie and Clayton stand slightly behind him. "Hey, sis," he says, forcing a small smile. "Liam. What are you doing here?" I pause. "Please, come in." I stand back and hold the door open as they all enter the house. "What do you mean, what am I doing here? My niece is missing. I came to be here for you." "Did someone call you? Did mom and dad tell you to come?" "Can't you just be happy that I'm here and accept that?" He stares at me. "Give me a hug, it's been ages." He leans in and wraps his arm around my neck. Just like old times. My parents must have heard his voice because before our new arrivals can even get their shoes off, my parents are hurrying down the hallway, coming right at us. "Liam, honey!" My mother grins as she walks over and embraces her son. She then makes her rounds, giving Lianna a kiss on the cheek, picking up Sophie and Clayton for a hug and kiss. We walk together from the doorway into the living room where I was just sitting, alone. Clayton chases Sophie around the coffee table and the adults stand around awkwardly before I motion for everyone to sit. "I'm so sorry, Cordelia," Lianna says. "I can't imagine what you're going through." "Thank you. It's been really hard these past couple of days." "And months, I bet." She says. I eye her, wondering what she's implying. "Yes, the last couple of months have been difficult. But I'm much better now. Well, until Thursday, that is." She shakes her head. "I'm at a loss of words. I can't even begin to fathom how I'd feel if one of them were taken from me." She pauses, holding a fist to her mouth. "I don't even want to think about that." Liam reaches out and places his hand on top of hers, but doesn't say anything. Then he looks up at me. "Is Colton here?" "No, he went back to Evanston. Did you want to see him?" "No, I –" he stops. "I mean, if he was here, then, yeah, I wouldn't... sure." We all stare at him. "Alright," I say, then clear my throat. "Can I get anyone coffee or tea? Water maybe?" "No you sit, Cordelia," Lianna says, prepared to stand. "You've been through enough. I'll get the drinks." "No, really, it's fine." I insist. "Let her do it," Liam says to his wife. "Really." I turn from Liam and stare at her, waiting for an answer. "I'll have some water," Lianna says. "And maybe some juice for the kids." "Of course. Liam?" "Sure. Coffee's fine." I head back over the kitchen to get the drinks. I pass Detective Robbins again and she's staring at me. It's only now, in this dusk morning light, that I notice how crystal blue her eyes are. She could almost be pretty if she wasn't so rude. "What?" I say to her. She looks back down at her laptop. "Nothing." I glance back at my family who sit there awkwardly attempting to make small talk. "Do you have a problem?" I ask. "Am I not allowed to have family over?" She laughs slightly then shakes her head. But she doesn't answer me.

I sigh and head over to the coffee machine. Perhaps I should call Colton.

CHAPTER THIRTY-SEVEN

A FTER Detective Gerard Sullivan Sunday May 21, 2016

I came to the station early this morning, couldn't sleep at all last night. So many questions racking my brain, all of them without answers.

Perhaps I was wrong. Perhaps Rosella Collins had nothing to do with Emerald's disappearance and this is just one big coincidence that she turns up dead. And what about this so-called daughter of hers? Where is she? We put out an APB for a Clementine Collins last night, but we don't have much to go on. Did someone kill Rosella and take her daughter?

I grab another coffee and head over to Younger's office. Perhaps she can be of some assistance in finding out who exactly Rosella Collins was. Then maybe I can try to piece together her death.

"Hey," I say as I tap on her door. "Hey Ger," she spins around in her chair. "Heard you had a hectic night," "That's an understatement." "What can I do for ya?" "I need you to find out as much as you can about the deceased woman – Rosella Collins. Get me anything and everything on her." "I'm on it," she smiles at me, then spins back around to her computer.

I return to my office and pull out my notepad, flipping through the notes from the beginning. As of this moment, nothing is adding up or making sense and we still don't have any idea as to where the child is. I had a notion that Weston could have been in on it with Rosella; kidnapped the child and planned to run away together. Then something goes wrong and he kills her. But that doesn't make sense either, especially with his genuine need to find his daughter. I've seen men fake things before, and his desperation to find Emerald is not artificial. He doesn't know where she is. Which means that the kid is still out there somewhere. Doesn't necessarily mean that Weston is innocent, though. If he did kill his mistress, then I will prove it. But that still leaves the baby. Where on earth is Emerald?

I return to the original theory that Cordelia had a psychotic break and killed her daughter. Does that scenario still make sense? Perhaps. I must admit that I let my suspicions with Rosella Collins take me on a detour from our original theory. Should I return to that? Try to focus on the mother?

There are so many possible scenarios going on in my brain, so many questions and suspicions regarding everyone in this case. I worry that we won't find her. I worry that Cordelia killed her and we're too late. I worry that Rosella Collins took her and got rid of her before she was murdered. I worry that Weston is a much bigger part of this than he is leading on.

The worst part is not knowing. The uncertainty is what keeps me up at night. And because I don't have many clues or leads to go on, it's difficult to try and pin-point what the real story is. Who is lying? Whose story do I believe? It makes it a lot more difficult to solve a case when you can't trust anybody you speak to.

I lift the cup of coffee to my lips and take a long gulp. I need to stay awake. I need to figure this out. Today. Because if Monday rolls around and the child still isn't found, well, I don't know what I'll do. I can't let it get to that.

I decide to clear my head and start from scratch. Forget everything I know or any biases I may have towards certain people. Let's start from the beginning: the minute we got the call.

We went over to the Waters' home. Weston is pacing back and forth, frantically talking to Holden and Ashby. Honest or suspicious behaviour? He seemed genuine. I've seen people fake concern before, and I do admit, people have been good at it. But his reaction was real. I can tell that, if anything. Could he have known something more at the time? Well, yes, I know that now. He knew of his wife's meltdown earlier that morning and chose not to say anything. Perhaps he thought her psychosis was enough evidence to go on that she was to blame? He told us what happened: he got home from work, went to check on his daughter, found the empty crib.

Moving to Cordelia. She was sitting on the couch, looking stunned as she stared off into the nothingness. I brought her coffee and asked her questions. She seemed hazy, out of it. Possible behaviour for someone who recently had a psychotic break and murdered their child? Perhaps.

She did seem to be in shock. But then again, that's a mother's typical reaction when her child goes missing. They're either crying hysterically or frozen still. It was almost as though she didn't believe it was true. Weston was in a panic. Cordelia was numb.

I wish I could gauge a better reaction based on her past experiences. But unfortunately, I didn't know her at the time of her psychosis, and can only go off of what Doctor Wyatt has explained to me.

The days that followed don't help me much. All I can gather from Friday morning until now is that everybody lies. And I'm at the point where I'm not even sure who to believe anymore.

______

I'm sitting in my office staring at the blank computer screen when Holden rushes into my office. "Cassidy's here to see you. Says it's urgent."

Cassidy is the medical examiner in charge of performing the autopsy on Rosella Collins. I stand and hurry down the hallway, Holden at my heels. "Cassidy," I say upon reaching her. "What are we dealing with here?" "Well," she takes in a small breath. "Cause of death was blunt force trauma to the frontal lobe. Looks to me like she smashed it off the counter, perhaps. And I estimate time of death to be approximately thirty hours from the time she was found. That gives us an estimate of around Friday afternoon." "Okay, so definitely after the child went missing." "Right. But that's not why I'm here, Gerard. There's something else." "What is it?" She stares at me for a moment, trying to form her next words. "Rosella Collins was six weeks pregnant."

CHAPTER THIRTY-EIGHT

B EFORE Weston Waters May 10, 2016

I drive down Eastern Avenue until I reach the plaza containing Coffee Culture. Cordelia and I came here a couple of times when we first moved to town. I remember how much she loved their mocha lattes.

Rosella emailed last night asking to meet at Finnick's, but I suggested we meet here instead. This isn't the kind of chat you have in a bar.

I pull into the parking lot and spot Rosella's car right away, parked a few spots down from mine. As I walk towards the entrance, I try to peer through the window to see where she's sitting.

When I walk inside, it takes only seconds before I spot her long legs and jet-black hair seated in the far corner. She looks anxious, sitting up straight, legs crossed, staring out the window opposite to where I parked. I approach slowly, unsure if I'm ready to hear the news she is about to present.

"Hey," I say softly. Her head turns and she stares up at me, her blue eyes looking more worried than ever. This can't be good. "Wes," she forces a small smile. "Please, sit." I pull out the chair and sit so I'm facing her. I take in a deep breath. "Okay. I'm ready to hear it." She flattens her mouth. "Are you, Wes? Really..." I nod. She straightens up even further, taking in a deep breath. Here we go. "The doctor confirmed it. I'm pregnant." Even though I knew those words would leave her mouth, I can't help but feel as though I've been shot; a gaping hole directly through my stomach, blood and organs spilling out. I feel sick. Nauseous. I close my eyes and bring my hand to my forehead. She reaches out, her soft hand grabbing mine. I open my eyes and stare at her. Tears are forming in her eyes. "What do we do?" she cries softly. Fuck. I can't do this. I can't. "Rose," I start. "I know this is so hard for you. God, I can't even imagine," I take another breath, as though I can't quite get enough air. "We'll have to abort it. I'll take you to the clinic this afternoon if you want." Her eyes widen and she recoils her hand away from me. "What did you just say?" I know she heard me. I don't have to repeat myself. "Rose, this is the best possible option. We can't do this. We can't raise a baby together," "Fuck you!" She spits. "Are you fucking kidding me right now?" I'm taken back. I thought she would have mutual feelings. "You were actually planning on keeping it?" "Are you crazy, Wes!? Are you honestly that inconsiderate? This is my child! Our child!" she says the word child slow and steady, as if I don't know what a child is. "I'm aware, Rose. But it's not even a fetus yet. It's an embryo. It's not our anything." I watch as her face turns from sadness to rage. "Is that what Emerald was to you? Just a fucking embryo? Well guess what, Weston. She turned into a baby. Your baby. And this one will too." "What are you saying?" I snap, leaning in closer as I notice heads begin to turn our way. "You're going to keep it?" "What else did you think I was going to do? I can't believe you honestly think I would abort this baby." "We can't do this, Rose. It's wrong. You know it's wrong. Bringing a baby into this world, unwanted. Conceived from adultery and dishonesty. We can't do that." "You mean you can't do that. This was a choice, Weston. You chose to have an affair. You knew this could happen. This is what we did, together. We created this life. And I'm sure as hell not going to end it." "I never planned for this!" I motion between us. "It was supposed to be temporary. An escape from home. You knew that. You knew we were never serious. We weren't going to ride off into the sunset and live happily ever after. I have a wife and daughter." I pause, closing my eyes and shaking my head. "I can't do this." When I open my eyes, she's staring at me, disgust evident in her face. "You've already made your decision then, clearly." She takes in a quick breath and wipes the drip of mascara that's running down her face. "Fine. You can do whatever you want, Weston. Go live your fucking life with your psychotic wife and unwanted baby that she doesn't even want!" she raises her voice. "You go do that, okay! And tell me how that goes in ten years when Emerald is all by herself because you've left again and moved on!" She stops to collect herself. "You've made your decision. You can live with that for the rest of your life. But just remember, I will too. And so will this baby."

CHAPTER THIRTY-NINE

AFTER Cordelia Waters Sunday May 21, 2016

This day seems to be turning into a family reunion. I phoned Colton three hours ago, informing him that Liam and Lianna were here with the kids. Now I watch him and Jada, who arrived moments ago, as they sit together on the couch, immersed with the family.

Everyone sits in the living room: my mother, my father, Weston, Liam, Lianna, the kids, Colton, and Jada. I'm standing from a distance observing this odd scene, fiddling with my fingers. Why do I feel so uneasy? I should be happy to have my family together like this. Especially since Weston is here too.

I turn and glance at him, watching as he stands there holding a cup of coffee. I was sure he'd be up early and out of the house, just as he was yesterday and the day before. It's as though he can't stand being around me since she went missing.

I understand that he thinks it's my fault. I can't really blame him. But I don't care about that right now. I'm just glad he could put our differences aside and be here with my family.

I stand here, allowing my eyes to linger on him just a little longer. I don't want to turn away. The sight alone has the ability to make me feel even the slightest bit better.

Colton loves spending time with his niece and nephew. He's been chasing them around the house, playing games like hide and seek with them. They hardly know him due to the fact that Liam has been keeping his distance over the years, but they seem to be thoroughly enjoying his presence.

As soon as I called Colton and told him that they were here, he said he was on his way. I told him he didn't need to rush, but he said he wanted to. I guess he was eager to see everyone. Eager to see his brother. I know we've all had our differences, especially him and Liam for reasons that are beyond me. But despite all of the tension in the room, everyone seems to be getting along and catching up.

Nothing like a family crisis to bring everyone together.

CHAPTER FORTY

A FTER Detective Gerard Sullivan Sunday May 21, 2016

Rosella was pregnant. Six weeks pregnant. There's no question as to who the father is. It's Weston. Did he know? Or did he lie, as he has done countless times over the past three days?

We'll need to bring him in for questioning, once again. I swear to God if I don't get the truth out of him today, there's going to be consequences.

I'm about to head to my office to call Robbins and give her an update when I hear my name being called. I turn around to see Younger jogging towards me.

"What's up?" I say to her. "You're going to want to see this. Follow me." I turn and follow her back to her office. On the screen is an enlarged picture of Rosella Collins. "What did you find?" I ask. "Not much. Your girl is clean as a whistle. No criminal record, no history of abuse or violence, no bad relationships. She works as a nurse over at Davenport General. She's an active member of the community, she's on the elementary school's Parent Committee. She volunteers to help disabled children at the Athletic Center on Tuesdays, and often helps out with fundraisers around the city." She stops to let me take in all of this information. "So what are you saying? She's perfect?" "Yes." "That makes sense. I spoke to one of her neighbors yesterday and he basically confirmed all that you just said. He painted her as an honorable woman." "And she probably was," Younger says. "But get this, there's more." She pulls up another screen and types something in. "It seemed kind of irrelevant at first," she explains. "But if there's one thing I've learned being in this business, it's that nothing is irrelevant." I lean in closer to follow what she does. She pulls up an image of a young woman. Light brown hair, blue eyes, early twenties, maybe. "Who's that?" I ask. "That would be her sister," she says matter-of-fact. "She has a sister?" "Had. She died in 2005. Committed suicide. Her name was Antonia Collins." "Okay, I'm not following." "That's what I thought at first, too. But here's where it gets interesting," she pulls up another file. The death certificate and a birth certificate. "She killed herself just thirteen days after giving birth. She was only twenty-years-old." My pulse quickens. "But that's not all," she starts again, pulling up a school record. "You're not going to believe where she went to school," "Let me guess," I say, leaning forward to read the computer screen. "Northwestern." "Bingo. And I don't have to tell you who else went there." "Cordelia and Weston." "She was a year above Cordelia. Do you think there's a connection?" "Between Antonia and Cordelia?" I ask. "Yeah." "It's odd, that's for sure. But I don't know. They could have known each other. Maybe they were friends." "But the similarities..." Younger continues. "Antonia Collins gave birth to a baby, then killed herself two weeks later. They say it was postpartum depression." "Same as Cordelia," She nods her head. "But how does Rosella tie into this? Ten years later and she's having an affair with Cordelia's husband?" "Do you think she knew?" "That Cordelia and her sister knew each other?" "Maybe. Maybe she doesn't know and this is all one big coincidence," she says. "Meredith," I smile at her. "You know I don't believe in coincidences."

———

By the time I get to the Waters' residence, it's quarter passed one and it seems to be a full house. Her parents sit in the kitchen eating lunch, and a few other people stand scattered between the living room and the dining room.

I don't know what my plan of action thus far is. Cordelia doesn't know about the affair or that Rosella Collins was found dead last night. That sort of information is on a need-to-know basis. I have to be fragile with Cordelia, see what she knows. Perhaps she can provide me with some information on the sister – Antonia. And if that proves fruitless, then I'll have to take a more aggressive approach, and that includes bringing Weston down to the station, yet again.

Cordelia introduces me to everyone. Apparently Liam decided to drive in after all. And would you look at that, he brought the kids.

Colton has returned with his wife, Jada. I shake their hands as I make my way around the kitchen. I turn to my left and watch the two kids running around, chasing each other.

"And that's Sophie and Clayton," Cordelia smiles as her eyes turn to follow them. "Rambunctious." I remark. She nods her head. "Just like us," she turns to her brothers who smirk and nod their heads in unison. "Oh you can't imagine, detective." Lily laughs. "Raising these three, I ought to have some sort of award." "You did get a reward, mom." Cordelia says. "Just look at them." She turns her head back to the children. Lily smiles. "Of course. The most rewarding part of it all." The room goes quiet, almost as if everyone has just remembered that Emerald is still missing. "Do you mind if I ask you a few more questions?" I say to Cordelia, breaking the silence. "It will only take a few minutes." "Sure," she says, looking numb once again. "Do you want to step outside?" She slips on her shoes and we head out the front door. The air is warm and crisp, no signs of the rain storm that let loose last night. She looks around the yard for a moment, observing the flowers that are sprouting up in the garden. She crosses her arms over her chest and turns to me. I clear my throat. "Do you know of a woman by the name of Antonia Collins?" I watch her face as she searches her memory for the name. "No. I don't believe so. Why?" "Are you sure? It may have been from a long time ago. She was a student at Northwestern. A year older than you." Her face looks puzzled. "Antonia Collins?" she repeats, almost asking herself. "I don't think so. Honestly, I remember most people from university. Why? Does she have something to do with this?" "No. It's a bit of a stretch, really." "What happened?" I hesitate. How much should I tell her? "She killed herself two weeks after giving birth. Back in 2005. She was only twenty." She brings her hand to her mouth. "Oh my God," "It's terrible, really –" "I remember that!" she exclaims. "I didn't know her. Or her name, even. But I remember when it happened. My friend, Margo, told me about this girl who killed herself." "But you didn't know her personally?" "No. Only heard once it happened." "Do you remember anything else?" "Um," she tries to think again. "At the time, all Margo told me was that they thought it was homicide at first. But then they found the suicide note in the baby's crib. I don't even think it had a name." "Anything else?" She shakes her head. "No. I'm sorry. Like I said, I didn't know her." I nod. "Okay. Thanks." "Why are you bringing this up now?" I look into her eyes, can see the pain and worry inside of them. "Just an old case one of my partner's was working on. I saw she went to Northwestern and thought I'd ask you." "But not because of the postpartum, right?" "You knew about that?" "Well, why else does a mother kill herself two weeks after giving birth?" I pause. "No. I didn't ask you because of that," I lie. "Just the Northwestern connection, that's all." "Alright," she nods.

We walk back into the house, Cordelia heading off towards the bedroom and I heading to the kitchen. Weston stands there holding a cup of water, talking with Colton. I approach them slowly, hoping I'm not interrupting anything too important.

"Sorry to interrupt," I say as I butt in, looking to Weston. "Do you mind if we have a word?" He looks up and meets my eyes, knowing he doesn't have much of a choice. "Sure. Yeah, I'll be right back," he says to Colton. We follow the same path Cordelia and I just did and end up on the front porch. "What's going on now?" he asks once I close the door behind us. "I have more questions. And you're lucky we're doing this here rather than down at the station." He stares at me. "What happened now?" "Do you know of a woman by the name of Antonia Collins?" As soon as I say the words, I see his face alter. "Antonia? No. I'm not familiar with that name. Why?" "You're lying." I say. "You're a bad liar. I can always tell." He turns his head and stares at the road, watching the cars drive by. "Weston." I say. "You knew her?" He turns to face me. "It was a long time ago." "I'm aware. Northwestern." He closes his eyes and tilts his head back slightly. He takes in a deep breath and exhales through his nose. "Toni," he says when he finally speaks. "She went by Toni." "And, the two of you were close?" "We dated for a bit. Off and on kind of thing." "And then what happened?" "Well, I'm assuming you know what happened since you're standing here asking me about her." "Why don't you tell me?" He sighs. "She killed herself. It was awful, really. She was a lovely girl. Very sweet and kind-hearted. But why are you asking about her now? After all this time?" "You don't find the coincidence a bit striking?" I ask him. "What coincidence." "You and both sisters." "Sisters?" he seems genuinely confused, as though he's not following. "Oh don't feed me anymore bullshit, Weston. You dated Antonia in university, and then eleven years later end up having an affair with her sister." His eyes widen. "What did you just say?" I pause for a minute. Does he really not know? "You must have been aware..." "What are you trying to say? That Rose and Toni were sisters?" "How did you not know that?" I say. "Collins?" "It's a common last name!" "But surely there would have been similarities," He doesn't answer. He seems distracted, sorting through his own thoughts. Suddenly his lips part. His eyes widen and flicker back and forth, putting together the pieces in his head. He stumbles backwards, gripping the railing beside him. I reach forward and grab his shoulder to help steady him. "Weston, what is it?" He stares straight ahead, wide eyed, face white, as though he's just seen a ghost. I look down and notice that the hairs on his arm are standing up, covered by goosebumps. "Weston!" I say again. That gets his attention. He turns and faces me. "I have to go." He turns around and grabs the door handle. I pull him backwards. "What did you remember? Where do you think you're going?" He shakes his head frantically, and it's then that I notice there are tears forming in his eyes. "Weston!" I say again. He's panicky, out of breath when he speaks. "How long ago did you say it was? That Toni killed herself?" "Eleven years." His eyes dart back, meeting directly with mine. "Clementine." He breathes, tears falling down his cheeks now. "Oh God. Oh God," "Weston!" I yell, getting tired of whatever he's pulling. I grab him by his arms, forcing him to stop shaking and look me in the eyes. He stops, closes his mouth, and stares at me. "She's mine." He says quietly. "Who's yours?" "Clementine."

CHAPTER FORTY-ONE

A FTER Detective Gerard Sullivan Sunday May 21, 2016

I'm back at the crime scene – Rosella Collin's house – trying to put together this puzzle and figure out what exactly went on here. The crime scene unit is here as well, searching the house for anything that may be able to help us with this investigation. The life and death of Rosella Collins is an enigma I tend to solve.

"Any word on the kid?" I ask Robbins. She puts her phone away and faces me. "Nothing." "Dammit, now we have two children to find." "Do you still think Weston killed her?" "I have no idea what to think right now. She was pregnant with his kid, after all. And apparently was raising his other one." "That is so messed up. How did he not know that they were sisters?" I shrug. "It's beyond me, really. I guess Rosella never mentioned anything to him." "Isn't that a bit suspicious on its own? I mean, your sister kills herself, you raise her child, and then eleven years later have an affair with the father of that baby?" "None of this makes sense." It's quiet for a moment, both of us thinking. "It's weird, right?" she says. "One of his daughter's goes missing on Thursday. The other one – who he didn't even know existed – goes missing Friday." "She must have known who he was," I conclude. "There's no way that this is just one big coincidence." "Did Antonia not tell him?" Robbins asks. "About the baby, I mean. Back at Northwestern." "He seemed to be clueless on that aspect. Although, he did put two-and-two together about Clementine pretty quickly. So he must have known something." "But it doesn't make sense – why would Weston take Emerald, kill Rosella Collins, and then take Clementine? If what he claims is true, he had no idea the kid was even his." I nod, thinking this through. "You're right. So perhaps Weston isn't at fault here, although he is the only common denominator." "And Cordelia," "What?" "She's the only other piece of the puzzle that links everyone together." "You think she knew?" "Maybe. Perhaps she knew about Antonia, the baby, the affair – everything." "And does what, exactly? Kidnaps her own child? Kills Rosella and takes Clementine?" "Maybe." "That's reaching." "I've seen worse." I shake my head. "None of this is adding up," I stop and look around the room. "We need to find that girl. Both of them. God only knows where they are at this point." We both stand there, dumbfounded. A voice calls from upstairs: "Found something!" Both Robbins and I turn our heads and follow where the voice came from. I run up the stairs, two at a time.

When we get to the top, one of the crime scene analysts stands in the hallway, directing us to a bedroom at the end of the hall. Upon entering the room, my eyes immediately sweep the walls, taking in everything in front of me.

Photographs, newspaper clippings, maps, drawings, all spread out and pinned to the wall. I edge closer, walking up to the wall to read the text. I turn and look at the desk that sits adjacent to the wall. The analyst approaches me, hands me two plane tickets he discovered in the desk drawer, Chicago to Sacramento, for the passengers Rosella and Clementine Collins.

I return my gaze to the wall. My eyes immediately find a newspaper clipping of Weston from 2013 standing in front of his newly opened orthodontist practice: Waters' Orthodontics. Beside it, pinned to the wall, is a map of Davenport. There's a red sticker placed over the location where the Waters' home is.

I scan the paperwork posted across the wall, and finally, to the far left corner, an old, outdated newspaper clipping from 2005.

HOMICIDE RULED OUT: DEATH OF TWENTY-YEAR-OLD NORTHWESTERN STUDENT DECLARED SUICIDE.

Below the title is a photo of a young woman, blue eyes, light brown hair flowing over her shoulders. It's a class photo. She's smiling, looks happy. I don't need to read the article to know that this woman is Antonia Collins.

I walk back to the center of the wall, skimming over everything. But it's the calendar that catches my eye, the date specifically that's circled: Thursday May eighteenth. Emerald.

I turn around and see the analyst standing there, holding what looks to be a black book in his hands. "What's this?" I take a step toward him. "We found it amongst her things, hidden in the desk drawer." He extends his arm and hands it to me. I take the book, which upon opening, discover is some sort of journal or diary. I flip it over in my hands, examining it. "You may want to take a read, sir," the young man says to me. I look up and meet his eyes for a moment, then nod.

I open the journal, scanning through the pages, gathering key words and sentences, stringing them together to form logical thoughts. Everything she has written in here over the past couple of years. Every single entry starts the same: Dear Toni.

I flip through the pages, aiming to get to the very last entry. That's what will help us put together the pieces.

I nearly reach the end of the small book when the writing stops. I flip back a couple of pages and find the very last entry that was written.

Friday May 19, 2016

Dear Toni,

Something went wrong. He didn't show at our drop-off location last night and won't return my phone calls. I know I'm not supposed to call him. He made that clear. But I couldn't just sit there, clueless. I'm afraid something might have happened to him. Or worse: he's done something to the baby. We were supposed to meet at the warehouse by the river last night and make the exchange. But he never showed. And now I'm worried.

I don't know what to do. I can't call the police because they'd know I had something to do with it. I've been seeing the Amber Alerts all day. Maybe I'll just leave it up to the police and hope they find him themselves. I'll pretend I had nothing to do with it. They can't trace it back to me, can they? No, I didn't even give him my real name. But he knows where to find me. Oh God, he could tell them where I live. Then they'll know. They'll make the connection through you.

I lift my head to see Robbins and the analyst standing there, staring at me. They're waiting for me to speak – to say something. But I'm not finished yet. I look down and flip back a page, to the entry right before the last.

Wednesday May 10, 2016

Dear Toni,

I feel so stupid right now. Stupid and used. I told him today. And do you know what he did? He left. Just as he always does. I can't believe I let myself get sucked into his trap. Did I really think that things could be different? I did. That just shows how stupid I am. Fucking stupid. Please forgive me, sister. I know how ridiculous this all seems. But it will all make sense soon. Then you will see. I promise you.

I flip through the pages, going back even further. Messy writing, sporadic thoughts. Journal entries dating back months ago. I flip to the very back again and stop when I see a page titled: Antonia's Story.

CHAPTER FORTY-TWO

BEFORE Rosella Collins Wednesday May 10, 2016

Antonia's Story

Antonia was the greatest person I ever knew. Kind-hearted, friendly, determined. She was more than just a sister – she was my best friend. The sole person who I could share everything with. The person who was always there for me through thick and thin. The person I relied on the most. She may have been younger than me, but I looked up to her so much. She always knew what she wanted to do with her life, having ambitions bigger than I ever dreamed. She was going to be a lawyer. She wanted to bring justice to people who deserved it. Ironic, isn't it? She was far too young to be taken from this world. Only twenty-years-old when she took her own life. And it's all his fault.

This is the story of my sister, Antonia Collins, and the reason she ended her own life: Weston Waters.

Let me tell you about him so you understand what he did and why he is to blame. Antonia met him during her first year at Northwestern. He was cute and charming and she thought it was love. They dated for a couple of months, off and on, but she always suspected he was secretly seeing other people. She didn't want to believe it was true because she was so in love with him. But there was no denying what kind of man he was.

But then, in June, just after her first year of university was finishing, she told me that she was pregnant, and that the baby was his. It had to be – he was the only one she had been with. And when she tried to tell him, he disregarded her. He said that she knew his family had money, and that she was lying to get money from him. But as the months progressed and her stomach began to expand, it was clear that she wasn't lying.

She would cry to me at night because she didn't know what to do. She couldn't raise the baby on her own. Our family didn't come from a lot of money and our parents weren't supportive of her choice to keep the child. She was running out of options. And that man didn't even do anything to help. He refused that the baby was his. Said he couldn't be forced to pay child support. What a despicable excuse of a man.

So then, on February fourth, 2005, she gave birth to a little angel. She didn't have a name for her at first. I told her that she didn't need to rush. That she could wait and figure it out in time. But that time never came. Because only two short weeks after the baby was born, Antonia, my best friend and only sister, killed herself.

She overdosed on a bunch of pills. Left the bottle on the nightstand. I didn't believe it at first. How could she do such a thing? And why? I was convinced that she was murdered. That somebody broke into our home and forced the pills down her throat.

But a few days later, they found the suicide note under the baby's crib. She explained in the note how she couldn't do it; couldn't handle being a mother. It was all too much for her. The doctors said it was postpartum depression. But Toni wasn't depressed – she had simply run out of options.

The real reason she killed herself? Weston. He didn't support her or give her any money. No wonder she thought she couldn't do it on her own! I knew it was his fault. I knew it from that moment on. At the bottom of the note, my sister said the baby's name was Clementine.

My parents and I raised Clementine together for the first few years of her life, just until I could get my schooling and finances figured out. I finished my four years at DePaul University with a Bachelor of Science in nursing. I did my placement at Northwestern Memorial where I specialized in births. Once I had my life sorted out, I legally adopted Clementine and she became mine.

I raised Clementine to the best of my abilities. We moved on from the trauma of the past and created a good life for ourselves. But I never forgot what that man did to my sister. It's his fault, and his fault only, that she is gone. No longer will I remain silent and take this secret to the grave. It's time to expose that man and the truth that I've been holding onto for eleven years. It's time to finally bring justice to my sister.

It all started a couple of years ago when I saw his name in the newspaper. Clementine and I relocated to Davenport shortly after I graduated. We wanted a fresh start away from it all, and Davenport seemed like the perfect place. So you can imagine my surprise when I saw that he moved here and was opening his orthodontic practice. In my town, of all places.

I sheltered Clementine from this news. Yes, he may have been responsible for creating her, but he was not her father. I didn't want her ever knowing that such a despicable man shared the same genes as her. I had no plans of ever introducing the two of them, and so eventually, any and all thoughts of Weston Waters left my mind.

But then three years after seeing his picture in the newspaper, something substantial happened – he and his wife had a baby. I was working that day, running on only four hours of sleep from my nightshift. And that was when I saw him in the hallway, walking to the nursery.

I recognized him immediately; those broads shoulders, his blue eyes. He was obviously much different looking than he was in university, but still the same Weston. It wasn't difficult to find out which room his wife was in, which baby was his.

The sight of him alone was enough to bring back all of those horrible memories. I had forgotten all about him, put him completely out of my mind. But then here he was again, and this time, with a baby. His first-born. Or so he thought.

It enraged me that he was starting a family with this woman. He was so ignorant to everything he had done in the past. It was then – that night in the hospital – that my plan began to form.

I wanted to make him pay. I wanted to bring justice to my sister. So I began brainstorming ways I could execute this plot for righteousness. I knew the best course of action was blackmail. If I could extort money from him, I'd not only shake-up his perfect little world, but I could get some money from him – money that he never gave to Antonia when she needed it. If we're being honest, that money rightfully belonged to Clementine. All those years that he neglected to acknowledge her existence or pay child support. All the years he was missing from her life. The thought crossed my mind that I could have taken him to court years ago; get a judge to subpoena him for DNA evidence. But I had no money back then. And I'd have to be a complete idiot to go against a family as wealthy and as powerful as the Waters'. They'd take me down and make me look like the bad guy. It simply wasn't an option.

And then I had another idea: I could cause him the same pain and suffering that he caused me and my family after Antonia's death. And the only way to do that was to show him what life is like without your daughter.

I know what you're thinking: that I'm a horrible person. But you have to understand, I never intended to harm the child in any way. The baby was simply a means to an end. A way to get vengeance on Weston.

I obviously couldn't kidnap the child myself – I would never get involved in such an illegal matter. So I turned to the dark-web, where anything and everything is possible. It didn't take me long to find a guy for hire. It was the beginning of March when I became acquainted with a man named Teddy. I told him my name was Margery. We made a deal. In exchange for six thousand dollars, he would abduct the baby, bring her to me, and his job was done. I'd take it from there. Six thousand was a small price to pay, considering I'd make the money back from extortion money. Weston had plenty of that to go around.

From that point on, I would keep the child safe with me while simultaneously sending anonymous letters to Weston requesting large sums of money in exchange for his child. Once he transferred over one-hundred-grand, I would arrange a drop-off location where he would find his baby. It was the perfect plan – or so I thought.

In the beginning stages of my plan, I looked him up in the phonebook and easily found his address. Not many Weston Waters' in Davenport. And then I began following him, studying his every move, watching where he went every day. I had to know everything about his life.

You have to understand, I only ever intended to observe, never act. But one night, I followed him down to a bar, Finnick's Tap. I had been watching him go there twice a week for three weeks now. It was as though he was becoming obsessed. One night after following him, I decided to go inside. As I sat there staring at him, something clicked inside of me and I knew: I had to talk to him. Had to speak with the man who ruined my sister's life. And so, I started up a simple conversation.

I should have left it at that. I should have said good-bye and kept my distance from that point on to ensure the welfare of the plan. But that's not what happened.

I saw him again. And again. I kissed him. Had sex with him. All for what, exactly? My 'plan'?

I tried to justify my actions by convincing myself that I could use this to my advantage. I could embed myself into his life and get all of the information I needed. I knew he wanted me. Just by the way he looked at me, I knew. So we started something.

I told myself that I wouldn't develop feelings for him. Oh, I didn't even have worry about that. I knew I wouldn't. How could I? After knowing what he did? He'd fall right into my hands.

But sometimes even the most meticulous planning can end up disastrous. Because one thing I didn't account for was this baby. Not Emerald – the one inside of me. God dammit, I didn't plan for that. I also didn't plan to develop feelings for that horrible man.

But here's what happened: I got distracted. Just like my sister did eleven years ago, I fell into his hands. With his kind eyes and charming words. He knew all the right things to say. He made me feel special, wanted. As though I meant something. And I second-guessed myself. I told myself that he changed. It had been eleven years, after all. Everyone changes, right? And then I did the one thing I vowed to never do: I introduced him to Clementine. Oh what a mistake that was. Because he was so good with her. All I told him was that her parents died in a car accident years ago, and I raised her as my own. He adored her. Always made an effort to talk with her and ask her questions about her life and school. He was so kind and genuine, I truly believed he had changed. I let myself slip. I deviated from my plan.

How could I let myself become so stupid and desperate for his love and attention? He has the ability to make women fall under his spell. And I fell for it. I thought that perhaps things could be different for us. I was even going to call off my plan. Contact Teddy and tell him that the May 18 plan was cancelled.

What the fuck was I thinking? That he'd leave his wife and baby to come be with me, Clem, and this new baby? Idiotic.

All my prior thoughts and hatred towards him were resurrected today. We met at Coffee Culture so I could confirm the news of my pregnancy and have the chance to talk things out with him. I thought that things would go smoothly. That he would take my hand and tell me that we would be alright.

But you know what he did? The exact same thing he did to Toni, with his bullshit and excuses. He offered to take me to the abortion clinic. And when I refused that, he said he couldn't raise this baby with me. Backing out and not taking responsibilities for his actions. What a fucking scumbag!

He is the sole reason that my sister killed herself. Because he couldn't own up and take responsibility to be a father. And after eleven years, I can see that nothing has changed. He's still the same immature, selfish prick he was all those years ago.

I just don't know how I didn't see that coming. How did I allow myself to become so blinded by his flawless face and magnificent charm? He's a devil, alright. A wolf in sheep's clothing. I just can't help but feel stupid for falling for it all. I should have known better. Why did I think he could change? Why did I think things could be different?

The plan is back on. I should have never considered calling it off in the first place. After today, I am no longer distracted. My mind is focused and my eyes are set on revenge. I'm going to take him for all that he has and more. He owes it to me and Clem. He owes it to Toni. And he owes it to this precious little life inside of me. The little life that is Clem's half-sibling.

Ironic, isn't it? Half-siblings.

We will be fine without him, just the three of us.

Once I get the money, Clem and I will leave town and never return. This place will be all but a memory someday. A place where Clem lived and learned and grew up. We'll go somewhere else. Perhaps California. We've always wanted to go there. Start a new life where the three of us can live in peace and harmony away from that despicable man.

We'll go wherever Clem wants. Because I love her so much. I never thought it was possible to love another human being so much. But I'd do anything for her. She's my everything. And she's the last little piece of Antonia that I have left.

CHAPTER FORTY-THREE

I rush down the stairs, clutching the journal in my hands. It all makes sense now. Everything. How did I not figure this out before? I had all the pieces right in front of me. The name, the car, the affair – how did I not piece it together sooner? I can't help but think that maybe if I did, we'd have Emerald back by now. And Rosella wouldn't be dead.

Teddy must have gotten to her first. By the looks of things, she was supposed to meet with him on Thursday night. I guess he had a change of plans, kept the baby for himself, then killed Rosella. He's most likely taken Clementine as well.

I reach the bottom of the stairs, turn swiftly around the corner and end up back in the kitchen. The Chief Lieutenant, Frank Connelly, has arrived, and stands in the corner speaking with Holden. I head towards them, my mind blazing. They both turn and face me.

"What's wrong? Did you find something?" Holden asks as he gauges my face. I hold up the journal. "This," I huff. "Is our golden ticket. It explains everything." The chief reaches his hand out and I place the journal in his hands. "What's it say? Summarized." "She was getting retribution for her sister's death eleven years ago. Weston's the father of the kid, Clementine. He denied the child was his, left her on her own. This was Rosella's idea of revenge." His eyes widen. "You're kidding," "It makes sense now. All of it. She arranged to have the baby kidnapped and was planning on using her for ransom. But the guy never showed on Thursday night." "Guy? Who is he?" "All she wrote was that his name is Teddy. I don't know if that's legit or not, it could be an alias. She used the name Margery, so we'll need to look into it." "I'll have an officer on it," the chief says. "My guess is that this Teddy guy had a change of plans and decided to keep the baby for himself. Then he must of come over here, killed Rosella, and took Clementine." "Dammit," Holden curses and turns away from us. "Now what do you suggest?" "Get a search on all possible Teddy's in the area. Last names, first names, anything. I want it all," I pause. "And lastly: someone get me her phone."

CHAPTER FORTY-FOUR

THE DAY OF Teddy White Thursday May 18, 2016

I keep an eye on the clock as it goes from two-fourteen to two-fifteen, then I slip the syringe into my pocket, lock the car door behind me, and head up to the front door. It's time.

I've been parked on the street for the past couple of hours, waiting for the perfect moment. The husband and another woman were here a little over an hour ago, some kind of commotion ensuing from inside the house. I had to wait for them to leave, then wait a little longer, just to be sure they weren't returning. The neighbor took his kid to school just before that. The other neighbor was out watering her garden, so I had to wait for her to finish. Now the coast is clear and it's my time to shine.

I knock twice on the door, waiting patiently for her to answer. I've seen a photo of her, so I know what to expect. White blonde hair, big brown eyes. Pretty lady.

She opens the door and looks surprised to see me. Of course she does – she doesn't have the slightest clue who I am. I put on a large grin. "Hello, Mrs.

Waters," I beam. "Do you remember me?" She looks confused. "No, I'm sorry, should I?" "I work with your husband. We've met once or twice at one of the gatherings," "Oh. I'm so sorry I don't remember. What's your name?" "Andre! My wife is Cynthia." She smiles softly. "My apologies. Usually I remember a familiar face. Is there something I can help you with?" "Weston actually just sent me over to pick up something he left here. Do you mind if I come in and grab it?" I've been in this business far too long to be an amateur at this thing. It always takes research and careful planning. "Oh, what did he forget?" I hesitate. "Oh, you know Weston," I joke. "Something in his brief case, I believe? Said it was in his office. I can call him and ask." She raises her eyebrow. "But he was just here. What could he possibly have forgotten now?" "I'm not sure." I force a laugh. "Do you mind if I come in?" She stares at me intently, studying my face. "Where did you say we met again?"

In one quick motion I bring my left hand out of my pocket, clutching the syringe, and step forward into the house, sliding the needle into her neck. Eszopiclone and zaleplon, a sedative that, with a high enough dosage, will cause loss of memory. She won't even remember me. My face can never be identified.

I hold the back of her head in my palm, carefully steadying her while simultaneously shielding her limp body from the outside world. I step inside and kick the door shut behind us. Her eyes are fluttering shut. She's almost out.

After lying her body down on the couch, I head straight for the baby. Fortunately for me, they live in a large bungalow and the baby's room is easy to locate, just down the hall. What a cute little thing. Looks just like her mother. She's lying on her stomach, sound asleep. I grab the pacifier and blanket that rest beside her. These will come in handy later.

I wipe down the place to ensure there are no fingerprints or footprints that can be traced back to me. Then I wrap the child in my jacket, holding her carefully to ensure she doesn't wake. I take one last glance at the sleeping mother and head out the front door, disappearing as though I was never there.

As I drive down 53rd street, I glance in the rear view mirror, keeping an eye on the baby as she remains asleep in the car seat. I put my phone on speaker and dial Andy's number. I tell him that the plan has been successful thus far, and I'll meet him at his place later tonight.

Andy and I run a business together, you see. We discovered long ago the valuable price of children on the market today. Some may say it's an unethical business, but we get the money for it and that's all that really matters.

We've already found a man out in Wisconsin who's going to purchase the baby. He's giving us ten grand for her. But little does Andy know, I have another plan in store for us tonight. I'm going to take the other kid, the eleven-year old. She'll be a perfect sell. Young and cute, ideal age for certain buyers. Someone will love her. And will pay big bucks for her. I just gotta get the money from the mother, then dispose of her. She's collateral damage.

It always baffles my mind how clueless some people are. She honestly thought I was going to give up the baby, just like that? Does she not know how valuable this little girl is?

I'm not even sorry. It's her fault for getting involved with a guy like me. She should really do her research before hiring strangers from the dark-web. Because guys like me are bad news. And I only got one goal on my mind.

The baby yawns and I smile to myself, knowing how much money I'll be getting tomorrow.

CHAPTER FORTY-FIVE

AFTERTeddy White Friday, May 19, 2016

It's after three o'clock when I leave Margery's house with the girl. And I just had the biggest favour handed to me.

After taking the baby to Andy's place last night, I drove around and grabbed some dinner before heading back to the motel to crash. This morning when I got up, I decided to continue with my most recent plan on taking the eleven-year-old. My plan was to go to Margery's, knock her out, then wait for the kid to get home from school so I could take her. But it looks like someone already took care of that for me, because when I got here, I discovered that Margery was already dead.

It's as though someone knew my plan and had it taken care of for me! Now I don't even need to get my hands dirty! From there, everything else happened seamlessly. I waited for the kid to get home from school, then sedated her and put her in the trunk. I'm sure no one will even notice that she's gone.

Her dead mother sure as hell won't.

CHAPTER FORTY-SIX

A FTERDetective Gerard Sullivan Sunday May 21, 2016

One of the crime scene analysts brings me over a plastic zip-lock baggy containing her cell phone. I pull on a pair of latex gloves and slide the phone out of the bag. I power it on, waiting for the screen to load. Once it's on, I see the two missed calls from my own number.

I go immediately to the text messages, hoping there's something there. I scroll down, but there's no Teddy's. Perhaps she has him under a different name?

I open each and every text message, but there's nothing out of the ordinary. Text's to friends, family members, mothers from school.

Suddenly I remember something she wrote in the journal. I move my finger back to the home button and click outgoing calls. Sure enough, there are thirteen outgoing calls made from Thursday night up until Friday morning. This has to be him. She was probably calling all night, desperately trying to get a hold of the guy.

"Hey," I call out to one of the men standing beside the counter. "Can you get a trace on a number for me?" The man walks over. "What's the number?" he asks. He brings out an iPad and I recite it to him. After a moment of searching, he turns to me. "It's a payphone. The corner of Kimberly and Utica." Dammit, of course it's a pay phone. "Robbins!" I wave her over. "We're going for a drive."

CHAPTER FORTY-SEVEN

A FTER Weston Waters Friday May 19, 2016

This is a nightmare. I'm living my real life nightmare. The thought that something like this could ever truly happen never crossed my mind. You see it on the news all the time, but you never actually think something that horrible could happen to you.

It's surreal. I've been in a state of shock since I found the crib empty last night. Why? The question I keep asking myself, over and over again. But no one's going to answer me. Nobody knows why.

From the moment I walked through the door and saw that empty crib, my heart was ripped out of my body. I didn't know it was humanly possible to feel such immense pain. I didn't know what to think. Did Doctor Wyatt come over and take her out? Is she on a play-date? Did she have an appointment I was unaware of?

My spirit remained hopeful – that perhaps my fear was a mistake and everything was fine after all. I was just being a paranoid father. But when I saw Cordelia asleep on the couch... Something inside didn't feel right. And when she was just as clueless as I was about our daughter's whereabouts, the dread was back.

My initial thought – which partially remains in my mind today – is that Cordelia did something to our baby. It's the most likely possibility out of everything that could have happened. She's been better the past two months, no longer crying and having meltdowns on a regular basis. She was better. I honestly believed that she was cured.

I guess no one can truly be cured from something that extreme. But regardless of all the trauma she went through, how could she have done something to her own child? Was her state of mind that bad that she finally had enough? Did she snap? Drop Emerald? Strangle her? Smother her with a pillow?

I can't help but envision the worst. Cordelia kneeling over Emerald's tiny lifeless body, unsure of what to do next. The chills run down my spine just thinking about it.

Did she kill our daughter? I'd like to believe otherwise. But how can I be sure? I don't even know her anymore. And she doesn't even know me.

I've been driving around since early this morning, trying to think and clear my head. What can I do to help my baby? Is she even alive right now?

I feel like a failure, letting her down when she needs me the most. I'm her father for God's sakes, I'm supposed to be there for her! But where was I when something happened to her?

The hardest part is simply trying to analyze the situation and distinguish between what I think happened, and the truth. Is it a possibility that Cordelia killed our daughter? Yes. And that frightens me. But there could be other factors involved. What if she was kidnapped? Who would do such a thing, take a six-month-old baby from her crib?

It's not fair. Why did this happen to Emerald? She's so small and innocent. I yearn for the power to do something about this. If only I could fly to her, scoop her up in my arms, tell her that daddy's here and everything will be all right. But I can't do that.

The feeling of anxiety has been pressing in my chest since yesterday morning after Cordelia's latest break down with Savannah. I thought she was fine. I truly and honestly believed that. Could something have happened after I left? Did she have a break down and do something to Emerald? Could all of this be my fault? I should have never left her alone with our daughter. I slam my hands down on the steering wheel and try to fight back the tears as they come.

I haven't spoken to Rosella since last Wednesday at the coffee shop. God, just thinking of her brings back memories of the terrible conversation.

We left things on a bad note. She's pissed, I get that. But it's not my responsibility anymore. I told her what I thought we should do – the right thing to do – and she didn't listen. That's not my fault. If she wants to keep the baby, then by all means, she can. I told her it won't be possible for me to take part in the child's life. She has to understand that. I told her what we were getting ourselves into from the beginning. I have a wife. I have a daughter. If Cordelia ever finds out about the affair, she'll take Emerald away from me. I know she will. It will break her. I can't do that to either of them. I may not have been the best man in the past, or even now, but I can be a good father to Emerald. I have to.

With Rosella, it's different. I never planned for things to go as far as they did. Would I go back in time and take it all back? Of course not. We had fun. But it was just a fling, spur of the moment. Temporary. Lust, not love. She helped me realize who I am at this point in my life and what I need to make myself happy. I know now that Cordelia and I can't stay together. I fear she will only bring me down. Perhaps I'm doing the same to her. We're bringing each other down.

There was once a time when we were young and in love. And it may have taken going through hell and back to realize our true feelings for each other, but at least now I know where I stand. I can't stay with Cordelia. But I will fight my hardest to be the primary figure in Emerald's life. Because she is the most important thing in mine.

Just like that, I decide to detour and go to Rosella's place. Maybe she'll talk to me. I do feel partially responsible for her anguish. It's been a week since we last spoke, her words still lingering fresh on my mind. The way her eyes looked so angry yet sad all at once.

Is she in love with me? I've never wondered that before, but right now, the thought crosses my mind.

She has to talk to me. I need to tell her about Emerald, maybe find some solace that I can't find at home. She was the one person I could talk to for all those months. Every time Cordelia had a breakdown or couldn't cope, I'd turn to Rosella. We may not be on good terms, but she's the only person I want to be with right now. What does that say about me?

I pull into the driveway, eyeing the Impala as I get out of the car, and hustle up the steps. I ring the doorbell three times, hoping she'll answer quickly.

Within minutes, she's at the door pulling it open, staring at me. Her face is a mixture between anger and disgust. She wants nothing to do with me.

"What do you want?" "Can I come in?" I ask. She glares at me, then takes a step back, allowing me to enter her home. She stands back and crosses her arms, waiting for me to say something. "Emerald is missing," I say. I try to watch for any flicker in her eyes, but her facial expression doesn't change. She stares at me with that pissed-off glare. "Did you hear what I said? My daughter is missing." "I heard you. What do you expect me to do about it?" My jaw twitches and I try to contain my frustration. Here I was thinking she would care even the slightest. Perhaps show some concern for an infant, considering she once raised one and could now possibly have another. "Are you fucking kidding me right now, Rose? Show some compassion." "Oh, that's gold, Wes. Where the hell was your compassion during our conversation last week, huh? You heartless piece of shit." "Don't turn this on me. This has nothing to do with us," I say. She turns away from me and begins walking towards the kitchen. I follow behind her. "Don't walk away from me." I raise my voice. She reaches the fridge, swings open the door, and pulls out a bottle of water. I watch as she unscrews the cap, tilts the liquid back into her mouth. I stare at her, breathing heavily through my nostrils, trying to stay calm as she swishes the water around in her mouth, then swallows. She glares back at me, not saying a word. "Do you not care that my child is missing?" "What happened, Wes? Your wife finally snap and kill her?" I feel my heart sink in my chest and I'm suddenly filled with rage, but also dread, because I fear that she's right. "Don't say that." I never should have confided in her about Cordelia's past. "Why? You don't think it's possible? Come on, Wes. Why are you really here?" "We haven't spoken since last week. I wanted to see if you were okay." "Bullshit," she spits. "You could care less about me or this baby." She glances down at her flat stomach. I take a step forward and she flinches back. "Don't touch me." "Rose. Please," I say. "We can work this out." "By 'work this out' you mean take me to an abortion clinic," she says. I don't respond. "Get out of my house." "Rose, please. Emerald is gone," "I don't care, Wes! Get out!" I take another step forward and reach for her arm, but she pulls back. Then, in one swift motion, she steps forwards and slaps me across the face. I stand there, staring at her, feeling the sting on my cheek. "Fuck you," she says. And then something inside of me ignites. I'm not sure what it is, but I know I've felt it before. Illuminated rage and aggression. My palms begin to sweat and my heart rate accelerates. My adrenaline is pumping and I can't contain myself. I feel as though I'm going to explode.

Before I can even think about what I'm doing, I'm lunging forwards, grasping for her body as she jumps back and tries to run from me. I grab her by the arm and yank her towards me. She lets out a scream and kicks me in the shin. I topple forwards, trying to ignore the sharp pain in my leg.

She turns around and begins to run forwards. I lunge after her once more and grab her by the hair, yanking her backwards. I ease up on my grip, and at the same time, she pushes forwards, launching herself directly towards the counter.

It all happens so fast. Her thick, dark hair leaving my hands, falling forwards, bashing her head off the edge of the counter, collapsing face first to the ground. She lies there on the kitchen floor, motionless.

"Rose," I say gently, realizing that she may be seriously hurt. I kneel down and crawl over to her. "Rose," I say again.

I place my hand on her back to shake her, but she doesn't move. I grasp her shoulders and roll her over so she's facing me. Her eyes are open and there's a pool of dark red blood gushing from a large gash in her forehead.

"ROSE!" I frantically pull her onto my lap and shake her, trying to bring her back into consciousness. I lean down, placing my ear to her chest. She's not breathing.

My heart is beating faster now, as though any minute it's going to jump right out of my chest. I bring two fingers to her neck, trying to feel for a pulse, but there's nothing.

My body begins to tremble and I feel a large pit arising in my stomach. Oh God, what have I done? What the fuck have I done...

CHAPTER FORTY-EIGHT

A FTER Detective Gerard Sullivan Sunday May 21, 2016

It's quiet in the car, the only sound being the intermittent updates coming in from our radios. If we can find this Teddy guy, then we can find the kids. I just pray that they're still alive.

Once we get to the intersection, I park the car beside the curb and instantly spot the phone booth. We walk over and examine the surroundings. Robbins begins to check for any possible prints while I walk around the outside to see if there's something that can point me in the direction of Teddy.

It's a standard industrial area; shopping centres, government buildings, banks. I lift my head and my eyes connect with a Rogers store directly across the street. There's a security camera just above the sign. "Stay here." I shout to Robbins. "I'll be right back." I hustle across the busy street.

Once inside the store, I walk up to the counter. A petite brunette is working, mid-thirties perhaps. She has light wrinkles under her eyes. I flash my badge. "Are your cameras out front working?" "They are," "I need to see the footage, immediately." She leads me behind the counter to a room in the back, containing two computer screens with multiple different live images flashing. "Rewind it to this past week. I need to see if there's a recurring pattern at all." She clicks away at the keyboard, and the screen plays out in front of me. After sitting in the chair and watching the tapes for over seven minutes, I still don't see anything. "Can you keep rewinding it back over the past month?" I ask. She nods her head, and eventually we're watching the entire month of footage.

Finally I see something: a pattern. Twice a week, a black Chevy Cruze pulls up slightly in front of the phone booth, stays there for five minutes or so, then drives off.

I ask the woman to slow down the tapes so I can get a licence plate. Could this be our guy? Why else would someone come to a pay phone twice a week for over a month? It has to be him.

I call the Chief and recite the licence plate: FC6 BH1, registered in Missouri. I end the call, thank the woman for her help, and head back across the street to Robbins.

Now all we have to do is wait.

———

Not an hour after we arrive back at Rosella's home, I get a call from the station saying they've tracked down the car, which is registered to a Theodore White. Younger is watching the CCTV footage as we speak, trying to piece together a time line.

I race out the front door and straight to the cruiser, Robbins, Ashby, and the Chief Lieutenant following close behind. Frank gets in the front and starts the car. A few officers remain at the crime scene, but the rest of us take off in unison. We all want to be there for this.

Holden radios in and tells us that they've spotted the car at a residential home just off of Division and 2nd Street. SWAT is already on scene, waiting for the go-ahead. The chief tells them to wait for us to get there, we're five minutes out.

We pull up out front and I see SWAT armed and ready to enter the home. It's a small, shabby-looking place. The windows are covered with curtains from the inside and the roof looks as though it's about to cave in. Definitely somewhere to come if you're hiding abducted children, I assume.

The chief walks towards Holden who hands him a vest and removes his gun from his holster. "You coming in?" he asks me. I nod and slip on a vest as well. "We believe the vehicle has been here since this morning," Holden says as we walk towards the SWAT team. "We're unsure if the suspect is inside the house or not, but we're taking extra precautions if he is because he'll have the kids with him." I nod, look down, and remove my gun.

It's time.

CHAPTER FORTY-NINE

A FTER Cordelia Waters Sunday May 21, 2016

I've been waiting around the house for hours, pacing back and forth, biting my nails. It's almost three o'clock and I haven't heard from anyone in the past two hours.

After Gerard came over earlier to speak with Weston and me, he left in a hurry without telling me what was going on. Weston locked himself in the bedroom and wouldn't talk to me either. I know something happened. I thought they might have found Emerald. But Weston said that they didn't. I have no idea what to think.

My parents are in the kitchen, working together to prepare a Sunday night dinner for us all. I tried to explain to them that they didn't have to do that, but of course, they insisted. Dad ran out to the grocery store to stalk up the fridge and cupboards. It's been so hectic these past couple of days that food has been the last thing on my mind. I've been barely scraping by, eating soup and bagels whenever I feel my stomach growl. But honestly, how can one even think about food in a time like this?

My mother puts on one of my old aprons and stands in the kitchen, boiling pasta and cutting up vegetables. I'm glad that she's putting the effort in. With everyone here especially. It will be nice to eat together as a family.

Liam is in the other room taking a phone call. He and Colton have been talking and catching up all morning. It gives me hope that they can work things out and perhaps find some common ground once again. These past few years of mutiny have been unbearable on our family. Perhaps today will change that.

Clayton fell asleep watching a movie on the couch with Colton, and Sophie is on the floor putting together a Barbie puzzle. Lianna and Jade sit at the kitchen table, drinking coffee and discussing home décor.

And then there's me, standing here, anxious and falling apart. I can't deny that having everybody together makes me happy, but we're still missing a piece to this puzzle. I need my daughter.

—————

When I hear the doorbell, my heart sinks further into my chest. My hands are quivering, and when I bring them together to stop the shaking, I realize that they're ice cold. I stand up and make my way to the front door, praying that it's someone who can tell me what is going on. Everyone else watches as I make my way over.

When I open the door, all of the tension in my body falls to the ground. Am I dreaming? Did I fall asleep on the couch again?

My bottom lip parts from the top and I stand there, stunned. Gerard gives me a small smile and turns to Detective Robbins, who is holding my baby.

I scream for my husband as I fall forward, grabbing Emerald from Detective Robbins. Behind me I hear the sound of doors opening and multiple feet rushing towards me. The tears are streaming down my face and I'm sobbing into Emerald's tiny neck. I hold her tightly. As though if I ease up my grip, she will be taken away from me again.

When I turn around and open my eyes, my entire family stands there, completely awestruck. Weston looks as though he's witnessing a human resurrection. Face pale, eyes wide. The tears come for him, then, as well.

He reaches forward and together we meet and hold Emerald between us, loudly sobbing for everyone to hear. But it doesn't matter that I'm being loud or crying like a fool. I don't care. Not one little bit. Because she's here. She's back. And we're finally together again.

———

Emerald makes her rounds being passed around, receiving hugs and kisses from all of her family. Only six-months old and she already has more love than some people have in their lifetime.

Once my baby is back in my arms, we sit in the living room, talking quietly amongst ourselves. We're all in a state of shock, really. These past few days have felt like a nightmare. A foggy haze of wandering aimlessly. But now my compass is facing north again, and rightfulness has been restored.

I invited Gerard and Detective Robbins – who told me to call her Claire – to come inside and sit with us. The news anchors and TV crews are beginning to pile in our front yard, all yearning for the first footage of the baby's return home, the first interview from the parents. They've commoditized her abduction, monetized our tragedy. I let them wait a while. I don't care what they want right now. All I want is my baby.

Gerard turns to me. "Listen, I just wanted to apologize –" "Don't," I smile and hold up a hand. "It's fine, really. You were just doing your job." "I know, but I wasn't fair to you. I treated you like a criminal." "You had every right to. I understand. I'm just glad that you brought my baby home. I can't thank you enough for that." Claire turns to me, then, her crystal blue eyes revealing sympathy rather than suspicion. She doesn't say anything, just gives me a small smile. I know that's her way of apologizing as well. But she doesn't need to. She helped bring my baby home and that's all that matters. It's quiet again, and I can see Gerard looking at Weston, then back at me. He speaks up. "I don't want to interrupt this moment, but do you mind if I speak with the two of you for a moment?" We look at each other, and I can almost feel the tension and unease. I hand Emerald to my mother and stand slowly. Once we make our way down the hall and into the office, Gerard closes the door behind us. Our first moment alone since she's returned. Weston turns to me and I notice he's on the verge of tears. "What's wrong?" I step closer, bringing my hands to his face. "I'm so sorry, Cor. I'm so sorry," he starts to cry. "This is all my fault," I reach forward and take him into my arms. "What are you talking about? What happened?" I hold him with one arm and stroke his hair with my free hand. I wait patiently as he sobs into my neck, trying to gather himself. Finally, he looks up and meets my eyes. "I don't even know where to begin." Gerard speaks up, then. "Why not from the beginning?"

CHAPTER FIFTY

A FTER Weston Waters June 1, 2016

The worst is over and behind us. Emerald's abduction, Rosella's plot for vengeance – everything.

The police initially suspected that I had something to do with Rosella's death, as to be expected. But once they found both Emerald and Clementine being held with Teddy White, the blame fell to him. Once he was arrested, he admitted to taking the children, but denied any involvement in Rosella's murder. Told them he found her like that.

They didn't believe him, of course. Why would they believe anything that man says? It works in my favour, though. No one will ever know what really happened that morning.

After she fell, I felt for a pulse, but there was nothing. She was gone, just like that. There was nothing I could do. I weighed out my options. I could call an ambulance, but there would be no point. She was already dead. I could have called the police, but I knew how that would look, especially with all the factors: Emerald going missing the day before, a full analysis of the body would have shown she was pregnant. I knew I would be found guilty, even if it was an accident. No one would believe me.

I had to leave. I had no choice. I had to find Emerald, save my daughter. And I couldn't do that from a prison cell. So I left, headed out the front door, and tried to pretend it never happened. Which proved quite difficult with Cordelia constantly nagging about my whereabouts and bringing Detective Sullivan into it.

If I would have known then that Emerald's abduction was all because of Rosella... God, I can't even fathom what I would have done. But I have to move past that.

This all started with me, and end with me it shall. I take full responsibility for my mistakes. I understand now that what I did eleven years ago was terrible beyond words. I was young, stupid and irresponsible – but that's no excuse. I cannot change what happened in the past, but I can sure as hell make sure I do better in the future. I've already ruined every good relationship I've ever had. Antonia has been gone a long time, but our daughter, Clementine, has lived on in her place.

Cordelia was absolutely devastated after I told her what happened. She said she could never forgive me for what I did, and I honestly didn't know if she meant with Antonia or Rosella – but thinking about it now, she meant both. She meant everything.

I deserve that, I really do. I was a terrible person. I don't know how I could allow myself to become such an awful human being. A man does not behave that way. A man does not abandon the women in his life. If I could go back in time and change what happened to Toni, I would in a heartbeat. She didn't deserve to die because of my mistakes.

I've made so many mistakes in my life – too many to even count. But from this day forward, I vow to be the best man that I can be. And that means being the best father to Emerald, as well as to Clementine. Even though I wasn't a part of her life for eleven years, and she didn't even know I existed, we're working on building a relationship.

Since Rosella is gone, and her grandparents are deceased, she has no living family members to look after her. I asked Detective Sullivan to help me with my case to the courts to gain full custody of Clementine – with her permission, of course. It would kill me to see her have to go into the foster care system when she has a perfectly well and alive father ready to finally look after her.

I'm fortunate that Rosella never told her the truth about me. Clementine believes that her parents died in a car accident all those years ago, just as Rosella said. In Clementine's mind, I'm just her aunt's boyfriend. She has no idea who I really am, and she doesn't know all of the horrible things I've done in the past that put me in this situation. What I did to her mother, to her aunt. But the time will come when I will have to tell her that I'm her father. It will be complicated and messy, and I don't know how she'll react. But I'm praying she'll accept me.

Cordelia is filing for a divorce. No surprise there. I expected that. But the one thing I didn't expect was her agreeing to full joint custody of Emerald. I thought she would take me to court and fight for full custody, given everything that I've done and the mess that I caused this family. But she's seemingly okay with sharing custody of our daughter.

I won't question her motives. I'm just glad she still thinks I can be a good father to Emerald. However, if Cordelia wasn't so understanding, I would have fought for full custody. And I would have won, given Cordelia's history. I'm the most eligible caregiver for Emerald, and there's no denying that. I'm just glad we could come to a mutual understanding.

My feelings towards Cordelia haven't changed, even after all of this. I still love and admire her as a person. But we don't work together anymore.

We've grown apart as people and it's unfortunate that it had to come to this. But we will be better off on our own. She is so strong for overcoming her past and fighting to prove us all wrong when we accused her of hurting Emerald. Even when everyone doubted her, she was determined to find the truth. And that truth happened to be all my fault.

I can't describe the immense happiness I felt when they walked through that door with Emerald. There came a point where I honestly believed that she was dead. From initially thinking that Cordelia killed her, to then thinking that Rosella killed her, my thoughts were consistent that she was dead. And it was the biggest relief in the world to see her alive and well, back in my arms. I love her so much and will never let anything happen to her again.

As for the guy who was working with Rosella, Teddy White, he'll be in prison for the rest of his life. It turns out that he and a bunch of other men are responsible for the online human-trafficking website that allows people to buy and sell children. Detective Sullivan said this group has been wanted for a while all across America, but they're constantly crossing state lines and are virtually untraceable. All it took was one little slip-up – Rosella's journal and cellphone – and they found him. I feel safer knowing that predator isn't out there lurking around children anymore.

Once they busted Teddy, they were able to gain access to the website and shut it down completely. They offered him a deal: release the names of all other website admins and accomplices in exchange for a lower security prison facility.

He agreed. From there, the police were able to track all of the buyers down and subsequently return a variety of other missing children home to their families.

All in all, everything worked out. Except with Cordelia and me, that is. But I'm okay with that. Perhaps we weren't meant to work out. Perhaps we were supposed to move on from each other. Cordelia may hate me now and never want to speak to me again, but I have a feeling that everything will be okay. Maybe slowly, eventually, after everything is sorted out, she will forgive me and we can develop a friendship. That would be best for Emerald.

I don't expect her to forgive me right away. First I have to find a way to forgive myself. Because right now I'm still trapped in this vicious cycle of blame. I know that none of this would have happened if it wasn't for me and my irresponsible mistakes from eleven years ago. I keep beating myself up and regretting things I did a long time ago. But none of that is going to change what already happened. My therapist tells me that I can't continue living in the past. I have to live in the present and focus on the future. I can only hope my journey goes upwards from here. Emerald is home again, and hey, now I have a second chance to be a father to Clementine.

That's all I really need. That's all I could truly ever ask for.

CHAPTER FIFTY-ONE

AFTER Cordelia Waters June 12, 2016

I sit on the park bench and sip my coffee, watching as Ainsley pushes Emerald around in her stroller. It's a beautiful day; sun shining, not a cloud in the sky. The forecast was showing rain all week, yet all we've had is sun. Funny how things work out.

It's been three weeks since Emerald was taken and returned to me. Three weeks since the most stressful ordeal of my life. Those three days were such a roller coaster. From initially being blamed for the act, to having the suspicion switch to Weston, both of us went through so much. But they found her. They found my baby and brought her home, alive and well.

June sixteenth would have been mine and Weston's four-year anniversary. I can't say that I'm even remotely close to getting over what happened last month, but I'm getting there. The wound is still open and stings quite a bit. But even I know that all wounds heal eventually.

It's taken me a long time to come to grips with this reality. I couldn't understand how my husband could be responsibility for such a horrific incident in our lives. But he was. He is. I need to keep reminding myself of that. Because there are days when I miss him. There are nights when I lie in bed alone, tossing and turning because of his absence. And it is in those times that I want to forgive him; reach out and tell him to be there with me. But I can't do that. Because what he did is unforgivable. I need to learn to move on from this.

Other than that, life has reverted back to normal for me. I told my boss that I need to spend more time with Emerald, so until further notice, I'm only working three days a week. This allows me to be the mother that I should have been six months ago. I wasn't in my right state of mind then, and it's taken a lot – going through hell and back – to finally make me realize what she's worth. I never want to lose her again. I will never take her cries for granted again. Waking up in the middle of the night to rock her back to sleep only seems like a fair price for having her in my arms again.

Although I truly and honestly felt that I was stable again, Doctor Wyatt obviously had some concerns. She had me speak to another psychologist who deals with childhood trauma. We re-visited the issue of Samuel and how I needed to come to terms with this reality. In all honesty, I remembered bits and pieces from that year, but not much. I remembered Samuel. I remembered hanging out with him and the other children on my street. But even when my parents told me about the horrible things they uncovered from that year, I still have no recollection of it. As though my mind managed to completely block it out. I guess it's all for the better, then.

Since there are no medications to help with dissociative amnesia, the best remedies are to learn to cope and deal with stress, and also to talk with someone on a regular basis. That is why I'm now seeing Doctor Nash once a week – to ensure that I keep my life on track and never have a dissociative episode again.

I've been trying to get involved in the community more. I'm working on organizing a fundraiser for this July. It's a benefit to raise money and awareness for postpartum psychosis. No one should have to go through what I went through. And although there is no prevention for the illness, there are many remedies that can aid in one's recovery. That is why I'm hosting the benefit. More people need to be aware of this sort of thing. If you ask somebody on the street what postpartum psychosis is, they'll think you mean postpartum depression. But there's a difference. And that difference needs to be established.

Gerard's been helping me with it, gathering information and research on the subject. He's even helping with the venue. Something tells me that he's just as passionate about this topic as I am. He doesn't want to see anyone suffer from this either. There are remedies out there: medicine and therapies that can help combat the psychosis. And I want to offer myself to any woman out there suffering. I want them to know that I went through this. I suffered. But I also beat it. I worked so hard every single day until I was better again. I want to be that hope for people. The light at the end of the tunnel. If I can survive it, so can they.

As for the rest of the family, everyone seems to be doing great. We all learned of some rather shocking news within the last few weeks. It turns out that Colton and Lianna had an affair four years ago. And even more shocking: Colton is Clayton's father.

Everyone thought that Liam and Lianna were going to separate. But according to Liam, he knew all along. Lianna told him about the affair all those years ago, but she never told him about Clayton. But Liam isn't stupid. He admitted to knowing early on about the truth of Clayton's conception. But rather than tearing their family apart, he decided to stay with Lianna and try to make it work. However, that is why Liam ceased all contact with Colton. He didn't want to face him, knowing that he was Clayton's true father.

What's even stranger is that this whole mess brought everyone closer together. Liam knew the truth all along, so all it took was Colton opening up and confessing to him for them to come together again. It's an interesting familial situation – I have to admit that. Liam will always be Clayton's father, but now at least Clayton will have an uncle that he's close with, although the truth about who his biological father is will never be revealed to him. It's simpler, that way. Jada, on the other hand, didn't take the news too well. She packed up her things and filed for a divorce from Colton. I guess not everyone can be as understanding as Liam and Lianna.

I'm not one to talk – I did file for a divorce from Weston, after all. But our situation is different. Not only did he have an affair which would have torn this family apart, he ruined that poor girl's life all those years again. I didn't know what kind of man my husband truly was and that frightens me. If he was capable of such ignorance and malice, who knows what else he is capable of? Yet still, I granted him the one thing he wanted: equal custody of Emerald. Because I know that she is his life, and regardless of my ill feelings towards him, I couldn't take that away from him.

Savannah comes to visit me a couple times a week, bringing with her coffee and a new type of chocolate each visit. We didn't talk for a little while after the whole situation occurred. I did accuse her of kidnapping my daughter, after all. But fortunately for me, Savannah was very understanding. She told me that none of that was my fault, and I love her for that. She's one of the closest friends I have and I never want to lose her. We bring Emerald out with us now on our lunch dates. I bring her to work sometimes, too. Everyone at the office adores her. Everything I do now, I do with Emerald. She wasn't an integral part of my life before, which is horrible considering she's my daughter. But she sure as hell is now. And I'm never letting her out of my sight again.

It all still seems so surreal to me. The fact that my husband had another daughter out there that he didn't even know about. Well, I guess he knew about her, yet failed to accept the validity of her existence eleven years ago. And then there was the mistress – Rosella. What are the odds that he went and got her pregnant, too? I mourn the loss of her. I mourn the loss of both those sisters. Even though it was Rosella who stole my baby and almost ruined my life, I can only pity her now that she is gone. The poor woman was only doing what she believed was right. She was only trying to right the wrongs of my husband. I can't blame her for that. I can only sympathize. May she rest in peace, both her and her sister.

But that's all in the past now. Whatever happened, happened, and there's no changing it. The only way to live from this point on is to keep going forwards without looking back. I have my baby back and nothing will ever come between us again.

I turn to my left and see his car pull into the parking lot. I watch as he gets out and walks towards me, carrying a paper bag.

"Hi," he says once he sees me. "Hi," I smile. He takes a seat on the bench beside me, handing me the paper bag, along with a stack of paperwork. More information on the benefit, I assume. I open the bag to see an assortment of cookies and baked goods. "I got your favourite," he says. "Oatmeal chocolate chip." I stick my hand into the bag and pull one out. "Thank you." He takes the bag and places it on the bench next to him. Together, we sit there in silence and watch Ainsley as she takes a spoon to Emerald, feeding her the apple sauce that I packed earlier. "How is she today?" Gerard asks me. "She's good. Smiling and laughing as always." "That's good," he says. "Two more days until she's officially seven months." "You're right," I smile. "We're going down to Evanston this weekend. I thought it would be nice to see my parents." He nods. "Will Colton be there?" "Most likely. I'm trying to get Liam and the family to come down as well. It will be nice." "How are things with him and Jada? She's still set in her ways?" I take in a breath. "Yes, unfortunately. He may have lost a wife, but at least he gained a brother. And a niece and nephew. That's something, isn't it?" "It is." He says. I smile and nod. It's quiet for a moment. We sit there in silence as we watch Ainsley and Emerald. "Have you heard from him?" Gerard asks me. "Not recently, no." "I heard he's doing well." "That's good. I'm glad," I smile. "It would have been our four-year-anniversary on the sixteenth." "How does that make you feel?" I hesitate. "I'm not sure. I feel a mixed array of emotions. Confusion. Sadness. Loss. But I can't dwell on those feelings. I have to understand that this is for the best." "You're allowed to feel those things as well, Cordelia," he turns to me. "It's only normal. You're grieving the loss of a marriage. That's perfectly acceptable." "Thank you," I smile at him.

He's been a great help these past few weeks after everything that has happened. From constantly coming by the house to check up on me, to helping out with Emerald, Gerard's presence in my life has become a normality. And now, I don't want him to leave.

Who knows where life will take us next? I've learned not to live my life wondering these sorts of things, but rather, by taking each day as it comes. There are no guarantees in this life, and I have absolutely no idea what tomorrow will bring. But I have today. I have this present moment. I have this beautiful, sunny weather. I have Ainsley watching Emerald. I have Gerard by my side, bringing me oatmeal chocolate chip cookies. What else could I possibly ask for?

***

THE END